MANDY HUBBARD

razOr
bill

An Imprint of Penguin Group (USA) Inc.

You Wish

RAZORBILL

Published by the Penguin Group
Penguin Young Readers Group
345 Hudson Street, New York, New York 10014, U.S.A.
Penguin Group (USA) Inc., 375 Hudson Street, New York, New York 10014, U.S.A.
Penguin Group (Canada), 90 Eglinton Avenue East, Suite 700, Toronto, Ontario,
Canada M4P 2Y3 (a division of Pearson Penguin Canada Inc.)
Penguin Books Ltd, 80 Strand, London WC2R 0RL, England
Penguin Ireland, 25 St Stephen's Green, Dublin 2, Ireland
(a division of Penguin Books Ltd)
Penguin Group (Australia), 250 Camberwell Road, Camberwell, Victoria 3124, Australia
(a division of Pearson Australia Group Pty Ltd)
Penguin Books India Pvt Ltd, 11 Community Centre, Panchsheel Park,
New Delhi – 110 017, India
Penguin Group (NZ), 67 Apollo Drive, Mairangi Bay, Auckland 1311, New Zealand
(a division of Pearson New Zealand Ltd)
Penguin Books (South Africa) (Pty) Ltd, 24 Sturdee Avenue, Rosebank,
Johannesburg 2196, South Africa

Penguin Books Ltd, Registered Offices: 80 Strand, London WC2R 0RL, England

10 9 8

ISBN: 978-1-59514-292-4

Library of Congress Cataloging-in-Publication Data is available

Printed in the United States of America

FOR BROOKE

May all of *your* wishes come true,
as long as none of them are for a puppy.

1

PEOPLE SAY I'M a glass-half-empty person. I guess they're right, because I've never understood why anyone would see it as half full, when clearly there's something missing. But then again, maybe that's because I spent last summer working at a diner, and a half-empty glass meant I was falling behind.

So maybe it's my pessimist nature, but as I sit in biology, two rows behind my best friend, Nicole, I can't stop thinking about the secret she is so obviously keeping. I'm holding my bite-mark-covered pencil in a death grip as I watch her, when I should be using it to copy down the cell diagram on the front wipe-off board.

See, Nicole, in all her glass-half-full glory, is not good at keeping a secret. At the moment, she's completely avoiding my looks, instead taking biology notes like they're going out of style, the toe of her trendy gray-suede ankle boot tapping on the tan linoleum more rapidly than a hummingbird's heartbeat. She's playing with her long blonde hair, pulling it in front of her face so that I can't see the expression in her blue eyes.

I haven't decided whether or not I'm going to ask her what it is, either. Because my birthday party is tonight, and her secret might be something amazingly spectacular, which means it would be better as a surprise.

Although this brings me back to the glass half empty and the fact that I highly doubt it's something spectacular. Nicole is one of those people who reads like an open book. And right now, that book is open to the definition of *nervous*. The rest of the classroom looks half asleep, leaned over their desks and notebooks. In fact, I'm pretty sure the guy in the dark-blue hoodie in the back row actually *is* asleep.

But not Nicole. Nicole is exuding more energy than a two-year-old on a sugar binge. She finally lifts her head and glances back at me, and those startling blue eyes widen when she catches me staring. She returns to her notebook, scribbling furiously. Either she's taking some serious notes or she's writing the next *War and Peace*.

I sigh and turn back to Mr. Gordon, who is now labeling the components of his cell drawing. The faded red words are smashed and crooked, barely legible. His red-and-blue-plaid sweater-vest is slightly askew, and he's sweating already, periodically wiping his bushy gray brow with the back of his hand.

I stopped listening somewhere around mitochondria, so now I'm hopelessly lost. Biology as a first-period class should be outlawed, because there's no way my brain is up to full speed at 7:50 a.m.

I bite back a yawn and stare out the window, willing something crazy to happen, like the big, bare willow tree in the courtyard falling over. Or maybe the freshman scurrying across the space will slip on one of the dew-covered orange fallen leaves, and I'll have to rush out there and make sure she is okay. Anything would be better than sitting here. We're only a month into our sophomore year, and already each day is going by more slowly than the last. And Mr. Gordon's monotonous voice and squeaky whiteboard markers aren't helping matters.

I reach down and scratch at the fishnet stockings I'm wearing. There's a seam on the inside of my knee, and it's driving me batty. I've never worn these things before, and I'm already regretting it. I think I might take them off in the bathroom.

It's not that I'm trying to be full-on goth or emo or anything, either. I just enjoy being a little less like the sheep at the top of the social ladder, if you know what I mean. Last spring, when Old Navy started airing those sundress commercials, they all showed up in a rainbow display of femininity. I can predict their clothing as if I have an actual tide table of it. All I need is a Gap ad and an issue of *Seventeen*, and I'll have all their outfits mapped out for the next week.

On occasions when I'm feeling particularly brave, I even bleat at them like a sheep, though none of them seem to understand what I'm doing. Nicole usually hides behind a locker bay or the trophy case and laughs hysterically, egging me on.

So I bought these stockings to wear with *my* Old Navy dress, except I bought the blue-and-white-striped sailor dress, the one that was 50 percent off after two weeks because no one was buying it. And there's definitely a reason no one was buying it, because whenever I wear it, I feel like someone is going to shout at me to "swab the decks, matey!"

Plus, since it's now September and not May, it's, like, forty-six degrees out. I probably should have worn leggings, not fishnets, especially not scratchy, annoying ones.

I open my binder and find my paper hall pass. I almost made it a whole month without using it, which is worth ten extra-credit points, points I could really use. But comfort is worth, like, fifty million points, so I'm going for it.

I walk toward the door and slide my pass into the box and then head in the direction of the bathroom, my black Converse sneakers silent on the carpeted hall. My feet are the only part of me that are truly comfortable, but I'm about to rectify that little problem. I know people say you're supposed to make sacrifices for fashion, but I'm sure that only counts if you're actually trying to be fashionable.

I'm just reaching the thick wooden door when it swings out at me, nailing my shin. It feels like my whole leg just shattered.

"Ow!" I jump back, sure that blood will gush at any moment. My calf pulses with pain as I jump up and down, howling a little bit. I know I'm prone to melodramatics, but dang, that really hurt.

Janae Crawford, queen of the Old Navy dress clique and most evil person I've ever met, emerges from the bathroom and gives me a bored look. I guess stomping all over her classmates fails to get her excited anymore.

Today she's wearing jeans that are so tight I think she must have used a shoehorn to get into them (is there such a thing as a butt horn?) and two layers of lacy tank tops with a pink cardigan over the top. Then she has a strand of pearls so long they reach her belly button. As if the pearls were going to make her whole outfit seem classy or something.

Her sneer morphs into an amused smile as her eyes travel down my legs and take in my fishnets.

I groan inwardly, though I totally don't let her know I'm worried about what she's going to say next. The key to being a black sheep is acting as if you love every minute of it, even when the whitest of the white sheep is about to rip you to shreds.

"I'm sorry, is it Halloween already?" She waggles her head in this totally annoying way as she speaks. Like she's on a daytime talk show saying, "Oh no, you didn't."

"Ahoy, vapid wannabe." I do a mock salute and walk right past her toward the sink.

She rolls her eyes. "You're *so* weird."

I slap my hand over my heart, trying to look as theatrical as possible. "Ay, it be the scurvy," I say, screwing my mouth up to the side and crinkling one brow so low my left eye is almost closed.

That sentence probably doesn't even make sense, and Janae makes a noise that sounds like a combination of a snort and a gurgle and then pushes past me, ramming into my shoulder and making me bounce off the cinder block wall.

I holler after her, "Does this mean tonight's pillow fight is canceled?"

I'm not even sure where that came from, but by the look she gives me as the door swings shut, I figure it's a victory. Even with the door closed, I can hear her thick wedge sandals as she stomps away, making enough noise to rouse the dead.

I laugh to myself as I enter a bathroom stall, but now I know that I can't take the tights off. There's no way I'm giving her the satisfaction, even if changing had nothing to do with her. Damn. Now I've wasted my extra-credit points and my legs are still going to itch all day. This is shaping up just perfectly.

Did I mention that today is my birthday? Well, it is. I'm officially sixteen. Sweet? Not exactly. I stopped being sweet when I stopped eating a dozen gumballs a day, back in elementary school.

Every birthday seems to be worse than the last one. By the time I'm seventeen, I'll probably be having an eighth life crisis.

I finish in the stall and head to the sink. I have no desire to get back to history, so I spend what must be a full five minutes washing my hands. A few mousy-brown strands of hair have escaped from my still-damp-from-the-shower ponytail. I'm wearing zilcho makeup, because even designer mascara wouldn't make my plain brown eyes any more alluring, and my thin lips aren't going to get any bigger no matter how much I spend on plumping lip gloss. My dress sort of hangs off me, because I'm probably a little too thin and a lot too boobless to pull it off.

Before I can decide that I hate my ears, too, Nicole walks in, her cute little ankle boots clacking on the white bathroom tiles. "Oh, good!" she says when she sees me, as if she didn't spend all of biology ignoring me.

"Hey," I say, grabbing a couple scratchy paper towels. "What's up?"

Nicole heads to the sink and starts washing her hands, even though she hasn't used the bathroom yet. Very suspect. Then she leans forward far enough that her blonde bangs fall into her eyes and she doesn't have to look at me. I watch the silver bangles on her wrists flutter around as she runs her hands under the water. Nicole got really tall over the summer, so she has to sort of lean over. She's still working her way through her gigantic new fall wardrobe, and today's jeans look like two hundred dollars' worth of perfection.

"Not much." She starts pushing the soap dispenser over and over, until the soap begins to drip from her hands.

I stop watching her and pretend to fix my ponytail. "I am really, *really* not looking forward to tonight. I wish I could get my mom to cancel it. It's going to be so lame."

She looks up at me in the mirror. I notice her skin looks really nice today, almost glowing, with only a few blemishes on her chin and one on her nose. Her mom probably dragged her to the dermatologist again, part of her never-ending quest to fix Nicole's acne. "About that," she says.

I meet her eyes and wait for her to finish.

"I kind of forgot your party was today. I mean, just for, like, a second. Ben and I went out last Saturday and he told me about this great idea he had for our three-month anniversary and I kind of agreed before I realized it was the same day as your party," she says, all in a rush, and then flips the faucet on full bore, so that the water hits her hands and starts splashing big sudsy drops all over the black-freckled counters.

My heart twists around and drops to my stomach. Just before school let out last spring, Nicole got her first-ever boyfriend. For a while things were just as great as ever, but then August hit, and it's like now there's not enough room for a best friend *and* a boyfriend. That shy girl I've been best friends with for the last six years has *finally* been coming into her own, and I'm really happy for her . . . but I don't know what that means for me, if she's going to outgrow me, move on, forget me. Because I'm the same person I've always been, and she's not.

And something's gotta give.

I grip the edge of the countertop, even though it's all wet. "You're kidding, right?"

She shakes her head. "But I'll only be a little late, I swear."

"Where are you going?"

She probably has a really good reason for this. Like she just found out she won the lottery and she has to be there tonight to claim the check in person.

"He thought we could go to Anya's, that place on the waterfront, and do you know how cool that place is supposed to be? It will be my first real anniversary *ever* and it'll be super-romantic. I totally won't go if it's a big deal, though." Nicole is talking really fast, the words flowing out like they're falling over the edge of Niagara Falls. "But he's been at the track a lot lately and now that school has started, we haven't had as much time together, and I really want to go. I don't want to let him down."

All I can do is stare. It just seems so wrong that she's *asking permission* to ditch me, as if there's any way to refuse her without being a total brat.

I take in a long, slow breath, rubbing my eyes. "You know I'm dreading this party, Nicole. I mean yeah, I would ditch my own party too, if I could. But how am I going to survive the torture if you're not there to make fun of it with me?"

Here's the thing about my sweet sixteen: My mom is the one who wants it, not me. She's an event planner for a living, and she's been talking about my sweet-sixteen party for oh, a thousand years. When I was little, it sounded like great fun, and we'd sit around talking about how cool it would be.

But things change, and so do people, and the idea of a frilly party revolving around yours truly is now my worst nightmare. I've been telling her for over a year that I don't want my party anymore—that I'd prefer a quiet dinner—but it doesn't help. She's throwing me a party whether I like it or not.

The worst part is that Nicole is the only person I invited. I figured with her to goof off with, even a Miley Cyrus concert could be bearable.

My mom, on the other hand, invited every relative we have, plus some we don't, like the neighbors and my bus driver. Seriously—she invited my school bus driver. So the entire place is going to be filled with people I don't want to be around.

And there will be games. Oh, there will be games.

"We wouldn't miss the whole thing, I promise. Just the first hour, tops. But only if you're cool with it," Nicole says.

We stare at each other for a long moment, the faucet still running in the background, my hand still gripping the countertop. My evening begins to stretch out in front of me, like a never-ending desert.

I can make it through an hour, right? No biggie. Nicole will get there before everything gets unbearable, we'll laugh at the silly decorations, eat ridiculous hors d'oeuvres, and it'll be like she didn't miss a thing.

"Okay," I say. "I can handle an hour."

"Okay? Really?" she says, her voice rising an octave. It's almost so high pitched only cheerleaders could hear it.

I nod, my stomach sinking. She springs forward and hugs me, smearing her soaped-up hands all over my sailor sundress.

"You're the bestest best friend," she says. "I promise, I'll be there by seven."

I just nod. I'll have to suck it up and grin and bear it until she arrives. My birthday is just one night.

The real problem is I know that Nicole is spending more and more time with Ben, and less and less time with me, and there's nothing I can do about it.

That's not even the worst part.

The worst part?

I've been completely and utterly in love with Ben Mackenzie for three long, agonizing years.

And she has no idea.

2

I MAKE IT THROUGH the rest of biology without a meltdown and then move on to trigonometry and slide into my seat next to Ben's empty desk. By some act of God—or maybe the devil, I still haven't decided—the random seating arrangement ended with us next to each other.

Three months and four days ago—June 19, to be exact—I would have died of happiness to be seated next to Ben. I mean, finally, I'd have the opportunity to talk to him.

Of course, him becoming my best friend's boyfriend kind of changed that.

I never told her about my crush. If I'd only said something months ago, before she went out with him, maybe I wouldn't be in this mess. But I didn't.

Oh, sure, I told her how hot he was, how amazing he looked in jeans, how beautiful his blue eyes were. But there was no way I could *really* be in love with a guy I'd hardly spoken six words to, right? What else could I tell her? That we'd had a connection for a long time, only he didn't know it? That I knew, without a doubt, that he was my soul mate?

Right. And ponies fly. So of course we would always talk about how hot Ben is, and I'd never reveal my deeper feelings, and that was that.

Until June 19.

Maybe June 19 was the day Nicole decided she didn't want to be shy anymore, the moment of change. It's easier to see now, in retrospect, that there's the old Nicole and the new one, and June 19 is the day smack in the middle of it all.

I know Nicole better than anyone in the world, and so I know that though she comes off shy, once she's around someone long enough, she warms right up. And she got paired as Ben's partner in table tennis, and they spent two weeks playing together.

And I still have a hard time picturing it, but somehow, she got up the nerve to ask him out. She probably blurted it out and turned all red, but she did it.

And he said yes.

She was totally beaming when she told me, bouncing around as if she'd won the lottery.

I couldn't bring myself to tell her that I was almost positive I'd been in love with him for years. And now that I know him better— through Nicole—now that Ben and I talk and joke in class and he tells me all about his dates with her, I've only become more sure. More sure that he and I fit together.

Ben is that one guy for me, my perfect match.

Except he's already matched, and now they're celebrating their three-month anniversary. Three months is, like, a decade in high school years. I spent most of the summer at that stupid diner, so I haven't been forced to endure that much quality time with both of them at the same time.

Thank God.

For the next fifty-five minutes, I will hold my breath, my heart will beat erratically, and the hairs on my arm will stand on end. This is life inside Ben's orbit, and it is the height of every day of my otherwise meaningless existence.

My crush on Ben began a few years ago, the summer after sixth grade. Nicole and I were at Flaming Geyser. It's a state park just outside our hometown of Enumclaw, a tiny cow town about an hour southeast of Seattle. The park is at the north end of the Green River Valley, and you have to drive long, windy roads to get to it. It's surrounded by achingly tall fir trees, where the river is wide and slow and perfect for swimming and tubing. On a hot day, cars line up on either side of the road for almost as far as you can see.

That day, I was wearing the last bikini I've ever owned, a teeny pink triangle top with white polka dots, the sort of thing I'd never be caught dead in now. Nicole was in a matronly one-piece—plain navy blue, the kind of thing a high school swim team would wear. By then, she was at least a C cup, and she wore a white sarong over her suit. I didn't tell her that it just made her chest look even bigger, because I didn't want to make her paranoid. She was even shyer back then, afraid to talk to just about anyone but me.

Nicole wanted to spend most of the day on the shore, lying out, eating Doritos, and reading one of her romance novels. Back then she was on this acne medication that made her skin really sensitive to light, so she was slathered in the thickest layer of 60 SPF I've ever seen. She was paranoid about actually swimming and letting it wash off. I guess the only thing worse than a face full of acne is a sunburned face full of acne.

I, however, could not tolerate sitting still. I guess you could say I'm a little impatient, forever ready for adventure.

So I swam across the river and then climbed up the reddish-brown clay banks, using tree roots as handholds, my feet getting muddy and slick. Although my hair was still dripping with the icy water, the short hike made me sweat. Even in the middle of summer, Enumclaw didn't often get hotter than ninety degrees, but that fateful day, it was ninety-seven.

There is a cliff on that side of the river, about twenty feet high. People jump in from up there, but you have to aim for this perfect little swimming hole; otherwise you'll slam into the rocks six feet under the surface of the water, likely breaking a leg.

Rumor has it someone died jumping off, years ago. I heard they drank too much and jumped headfirst. It scares a lot of people and they'll spend ten minutes up there, staring down, only to chicken out and climb back down the way they came.

Sometimes spectators, people smart enough not to climb up there at all, will tie their tubes up to the shore and just float there, waiting to see who has the guts to actually jump, mocking those who don't.

That day I met Ben, he was up there with three other guys, all of them staring down at the water with eyes full of worry. I guess he wasn't quite the daredevil yet, not the one he is now. I didn't recognize any of them, not even Ben, but I found out later they went to Thunder Mountain, the other middle school in town.

Once I realized they were a bunch of scaredy-cats, I wanted so badly to just walk straight up and jump over, no hesitation. Show them what I was made of. But they were so freaked out, and it leached into me, until the butterflies in my stomach were the size of seagulls. I had shivered a little, river water dripping off me, the sun blocked by the trees.

Ben, when he saw me, sort of snorted to himself and then tried to cover it up.

"What?" I had put my hand on my pink-bikini-clad, bony hip. I didn't have curves. Not back then, not now.

Ben's hair was even lighter back then, sun streaked and longer than he wears it now. Kind of a bowl cut, almost long enough to tuck behind his ear. He had on blue-and-red board shorts, his body lean, just a hint of the muscle he would later develop.

"Nothing." He crossed his arms and leaned against a tree near the edge. "Nothing at all."

My heart skipped a beat as his intense blue eyes bored into me, daring me, pushing me, doubting me. "Afraid I'm going to show you up? You've been up here a half hour." I raised an eyebrow, determined not to show him that he was making me more nervous than the jump.

Ben didn't say anything. He knew I had a point.

My lips curled into an enormous smile, and I stepped to the edge. The boys backed up a little, as if I was going to take them with me. Like my brand of crazy might be contagious. My heartbeat seemed to stop as I peered over the edge, looking down at that tiny little swimming hole. Suddenly I understood why they'd been standing there so long. It reminded me of those cartoons where the clowns climb up a ladder that extends into the clouds, then jump off into a tiny bucket of water.

I could have turned around, told the boys I was just as scared as they were.

But I didn't. I leapt, soaring through the air, the Green River rushing up toward my feet. As I fell into the river, the cold surface of the water closing around me, swallowing me, I knew I was already falling for Ben and that arrogant, adorable smile. There was something about the way he challenged me, stared straight at me, that twisted its way around my heart.

I spent the rest of the day watching him and his friends swim and splash and laugh, and yes, eventually they did jump off the cliff. I guess they *had* to, once I waltzed up there and jumped with no hesitation.

A month later, he moved across town, and that meant going to EMS with me, instead of TMMS with all of his friends. We shared an English class. But he didn't seem to remember me, and when I realized that, it was like a painful stab to the chest. I couldn't bring myself to speak to him when we sat so far apart, and the other girls were already latching onto him. He'd looked even better in his new fall school clothes than he had in his board shorts.

It was as if that moment at the river, when we stared right into each other's eyes, never happened at all. Sometimes I wonder if that's why I've never told Nicole about the crush. If it's embarrassment over the fact that the moment meant everything to me and nothing to him.

"Hey," he says three minutes later when he slides into his chair. His blondish hair is tousled with gel, and his skin has a natural, dark tan. Even his baggy jeans and loose T-shirt can't hide his now well-muscled body—one he's earned through a combination of working his butt off all summer for his dad's landscaping business and riding motocross every chance he gets.

That's the other thing about Ben. He races dirt bikes. He's

totally, completely amazing, and I could watch him all day. He has this bright-yellow motorcycle, and every time he launches into the air, my heart jumps right with him. It's mesmerizing to watch. Someday he'll probably go pro and get all these sponsors and stuff.

"Hi," I say, not looking up from last night's homework.

On an average day, we will exchange at least seventy-three words, his arm will brush mine seven times, and his knee will come in contact with mine on at least three occasions. He will look me in the eye and grin at least once, a grin that tells me in a half second that we would be a perfect couple.

If he weren't already one part of what is probably *the* perfect couple.

I will sigh inwardly at least once per minute and accidentally sigh aloud at least a half-dozen times. I will picture Nicole's face more times than necessary, trying to remind myself why I can't flirt with him. I suppose I should find it ironic that the very reason I can't date him is pretty much the only reason he knows who I am now. If he wasn't dating Nicole, I'm not sure he'd even recognize me in a crowd.

He leans closer to me. "Why are fish salesmen so greedy?"

I chew on my lip and stare forward, pondering. "Not a clue."

"Because their business makes them sel-fish," he says, slapping his desk.

Ben and I share the same horrible sense of humor. We like jokes. The lamer, the better. But that one? Beyond lame.

"I've got a better one. Why did the orange go to the doctor?" I say.

"To donate vitamin C?"

I roll my eyes. "Because he wasn't peeling good."

He chuckles. "Nice. You win."

I grin and meet his eyes. It makes my heart twist a little. He's too gorgeous for words. His perfect, tanned skin, the way his faded black T-shirt sort of clings to the muscles that seemed to be stretched tightly over his shoulders, the light calluses on his hands. "So you guys are going to some fancy dinner tonight, huh?"

"Yeah. Supposedly the food is amazing, and it's got a view of the water. It's supposed to be a pretty fun place. Nicole was excited."

"Cool," I say, turning back to my homework.

"Is it? Cool? I didn't know about your birthday until today. . . . We could always reschedule. . . . " He adjusts the silver watch on his wrist, and his arm brushes mine for the first time today.

I wave my hand in the air, as if it's no biggie at all, even though some irrational side of me wishes Ben had known it was my birthday. His is March 6. I've known that for two years, since I heard one of his friends wish him a happy birthday in the hall outside the gym. "Nah, I have a birthday every year. You'll only have one three-month anniversary."

I reach down and rub at the seam on my fishnets again. It's driving me crazy. I'd rather have a hundred ants walking up my leg right now than wear these for another minute. I reach down and rip a big hole in them so that the seam isn't rubbing against my knee anymore.

When I look up at Ben, he's staring at me, his perfect, dark eyebrows raised, his deep-blue eyes looking at my stockings.

I grin, my cheeks warming. "Sorry. These things are driving me nuts."

He shrugs and then slides down a bit in his chair and stretches his lanky legs out in front of him. His knee bumps mine. Twice. "They're kind of hot, though."

Oh no, he didn't. Ben has never, not in a million years, paid me a compliment. He reserves those for Nicole.

I suddenly wish I hadn't ripped a big hole in the knee. Then I shake my head. *Thou shall not covet thy best friend's boyfriend.*

"So, did you get your homework done?" I ask, forcing myself back to safer topics.

Ben flips open his binder and taps on the homework inside the front cover. His arm brushes mine again. "Barely. I finished the last two during homeroom."

Mrs. Vickers finally walks to the front of the room, a full ten minutes after the bell rang. She begins the day by writing down our assignments, and we all groan when we see that she's giving us another thirty problems.

Due tomorrow.

Ben leans toward me, so close I can smell his spicy cologne. It washes over me and I have to force myself to keep my eyes open instead of closing them and taking in deep, ragged breaths. "This woman is trying to kill us," he says. His breath is warm against my neck and minty fresh. If I turned my face, just half a turn, my lips would brush against his, and I'd finally know what it feels like to kiss him.

Instead I just nod and stare forward at the teacher as if I am totally unaffected by being closer to him than I've ever been.

Which I am. Unaffected, that is.

Because he's my best friend's boyfriend.

3

BY THE TIME my brother knocks on my door for the third time that evening, I've run out of stall tactics. I have no choice but to go downstairs and face the crowd of people who have gathered for my sweet sixteen. I've been listening to the hum of voices, hoping my mother would be so busy with the party planning she wouldn't even remember my presence was a required element.

I'm not wearing the outfit she set out for me. It was too girly. She knew well enough not to buy it in pink, but the blue skirt has white Hawaiian-looking flowers and a slightly asymmetrical ruffle. And she bought me heels.

It's either the dress or the heels, but there's no way I'm wearing both. I'm not in the mood to deal with a full-scale argument, so I hope she'll settle for the fact that I'm not wearing fishnets and these stupid white heels at least match my sailor sundress. I die a little inside as I buckle them around my ankles.

I survey the results in the mirror. The heels ruin the rebel, ironic side of my sailor dress and make me look like I actually take myself seriously. I look like I'm channeling a Ralph Lauren catalog. The kind with polo ponies and yachts. I take my hair out of the ponytail it's been in all day and brush out the indent from the rubber band, so now it just sort of hangs around my shoulders in big, ugly brown clumps. I never wear my hair down because I hate it. It has no shape, no color, and no curl.

I flutter my eyelashes at myself in the mirror. In a horrible southern accent, I say, *"Why, Kayla, I do declare, that is one hideous dress!"*

Then, in an accent worthy of the crocodile hunter, I add, *"Crikey, but that's an ugly pair of heels!"*

Although I usually prefer to mock *other* people, the voices have actually made me feel better. I sigh and flip myself off in the mirror and then decide it's now or never. And since *never* will get me grounded, it's time to give in.

I open the door to see my brother standing in the hall, his cell phone stuck to his ear. I am guessing that he's talking to his long-distance girlfriend. I'm not sure why she hasn't dumped him, seeing as he's a college dropout who now lives a few hundred miles from her.

Plus my brother is not that cute, if you ask me. He has the same medium-brown hair I do—as in, it's nothing exceptional. Mom has this beautiful deep-brown hair, and we have something between that and blond, which is completely blah. His is cut in a faux hawk. His nose used to be straight, like mine, but now it has a small bump in it, à la Owen Wilson, because he took a soccer ball to the face, or so he claims. I still think that's a cover-up for getting sucker punched when he poached another guy's girlfriend.

We both have those thin, kind of boring lips, and even if I add a pound of lip gloss, mine still don't look that kissable.

We're also both flat chested. I think I've got maybe a half inch on him in that department. Totally pathetic.

"Mom says if I get you to come downstairs *now*, I can use the truck tomorrow."

"And that's supposed to inspire me?"

He tips his head to the side and gives me an *I wish I was an only child* sort of look. "It's not like she's going to let you skip the whole party, so just go downstairs and spare us all a headache, will you?"

"Argh." I roll my eyes and stomp past my brother, heading down the hall and the stairs and through the family room. By the time I'm standing on the back patio, I feel like I've exited the house and stepped into a Selena Gomez movie. I don't even recognize the space anymore. On a normal day, our nondescript house is perched in the middle of a big half-acre corner lot, the perfectly green lawn framed with a tall cedar fence.

Today, though, instead of the empty grassy expanse, there is a big white tent in the middle, long strands of pink and white lights draped between it and the house. There are pink flowers tied to the cedar fence line and some kind of punch fountain near the door, already pumping gallons of pink liquid. Pink and white confetti litters the tables.

A DJ is playing really bad pop music under the tent, a strobe light and disco ball flashing out onto the empty floor. The round tables, flanked with folding white chairs, are perched all over the place, each of them with a pink floral centerpiece.

My mom is one of those super-feminine women who love pink.

Once my dad was gone, she completely redid the master bedroom in pink wallpaper, with a bunch of pink and white pillows on her pink-and-yellow-plaid bed set.

In other words, we totally don't get each other.

She told me about a hundred times how she'd never had a sweet-sixteen party. And now I think I know what it would look like if she'd had one.

I wonder how many episodes of *Sweet Sixteen* she watched in order to pull this off.

Seriously. This is a bit . . . over the top, even for my mom. It's like something from *High School Musical*. The pre-packaged version of a sweet sixteen. Just add water. And, well, a birthday girl who belongs on Disney, not the one standing in the yard right now, staring at the middle-aged DJ.

"What do you think, honey?" my mom says, appearing beside me like a magician, except without the puff of smoke. My mom normally does bar mitzvahs and corporate events. It's clear this one is a little out of her comfort zone, and by the tension in her voice, she knows it.

"Now you know I've never done a sweet sixteen, so you'll have to bear with me if the details aren't just right. You just let me know, and I'll fix everything I can, okay?"

Ugh. The harder she tries, the more awkward I feel. I blink a few times and keep staring at the backyard. Or what *was* the backyard. There are guests milling about, only a few of whom I recognize. I'm starting to think my mom may have put something like *Pretty in Pink* on the invitations, because there is an absurdly high ratio of pink clothes on the guests.

"It's, um, great." I chew on my lip. I'm certain I don't know some of these people. "Who is that?" I ask, nodding toward a tall guy in a suit with a bright-pink tie and a matching pink handkerchief sticking out of his pocket. He's wearing thick glasses and his gray hair is slicked back in a no-nonsense way. It somehow makes the pink accents seem all the more hilarious. He does not look ready to party. He looks like he's going to negotiate a better rate on his mortgage.

"Oh, I invited a few clients out. The sweet-sixteen market is huge, and I think I can really get my name out there. I hope you don't mind?" she says. Her eyes dart over to me for approval. "I thought if we were throwing this big party anyway, it would kill two birds with one stone."

My heart sinks. It's all for her business.

These last few weeks, I've been trying to convince her to cancel the thing and just go to Red Robin, but she's been oddly insistent. And now it makes sense. Because she needed this event. It's about that stupid day planner and BlackBerry.

It didn't used to bother me that she was so wrapped up in it. If the phone rang while we were having dinner, I didn't even roll my eyes when she answered—even though she won't let me or my brother answer our cells at the table. Because the thing is, there was a time that my dad being MIA really tore her up, and she moped around for months. Then she threw herself into creating a business so that she could return my dad's alimony checks, a big *refused* scrawled across the envelope. The first time she did it, we all went out to celebrate.

But it's been years since that happened, and now nothing is ever good enough—if she builds her name in one event, she has to add another and another, until every single day of the week consists of her running around in a frenzy. The fridge is filled with leftover pizza and Chinese takeout, and her bed is hardly ever slept in. I don't think she's ever slowed down long enough to use that big Jacuzzi she had installed in her showpiece master bathroom.

I shrug, biting back the words I want to say. There's no point in fighting with her. I'll just have to make it through tonight and pretend this ridiculous party never happened. In an hour, Nicole will be here, and we can entertain ourselves. "It's okay."

Or at least . . . it was. Until I see a slim, petite woman walking toward me, a blinding smile on her face. She's wearing crisp khaki pants with a bright-pink paisley-print top, her hair coiffed in a style that must have taken at least a half gallon of Aqua-Net. She's still a good thirty feet away, but she's throwing her arms out to give my mother a hug.

It's not this woman who concerns me, though. It's the girl walking behind her, her arms crossed and her black strappy heels sinking in the lawn. She's not wearing pink at all, just a simple black halter top and a pair of expensive, well-fitted jeans.

I swallow, trying to maintain my calm as the bane of my existence looks up and meets my eyes.

It takes her a moment to realize it's me standing on the patio, but when she does, her scowl transforms into a look of surprise . . . then delight.

I am so screwed.

My mom beams when she sees the woman. "Jean! So pleased you could make it."

The woman does one of those weird air kisses, like she's in France or something, and my mom doesn't miss a beat. "Of course! This is beautiful, Linda. Just beautiful. Although we'll need more flowers for Janae's party. And we were just saying that the punch fountain seems a bit . . . outdated?"

Oh God. They're critiquing my party. Janae is standing to the side of her mother, her lips quivering as if she can't believe how lucky she is to be here, seeing me in this girly outfit, pointing out my outdated punch bowl—er, fountain.

My mother is nodding as if she totally agrees that it is outdated. But I know she picked it out herself because I heard her on the phone. "Yes, Kayla wanted the fountain. You know how our girls can be, don't you?"

My jaw drops, but my mom doesn't even notice because she's already turning away from me, her arm entwined with Jean's. "We can talk more specifics later this evening. You're going to stay for a bit? I'd like to discuss the sort of theme we might do for Janae's party. I've heard *Twilight* is very popular. We could do vampires."

I swallow. She has *got* to be kidding me.

Janae steps toward me. "Oh, sure, vampires. Sounds hot."

My mom beams, totally missing the sarcastic tone in Janae's voice.

Where is Nicole? I glance at my watch. She promised she'd only be an hour late, tops. That means I probably have fifteen more minutes to go before she arrives. I can make it that long, right?

I *must* go straight back to my room and put jeans on. Right this minute, so at least I can feel normal. Standing out here with Janae is like standing on a pier and watching a tidal wave come roaring toward you. You know it's going to ruin everything, but there's nothing you can do about it unless a magical helicopter shows up and swoops in to save you. And since magical helicopters rank right up there with getting an A in biology and Ben professing his love for me, my outlook seems pretty dark.

"Let's leave these girls to chat, and I'll give you the tour so we can talk about your options," my mom says, throwing me to the wolves.

I watch them wind their way into the crowd, wondering when exactly I lost any hope of enjoying this party. It was somewhere between third grade and five seconds ago.

"Nice party. I feel so bad that I missed Pin the Tail on the Donkey." Janae motions to the punch bowl—er, fountain—and roses. "Although this does explain a lot."

I grind my teeth. It won't help to tell her it was all my mom's idea, because that just makes me look twelve years old.

The strange thing is, I once *wanted* to be friends with Janae. Back in elementary school, she was just a sweet, normal girl. I found her on the playground once, trying to get a fallen baby bird back into its nest. We combined forces and she distracted the janitor while I "borrowed" a step stool and raced out to the playground with it. I held on to the rickety stool while Janae climbed up and put the bird back in its nest, and then we patted ourselves on the back for our commitment to animal welfare.

For a couple days, things were a little different. We voluntarily worked together on a spelling assignment, and she even asked me to sit with her at lunch one day. But a few days later the school year ended and we never swapped phone numbers, and that's the summer she grew boobs and became a snob. I think she went to France or something, which explains her mom's penchant for air-kiss greetings.

I take a sip of the Diet Coke I've been practically crushing in my fist. We're just standing there, side by side, me barely breathing and Janae with one hand cocked up on her hip, and that's when the tidal wave officially swallows me whole. "So what, your *one* friend couldn't show up?" Janae turns and gives me a long, appraising look.

The edge of her mouth quivers a little as she crosses her arms and leans on one heel, her head tipped to the side.

For once, I'm at a loss for words. Janae's smile widens as she realizes that my usual quick-fire retort has not materialized.

"Why are you such a bitch?" I hiss. I can feel my face flaming and I don't even care.

Janae smirks down at me from her perfect, model, five-foot ten height. Is she wearing seven-inch heels or did I just shrink? "I'd rather be a bitch than a *Big. Fat. Zero.*"

I blink a few times, but I remain composed. At least on the outside.

"My mother dragged me here because your mom was her sorority sister. It's officially your fault I'm missing the scrimmage against Victor Falls High." Janae spins on her monstrous heel and stalks away, tossing her shiny, mahogany-colored hair over her shoulder as she walks into the crowd.

Well.

If I were a glass-half-full type, I might say the good thing about my sixteenth birthday is that every future birthday is bound to be better.

But right now I'm not even feeling like the glass is half empty—I'm feeling like I want to break the damn glass. Over Janae's perfect little head.

4

FOR THE NEXT two and a half hours, I stand at the edge of the patio, my arms crossed, trying desperately to keep from scowling at everyone, including my mom. She flashes me a thumbs-up and a wide, dazzling smile as she walks by, a stack of her business cards in one hand.

She's poised and perfect, just like always, not a hair out of place, not a speck of dirt on her tailored red suit jacket.

Somewhere between Taylor Swift and Miley Cyrus, I've realized that Janae will *never* actually let my mom plan her sweet sixteen even if her mom *did* pledge the same sorority as my mom. Janae thinks of herself as edgy, and the whole thing is far too 2007 for her tastes.

Mine too, frankly. And my mom should know that. She's trying so hard and has obviously done hours and hours of research.

But all she needed to do was ask me. Ask me what kind of decorations I wanted, ask me what songs the DJ should play.

But she'd never do that. Because she never talks to me, she just talks *at* me.

I've lost every ounce of patience. I don't want to talk to another random stranger who doesn't even realize I'm the birthday girl.

And I am so mad at Nicole right now. She should have arrived at least two hours ago, but there's no sign of her.

I flip open my phone and send her another text, what must be the twentieth one tonight:

Please tell me Timmy fell down the well and you're busy rescuing him.

Five minutes ago, I sent: *Did the birds eat your trail of bread crumbs and now you're lost in the woods?*

Ten minutes before that, I sent: *If you're late because Shia LeBeouf decided to join you guys for dinner, I expect pictorial proof.*

I've flipped open my cell phone about nine hundred times, but I haven't missed a call and she hasn't answered any of my snarka-licious texts.

She ditched me for some fancy dinner and left me to suffer through this party on my own, and she doesn't even have the cour-tesy to text an apology. If she were here, we could roll our eyes at all these ridiculous things, and she could pretend she doesn't feel well and I could act like I need to hang out inside with her. The DJ could keep right on playing this horrible music, and my mom could keep entertaining clients.

What is she doing right now that is so important she couldn't leave? Eating soufflé? Gazing into Ben's soulful blue eyes? Running her perfectly manicured fingers through his perfect, spiky blond hair?

Thank God, I've hardly spent much time with both of them. Because I bet reality is even worse than my imagination.

She swore she'd be here, and she's not.

On top of that, my mom just walked right past me and didn't even make eye contact because she was discussing ways for some guy to bond his employees through team-building exercises. Yeah. That *so* belongs at my party.

Even my brother has ignored me: He came outside for about forty-five seconds, long enough to fill a plate with food and disappear again. Not that I was going to hang out with him or anything, but he could have at least tossed a "happy birthday" in my direction.

I don't want to be here, I don't want to be here, I don't want to be here.

Every time someone rounds the corner of the house—entering the backyard through the side gate—my heart speeds up for a millisecond and I perk up, hoping it's Nicole and Ben.

But it never is.

Suddenly I hear my mother's voice, magnified by a microphone.

"Kayla? Will the real birthday girl please stand up?"

Oh God. Was she parodying "Slim Shady"? Please make this not be my life.

Now that everyone's turned in my direction, I make my way through the crowd, onto the parquet floor, underneath the disco ball. Everyone has gathered around, and the DJ, wearing a sequined teal vest over a white tuxedo shirt, is standing next to the biggest cake I've ever seen in real life.

It's pink. With white fluffy frosted flowers cascading down all four layers. Sixteen candles—four on each layer—are lit and glowing. I think I've seen this exact cake on an episode of *Made* on MTV.

My mom is standing next to it, a grin on her face so big that I think her face might crack. "Do you like it? It's custom," she says. "Cream cheese frosting."

I swallow and nod, staring at the pink mammoth of confectionary perfection. Cream cheese frosting is the only thing about the cake that she got right.

The DJ starts up the "Happy Birthday" song, and the crowd joins in. It feels like they're getting closer and louder as the song goes on, and I want to run away from it all. I'm not a center stage kind of person.

When they get to the part about my name, the crowd falters, and I hear at least a few of them call me Kelly, while the rest say no name at all, and it makes a lump grow in my throat, threatening to choke me. I feel like such a fool, standing here, surrounded by people who don't even know my name.

The song ends and I'm still staring at the cake, my eyes beginning to sting a little. When I finally look up, a movement catches my eye.

Nicole and Ben have finally arrived, three hours after the party started. They're standing near the edge of the crowd, overdressed for my birthday, so I know they came straight here from their fancy dinner. Ben looks a little awkward in a white shirt and red tie, while Nicole looks right at home in a sleeveless red dress and silver stilettos. She must be freezing, but she's standing there as if it's August and not late September.

She leans into him, her long blonde hair brushing against his shirt, and he wraps his arm around her, kissing her temple.

They look so perfect together: both tall, blond, attractive. And

I'm standing over here, looking totally dumpy in a reject Old Navy dress with a horrible hairdo.

"Make a wish, honey!" my mom says, completely oblivious to my distress.

I shake my head, not sure if I can manage actual words.

"Don't be a party pooper!"

Anger surges through me as I turn to look at her wide, happy eyes. She's hardly talked to me all night, and she hasn't even noticed I'm hating this. Fury boils up in my veins, welling in my chest until I spit the word out at her. "Fine!"

My mom steps back a bit at the sharp edge in my voice. Her wide smile turns a little plastic, and her eyes dart around to the faces of her potential clients.

I close my eyes to calm the anger boiling in my stomach and also to block out the crowd around me.

I wish my birthday wishes actually came true. Because they never freakin' do.

And then I blow out the candles in one long, lung-zapping breath. As I do, I feel as though I'm blowing my whole life away— like a pile of dried-up leaves.

5

WHEN MY ALARM rings out, it's all I can do not to smash it with a hammer. In fact, if I had an actual hammer handy, I might do it.

I slap it off and then sit up in bed, rubbing my eyes. My blankets are twisted around me because I've spent half the night tossing and turning, angry about the disaster of my party.

I'm dreading today. I don't want to know if Janae told everyone about how my party was like one bad eighties movie or how I was trying to look cute in my ugly sailor dress. Or if my mom is annoyed that I blew out the candles and then promptly left and retired to my room and locked the door, blasting Blink-182 so I didn't have to listen to the crowd outside.

I yawn as I stand and stretch my arms over my head, grumbling about the start of another day of my less-than-stellar life, when I see something bright flash across the lawn below my window.

Pink.

Are there still workers here, taking down the party decorations?

I wrap my neon-green-and-orange plaid quilt around my body even though I'm wearing a dorky flannel pajama set that covers me from head to toe and lean against the windowsill to get a better look. Below me, the backyard looks exactly as it did forty-eight hours ago: plain old grass. The cedar fence is no longer adorned with flowers, the tent has disappeared, and the punch bowl—er, fountain—has been retired. The aggregate patio below me is once again sporting the black, wrought iron patio set, nothing more.

So what was that flash of pink?

I yank the window open and press my forehead into the screen so that I can look to the right and left of the house. And that's when I see it again: a burst of pink as it rounds the corner.

Hmm. This reeks of my brother. He probably has a water-balloon ambush planned, and he's trying to lure me outside. It's probably fifty-four degrees out. He'd just *love* soaking me.

And there's no way I'm falling for it. He's one of those people who will try the same gag over and over, as long as it works. And he did this exact thing a month ago. He set up camp and then threw the balloons at my window. I went out the back door to yell at him, and he totally slammed me with an explosion of water.

Maybe I can go around the front of the house and use the element of surprise to snag his own weaponry and use it against him. Years of playing little sister have shown me that brains are more powerful than brawn, especially if you're talking about my brains and his brawn.

I throw on a fluffy blue robe with clouds all over it. It was a Christmas present, which is why I didn't get the black one with a cute lime-green skull-and-crossbones design.

I take the stairs two by two and am at the front door in seconds. I click it open as silently as possible and then walk across the slate-tiled stoop and down the steps. I hoof it across the lawn, the grass cold and dewy on my bare feet. I tiptoe into the backyard. My brother is probably on the other side of the rhododendron bush, staring around the corner of the house, expecting me to exit out of the back door.

As I turn to shut the gate behind me, I feel it: hot breath on my neck, whiskers tickling my ear. Ew, my brother has a serious five o'clock shadow. So gross.

I spin around to face my brother, but I see nothing but dead air. And that's when I feel it again: hot breath, this time on the bare part of my stomach, between the top and the bottom of my blue flannel pajamas, where the robe has fallen open.

And when I finally look down, I scream and leap back, crashing into the gate and hitting my funny bone. Pain ripples up my arm.

The pony—the *pink* pony—its dark eyes widening, sort of jumps into the air and then plants all four feet, as if *I've* startled *it*. Its nostrils flare, and it takes in a big, quivery breath. It's not very tall—its back probably reaches my waist. Maybe it's a miniature horse and not a pony. Or are they the same thing? Either way, it's not supposed to be pink, and it's *definitely* not supposed to be in my backyard.

We stare at each other, seemingly frozen, until it spins around and trots away, its blue-streaked tail dragging behind. It lets out a long, shrill whinny as it disappears around the corner.

Someone has seriously messed with that pony. I'm guessing it was white at one time, because that's the only way dye that pink would ever take. And the mane is mostly white too, except those crazy electric-blue streaks.

And I swear to you, it had an ice-cream cone painted on its hindquarters. Three scoops. Sugar cone.

I rub my eyes a few times. This isn't real, is it? Did the little guy escape from a local farm? Who did this to him?

Or wait. If it's pink, it's probably a girl.

I stomp after it, annoyed that I've gotten out of bed for something this insanely ridiculous. Who paints a pony pink? Shouldn't that be animal cruelty or something?

When I round the corner of the house, I get a full view of the backyard and the totally empty expanse of grass. Huh.

I walk around the garden shed and peek inside, but the pony isn't in there, either. The side gate is open on the other side, so I walk around to the front of the house and stand on the sidewalk. I look both ways, down the street, but I don't see her.

I close my eyes for a long moment, half expecting to feel warm breath and whiskers again, but there's nothing. The pony is gone.

It's official: I'm crazy.

I go back to the house and walk into the entry, where my mom is putting on a pair of sensible black pumps, her hair blow-dried and curled to perfection.

"What are you doing outside?"

I stand there dumbly. "Um, looking for the paper. For a current-events homework assignment."

"It's on the counter," she says, giving me an odd look. It is *always* on the counter.

"Oh."

She stands to leave.

"Mom?"

"Mm-hmm . . . "

"Did you rent a pony for my party?"

My mom laughs. "Of course not, honey. You're too big for a pony."

And then she walks away, toward the garage door, where her shiny Lexus awaits. I watch her go, wondering if I'm crazy or if the perfect events coordinator doesn't even know what kind of activities she booked for her daughter's sweet sixteen.

Shaking my head, I go back to my room. Clearly, my brain doesn't function properly without twenty minutes of a hot shower.

And I only have nineteen before I'm late.

6

THE SECOND I WALK through the double doors and into the wide carpeted hallways of EHS, Nicole ambushes me.

"I am so, so, *so* sorry," she says.

I don't say anything, I just keep walking, clenching my teeth a little.

She walks backward in front of me, her blonde hair blowing in her face a bit. She sweeps it back with a newly French-manicured hand and looks me in the eyes. She's wearing a diamond pendant on a fine, delicate silver chain.

I wonder if it was an anniversary gift. I try to remember if she was wearing it last night, but I never got within a hundred feet of her, so I'm not sure.

"I completely, totally lost track of time. I swear I freaked out when I finally looked at my watch. We raced straight to your house, but we got stuck in traffic. There was this semi-truck rolled over, and we had to go around and . . . "

She seems to realize I'm not really listening.

"What happened is not important. I swear, I will make it up to you somehow." She stops walking and I'm forced to stop too, to keep from slamming into her.

I stare into her blue eyes for a moment. They are crinkled up in concern, like at any moment I may tell her she's as good as dead to me. I cross my arms. "I sent you, like, a hundred texts."

"My phone was dead."

I twist a strand of my damp brown hair, resisting the urge to just yank it right out. "The whole thing was a disaster, you know. The *whole thing*."

She purses her pouty, perfectly glossed lips. "I'll do your bio homework for a week! I'll loan you anything in my closet. I'll go to the concert of your choice."

I raise an eyebrow. "*Any* concert?"

"Any concert where they won't throw me in a mosh pit or something."

I screw my lips up to the side and give her a long, hard look.

Maybe if I had ninety-nine other friends, I could at least give her the silent treatment for a day or two, but my resolve is already weakening.

I cross my arms. "Swear? You're not forgiven until you actually do it, you know."

She lets out a long, slow sigh of relief. "I swear."

"Fine." I uncross my arms. It's sad how fast I just gave in. But obviously, she didn't mean to be so late. And I'm more mad about the stupid party than I am about her. "How was your anniversary dinner?"

She brightens. "The food was so amazing. I got this risotto

thing and OMG, my mouth waters just thinking of it. And the view! It's right on the Puget Sound, near Point Defiance. They have a deck, but it was closed for the winter. But the windows look right out over the water, and you can see all the ferries and sailboats and stuff. I could have stared at it all night. And Ben said the funniest thing about the waiter! We kept laughing all during dinner about it and at one point I actually spit out my soup, but Ben was really nice about it and pretended he didn't notice. It was so cute. We talked about you, too, ya know. Ben thinks you're a rebel. That's his word, not mine."

A rebel? Ben *thinks* about me?

"So," I say, feeling a new flush of anger that she clearly had so much fun without me. "It was worth missing my party."

"Yeah—no, no, of course not."

Argh. "Whatever. I'm over it." Except I'm not. "But you owe me, like, a hundred of your mint-chip brownies."

Her smile brightens. "I'll commence baking tonight."

We pick up a walk again, heading toward biology. "And also, you might have to do my bio homework for the rest of the *year*. I'm lost already."

Nicole laughs. "My mom is making us all go visit my grandma tonight, but what if we get together tomorrow? We can go over the cell diagrams."

I nod, and we step into class, the fight over my party mostly forgotten.

If only the party itself was as easy to forget.

★ ★ ★

AS I SIT in photography several hours later, I can't stop worrying about Nicole and the inevitable moment she realizes she's totally outgrown me. We may have resolved our dispute, but what if it's just the first of many?

If she abandons me on my birthday, just about anything could be fair game, right?

I should be working on the assignment that is sure to sink the only A I have, but instead I keep flicking glances over at her.

Right now, she's standing over a tray of developer, a pair of tongs in her hand as she swishes her paper around in the fluid. Today she's been developing an entire roll of photos of Ben, stuff they took while at their dinner last night.

I saw a few of them. They went walking on the waterfront afterward. She took pictures of him on a pier, and the sun is just a sliver on the horizon. The water stretches out behind him, beautiful and serene.

She wasn't kidding when she said they lost track of time. Because when the sun was setting, she should have been standing in my backyard, but she was an hour away, totally oblivious, happily strolling along Ruston Way.

I'm still kinda angry. I'd never do that to her! But I'm also a mixture of other things: worried, annoyed, concerned, sad.

The thing with Nicole is that we've both changed a lot in the last few years. We're either going to grow closer or farther, and I think I know which way things are going.

See, Nicole used to be truly unfortunate looking. I never cared that her face was covered in acne, that she was at least twenty pounds overweight, or that she was unusually short.

But whatever she's been doing to her face is working, and in the last year or two, she's sprouted like eight inches, I swear.

Which, since she hasn't gained a pound, means she's thin now, though she's still got way more in the chest department than I do. Her hair has grown out of the truly tragic haircut she had throughout junior high, too. She still has that edge of shyness about her, but it's disappearing more every day.

She's figured out that she's not a geek anymore. So now I just have to wait for her to figure out that I still am, and then she'll probably ditch me. If yesterday is any indication, things are getting hot and heavy with Ben, while our friendship is getting more distant than ever.

I lean into the countertop where my enlarger is sitting, trying to focus on my project and get the negative adjusted so it won't look fuzzy or cut off anyone's head. Considering I've already had a few days to work on this project, I should be further along.

I mean, Nicole is so far along she's not even worried about it; she's developing photos of her boyfriend instead.

Mr. Edwards wants us to do a "self-portrait." But his definition of self-portrait is clearly skewed, because we're not allowed to take any pictures of ourselves. It has to be something "representative" of ourself. And then we have to use one of the special effects we've been taught to make it more creative, like reversing the negative or changing the focus or something.

I picked this class because it sounded less torturous than one of those FFA agricultural classes or drama or, God forbid, choir. But as it turns out, I kind of stink. Apparently I have no vision.

Mr. Edwards has given me reasonable grades because I've managed to keep the technical aspects just perfect, but he keeps harping on how I need to use my "inner eye" and "watch the world around me" and "blah, blah, blah." Then he assigned our first major project—half of our first semester's grade—with a big emphasis on creativity. Ouch.

The worst part is he's one of those teachers that you really like—the kind that actually cares about his students and spends a ton of time outside class talking with them and helping them.

So I guess I feel a little guilty, turning in utterly boring work, week after week. But what else am I supposed to do? Some of the other people in this class just look at something and click, and it becomes insta-art. I just don't have that natural talent.

So now I have less than two weeks to finish this project, and at the rate this is going, I'll have a big over-exposed nothing. What else can I possibly take pictures of that represents me? A big empty bedroom? A phone that never rings? My mom's day planner that has precisely zero time for me in it? The back of Nicole's head as she's walking away or worse—making out with Ben?

Nicole puts her photo into the dryer and then packs up the stuff scattered around her enlarger. Class ends in a few minutes.

"What time do you want to get together tomorrow?"

Nicole zips her backpack shut. She looks pretty in the red light of the dark room. It makes her complexion look clearer, more flawless, and her blonde hair shines. "Um, like seven? I have a doctor's appointment right after school."

"Sure, that works."

Nicole tosses a few rejected Ben photos into the trash between our enlarger stands. "Cool."

The bell rings, and I groan and start packing up my things. Another class period . . . totally wasted.

As I shove the last of my things into my bag and turn to go, I toss a ruined photo into the trash, except I miss and it flutters to the ground.

I kneel down and pick it up to put it in the garbage, but Nicole's discarded photos catch my eye.

They're not too bad, actually. The first one is too blurry, but the second, of Ben on the pier, has a soft, ethereal focus to it, like the clouds have parted to shine down just on him. There's something wrong with one side, like Nicole caught her finger in the frame, but the center, where Ben is standing, staring over the water, is perfect.

I glance around the room. No one is looking at me.

And then, feeling as if I'm stealing the *Mona Lisa*, I tuck the photo into my binder, my heart racing.

7

I TOSS AND TURN that night, dreaming of Ben and Nicole making out, giant cameras chasing me around with bright flashing lights, and thousands of punch fountains overflowing with pink liquid. Except the liquid is lava, and I spend the dream running from it. By the time I open my eyes, I'm in a decidedly grumpy mood. What I really need is an IV of caffeine and about a hundred Krispy Kreme donuts.

As I yawn and stretch, I swing my legs out of bed and start to stand, but something wobbles beneath me and my legs slide out in opposite directions and I slam to the floor, my face bouncing off the carpet. My teeth smash against my tongue, and I'm pretty sure I've nearly bitten it off, because the metallic taste of blood fills my mouth.

It all happens so fast I wouldn't have been able to save myself in normal circumstances, let alone four seconds after waking up.

What the?

Then I open my eyes and everything comes to focus.

I can only stare, my mouth hanging open and my eyes bugging out.

Gumballs.

Thousands of them.

Giant tubs and little packages and huge buckets. They're stacked up around me and they're rolling underneath my bed and I'm lying on at least fifty.

All I can do is stare, my cheek still smashed to the Berber. This many gumballs would cost hundreds of dollars. Did my brother rob a candy truck?

I sit up a little, wincing because that fall did *not* feel good, and get a better look at my room.

The gumballs are on my desk and windowsill and chair and stacked up against the walls and . . . there is not a square inch of my room that is gumball free. I try to swing my legs underneath me and am halfway to my feet when a few gumballs slide out from underneath me, I go down in the splits, then shriek in pain and fall over again, my thigh pulsing as if I pulled a muscle. A few gumballs shoot out the door and hit the hallway wall, then bounce out of view.

I decide to skip standing and crawl toward my closet, raking my hands back and forth in front of me to clear a path. It doesn't work very well, because they just roll in front of me again. It's like I'm in a sandbox, except the sand is gumballs. Or maybe it's more like the big ball pit at Chuck E. Cheese.

All I need is a change of clothes and I can go to the bathroom and get ready. Then I can go find my brother and strangle him.

I make it to the door and twist the knob, then realize belatedly

I've made a huge mistake: I've underestimated the size of this natural disaster.

Hurricane Gumball is clearly a category five.

The door flies open and nails me in the chin, and gumballs pour out in an avalanche of rainbow colors.

I roll back and then curl up and cover my head as they rain down, bouncing off my elbows and head and pooling around me. The sound is intensifying as they hit each other, bounding and ricocheting through the room.

This is so beyond ridiculous. How did he even do this? Did he slip some Benadryl in my soda last night to really knock me out? He must have had help, too. Because it would take a few people to get all this done in a few short hours.

He is so going down.

I settle for yesterday's jeans and a reasonably clean Pac Man T-shirt and crawl toward the exit, which could really use a neon flashing light just to spot it amid this mess. I hope my brother realizes that he is totally, completely responsible for cleaning this place. He'll need about a hundred trash bags and a snow shovel.

I roll out the door and head into the bathroom, shutting the door behind me. Whew. If I never see another gumball in my life, it will be too soon. I can't believe I was ever obsessed with those things. My mom used to say I was going to break my jaw from chewing so much.

I glance at myself in the mirror as I climb into the shower. I have a big pink spot on my chin where the door slammed into it and blue and yellow streaks all over my arms from the gumballs. Very stylish.

I take a long shower, totally ignoring the fact that I'll probably be late for school. I can blame it on my brother if my mom notices. After I'm totally prunified and I've erased the rainbow smears all over my skin, I get dressed and go to find my brother.

He's sprawled out on the floor in the den, staring at the coffered ceiling, listening to his iPod. His eyes are droopy, like he's barely awake, and he's wearing camo pants with a ratty thermal shirt. He really is a slacker.

He doesn't notice my approach. I don't say a word, I just yank the earbuds out of his ear. His eyes snap open and he sits up, rubbing at his ear. "Ow! What was that for?" he asks, glaring at me.

"Don't pretend you don't know." For good measure, I give him a little kick with my sock-clad foot. His hand darts out and he grabs my ankle and before I can get it back, he yanks and I end up on the ground next to him.

"I don't," he says, moving to put his earbuds back in. "Go take a Midol."

I reach for the earbuds again and he stops. "Fine. I'll play along. What did I do now? Scratch your *Superbad* DVD? Spit in your Cheerios?"

I cross my arms and glare at him. Why couldn't I have had a sister? A wise, helpful one? I can barely be in the same room with my brother without wanting to strangle him or at least take some tweezers to his unibrow. "One word: gumballs."

His look is totally blank. No satisfied smirk, no laughter, no twitchy eyes as he realizes I've figured it out. Hmm. This doesn't really add up.

"Argh! Fine, come with me," I say, getting up and yanking

on his T-shirt so hard it strangles him. He rubs at his neck and gives me another death glare, then sighs and gets off the floor. He knows just as well as my mom how stubborn I am, so he gives in easily.

We ascend the stairs and head to my room. I'm only halfway there when I see the first few gumballs in the hallway. I step aside and Chase walks past me, and when he gets to the doorway, he bursts out laughing.

I just stand there, glaring, as he continues to laugh, finally doubling over and holding his sides. He periodically glances up again, peering further into the room to see the candy, and that only sends him into more fits of laughter.

"Best. Thing. Ever," he finally gets out between breaths. Then he actually falls over, lying on the floor, still cackling.

"It is not! It's a disaster and you need to pick it all up!"

He stops laughing, though the grin never leaves his face. "Hey, I didn't do this. I'm not picking it up."

"Yes you did! I sure as heck didn't do it."

He shrugs. "Someone did, and as much as I want to take credit for it, I can't. It wasn't me. I'm not even sure where one would find this many gumballs."

He sits up and leans into the doorway again to get another look, then nods vigorously.

He has a point. And based on his expression, I almost believe him.

Almost.

"Whatever. I'm going to school. This better be gone by the time I get home. I know you're probably really busy with feeding the homeless and rescuing distressed kittens from trees, but I expect you to pick it up."

He sits up and puts his hands up to stop me. "Dude, I am not touching this. I have better things to do."

"Fine. I'll just tell Mom about that stash of magazines under your—"

"Okay! Okay, say no more," he says, waving his hands to stop me before I finish my sentence. God, does he think Mom has the place bugged?

I grin and turn around, triumphant as I descend the stairs and head out the door. It's a twenty-minute walk to school, and class starts in ten minutes.

Normally I find the walk relaxing, especially when the weather is nice like it is today. It's warm enough that I don't need a jacket, just a reasonably thick hoodie. The cherry trees that line Marrymoor Lane, where I live, are half bare, their leaves scattered on the sidewalks, crunching beneath my feet as I head to school.

But instead of enjoying the walk, I feel distracted and annoyed. I can't stop the nagging feeling that something strange is happening.

Because my brother never did ask me what I thought of his pink pony. Plus if the gumballs were from him, wouldn't he sit outside my door and wait for the payoff? Why would he play those pranks if he didn't even get to be there for his moment of glory?

Something isn't right here.

8

BY THE TIME school is over, I don't feel like going home. It seems like the whole house is becoming a disaster zone, and if my brother isn't done cleaning up the gumballs yet, I sure as heck don't want to show up in time to help.

Avoidance has always been my best coping mechanism. Why stop now?

So I make a rash decision: I'm going to Ben's motocross event tonight. It's nothing huge, but it's close enough that I can walk there in a half hour. I know if I go, I won't think about anything the whole time he's riding, and that is exactly what I need.

I'm going to test for my license Friday. With a little luck, this will be the last time I have to walk all over town. Especially if I get to use my brother's old Ford Ranger. So why not make the most of it and take a nice leisurely walk tonight?

The event is held at a privately owned outdoor dirt track, one filled with giant jumps and ramps and crazy things that no sane person would launch themselves off of but that Ben handles with ease. There's a set of stands about ten rows high and thirty or forty feet long, so it only holds a hundred spectators at best, and today it'll be less than half full. Wednesday nights are the weekly expo night, a day for the riders to practice without paying massive entry fees or stressing the competition. Basically, they goof off, and people come out to watch.

It's warm for fall, and I stop at a gas station along the way and buy a Mountain Dew. It'll go nicely with the Tupperware container filled with Nicole's famous mint-chip brownies. True to her word, she baked a batch just for me to make up for missing most of my party. I'm still pretty ticked at her, but the brownies melted a little bit of my anger.

I walk along the dirt shoulders of the country road, my snack in hand, feeling relaxed for the first time in days. It's hard to be uptight when you're walking along cattail-filled ditches, surrounded by big grassy fields filled with horses and cows, and the sun is shining, warm and bright, for what might be the last time this fall. I walk under a row of maples, the big orange leaves so thick on the ground they're ankle deep.

This was exactly what I needed—a night to get away from everyone and stop worrying about things.

I weave my way between the cars in a grassy field that doubles as a parking lot, my black Converse sinking into the mud. The trucks in the field outnumber the cars at least three to one. I shouldn't find it so amusing, but I do. In Enumclaw, trucks will always reign supreme.

I make my way up the rickety wooden stands, picking my way between a handful of strangers, and find a place to sit where the white paint isn't peeling. Winters in the Pacific Northwest aren't kind to structures like this, but on a sunny autumn day like today, I'd never want to live anywhere else.

The riders have already started goofing around. A guy on a bright orange two-stroke launches off a big dirt jump and clears several riders who are sitting below him, their helmets on, talking.

Ben is easy to spot: he has a bright-yellow bike and a blue helmet, plus a jersey with a black-and-royal-blue design on it. His number is 9, which has been my favorite number since the day I went to a race with Nicole.

Nicole says the expo nights and Ben's races are long and boring, loud and dirty. Ben doesn't care if she goes, because it's not like they get to talk any.

It kind of kills me that they have so little in common. I've spent so much time avoiding being around both of them at the same time that I don't really understand their relationship at all.

I don't even know if she loves him, like I do. And if she does love him, why isn't she here?

Although I recognize two people from school sitting in the front row, they don't look at me or talk to me. Nicole will never know I was here, because she'd never show up and Ben's wearing a helmet and riding by at a zillion miles per hour.

Ben rights his bike and kick-starts it in one try. It revs to life, a deep rumble that gives away all of the after-market parts he's painstakingly installed. I know, because he talks about it in math class. I feel like I know as much about his bike as he does. I wonder if Nicole knows he spent all of last weekend installing an extended swing arm.

His boots are almost knee high, with a color pattern that

matches the shirt and pants. He wears goggles over his big helmet, so I can't even see his face.

It doesn't matter that no one else recognizes him. I know what he looks like underneath all that gear. I've memorized it.

He takes off in a wheelie that lasts what must be a hundred feet, then drops the front wheel and shifts into a higher gear as the bank ahead of him looms closer. He rides around the half circle, going higher up the wall, until he's nearly sideways on it and the only thing holding him to the dirt is speed and centripetal force. By the time he comes out of the curve, he's hitting third gear and heading for a series of small bumps.

He launches off the first one and sails over the next two without touching the ground, then lands and quickly guns the engine. The jump ahead of him is sharp and angled, and as he hits the crest, the bike flies into the air.

Ben takes both his legs off the pegs and puts them on the same side of the bike—the right side—and does this crazy scissor walk. He manages to get his left leg back onto the correct side so he's straddling the bike again just as he lands. His toned legs bend with each bump and jump.

My heart is flying with him. I can't believe he can do all this and not die of fright or the adrenaline rush. I wonder if he would ever let me ride his bike, ever show me what it's like to be weightless for those precious seconds.

He slows only slightly as he rounds another corner and heads for the next part of the course, three large hills in a row. One after another he hits them, sails into the air, lands and rides another twenty or thirty feet, and then launches again. Occasionally, he throws in a trick, turning the wheel or letting go with both hands midair.

I don't even realize I'm holding my breath until my lungs start to scream for oxygen, and I have to take in a long, ragged gulp.

I don't know how Nicole could be bored by this.

Ben hits another jump and turns his bike sideways for a minute—on purpose—and then turns it straight again just in time to land. The crowd screams and claps. I get to my feet with them and holler at the top of my lungs, clapping and whistling.

Ben is one of the best racers in the area. He says he doesn't want to get into the really intense circuits yet, but he definitely could. The first day of math class, I saw all these stickers on his binder, and I asked him about them. He said the local bike shop pretty much gives him any parts he wants so they can put their sticker on his bike and a patch on his shirt. I believe it. He's that good.

My cell rings, and I flip it open without thinking. "Hello?"

"Hey Kayla," Nicole says.

My heart wrenches in my chest, landing somewhere in my feet. I totally forgot we were going to get together tonight to work on the cell diagram. If I left *right now*, I might be able to get home in time to meet her there. Maybe.

"Hi," I say. I put my hand over the mouthpiece. Can she hear the bikes in the background? Jeez, this is so shady.

"My dentist appointment was short. Do you still want to come over?"

"Dentist? I thought you said it was a doctor's appointment."

She pauses. "Sure. But a dentist *is* a doctor. Just a different kind."

I scrunch my brow. I guess it makes sense. But it seems weird. "Oh. Well, I'm, uh, I'm kind of busy now. What about tomorrow?"

Guilt seems to be swelling and building in my stomach. I put my hand back over the mouthpiece again as a bike rounds the corner and heads in my direction. I seem to hold my breath as the rider revs the engine.

"What was that?"

"The lawn mower," I say quickly. Too quickly.

"You're mowing the lawn? Doesn't your mom pay someone to do that?"

I close my eyes and take a deep breath. "Yeah, my mom says these landscaping guys aren't keeping up. So . . . I got stuck with it. Can we work on the diagram tomorrow?" I ask again.

"I can't. We'll have to do it this weekend or something."

I nod, then realize she can't see me. "Oh, sure. See ya tomorrow at school."

And then I flip the phone shut just as another group of riders is flying by the stands.

This is so . . . not right. I mean, if I'm hiding the sound of the bikes from Nicole, there's something wrong with this picture. If I feel guilty, it's because I'm one big liar, secretly coveting her boyfriend.

I shouldn't be here, watching the one guy I can never have. I mean, how long am I going to do this to myself? How long am I going to torture myself and watch him from afar and obsess over him, all the while hiding it from my best friend?

I'm not in the mood to be here anymore.

I have to stop this. I have to stop wanting to be with him. It's stupid to put myself through it. Maybe I could do some kind of out-of-sight, out-of-mind sort of thing. Maybe I could learn to just get over my crush and let Nicole be with him and just forget Ben Mackenzie even exists.

This ends. Now.

I get up from the stands and start to trek down them, carefully picking my way between the spectators. I'm only halfway to the bottom when everyone around me stands, and a rumble of laughter builds and surrounds me.

For a second, I think I must have something mortifying stuck to my butt, and I try to wipe discreetly at my jeans.

But then I realize they're looking out at the track.

And pointing.

I look up, and my stomach drops to my knees.

Uh-oh.

It's the pony. The pink freakin' pony.

THE PONY is racing across the track, leaping and bucking and having the time of its life. It kicks its heels up and twists and then leaps into the air, all four legs so high off the ground I think it could have cleared a three-foot jump.

My mouth goes dry.

It scurries up one of the larger dirt jumps, its little hooves digging into the clay, and then stands and whinnies with its head held high, looking rather proud of itself as it stomps and digs at the top of the jump, like it's king of the freakin' mountain.

Or queen, maybe. It is pink, after all. It prances around, its stubby little legs bouncing and dancing, merrily oblivious to the destruction it is causing to my poor, frail little heart.

A bike revs loudly, and I tear my eyes away from the pony. A racer, obviously unaware that a ferociously pink miniature horse is already occupying the jump, is gunning the engine of his big black bike, racing straight toward it.

"Stop!" I screech, scrambling down the stands and leaping off the last one, then racing to the fence line. I tumble over the white-painted rails, crashing to the ground and landing in a puddle of mucky wet clay. It immediately seeps through my pants and sneakers. Ugh.

I climb to my feet, my Converse reaching maximum saturation and soaking through to my socks. I race toward the jump, waving my hands, screaming at the top of my lungs. It's probably hopeless—he'll never hear me over the whine of his bike, and he'll just smash right into the horse. Body parts will probably fly all over the place.

By now, the racer is at the bottom of the jump. Just when I think it's time to close my eyes and hope a miracle happens while I'm not looking, his helmet turns, just a bit, and I know he sees me. He slams the brakes and jerks the handlebars, sending the bike toward the edge of the dirt mound. He flies off the side of the jump, straight into a group of riders who are sitting in the middle of the track.

He misses most of them but rams into the back tire of the last bike—Ben's bike.

The whole bike gets knocked over, Ben going with it, and the other rider falls to the ground in a heap.

I stand there, in the middle of the track, the silence engulfing me as I stare. The crowd on the stands are still on their feet, watching the whole graceful display of awesome.

Oops.

The pony whinnies again, a ridiculously high-pitched, shrill little blast of a whinny. And then it scrambles down the hillside and lopes across the track, its bright pink mane and blue tail flapping happily in the breeze.

It's loping straight to me, like I'm its long-lost best friend. The peanut butter to its jelly.

No, no, *no*. Not good.

Stay away! I try to channel my thoughts to the pony, hoping, praying that it runs back to wherever it came from. But it bounds right over and skids to a stop, shoving its nose up against me and nibbling on my hoodie.

There must be a hundred eyeballs on me right now.

I'm afraid to look up—in *any* direction—because I don't know what I'm going to say.

I really should have left the pony to save its own fluorescent butt rather than screaming at the top of my lungs and falling in a mud puddle. It's not like it's *my* pony, even if it was in my yard yesterday.

"Is that thing yours?"

I want to close my eyes and block out the voice—*Ben's* voice—but I know it won't make him disappear. So I look up at him. He's taken his helmet off, so his blond hair is all mussed up, and he's got one eyebrow raised as he regards the pony. His blue eyes are positively sparkling, like he's got about a hundred jokes he'd like to tell. One side of his jersey and riding pants are smeared with mud, thanks to the other rider knocking him over.

"Um . . . no?"

"Is that a question?"

"No?"

"It sounds like one."

"Well, it's not mine, per se, it just hangs out in my yard some-times. Once. Just once."

"Do pink ponies hang out in your yard often?"

"No."

He smirks. My cheeks heat up. Ben looks really pleased to be witnessing this utter humiliation of mine. Usually, I'm the one dishing it up. "Do you think maybe the Smurfs might want it back?"

I raise a brow and put a hand on my hip. "Seriously? That's the best you've got? I'm standing here with a hot-pink pony, and that's really the best you can do?"

Ben laughs, and the tension seems to unwind itself from my spine, and I find myself grinning right at him.

"Really, Ben, I'm disappointed."

"What can I say? Laffy Taffy has failed me with their utter lack of pink-pony jokes."

Someone at the other end of the track fires up their bike, and I realize we're standing in the middle of everything, and no one is moving.

"Oh, uh, I guess that's my cue to get out of here. I mean, I have homework and everything, and it's a long walk home, so . . . "

"You *walked* here?"

Er. Probably shouldn't have mentioned that part. Now I look really crazy.

"Yeah. It's only, what, two-and-a-half miles? Less than forty-five minutes. And the weather is nice." And maybe somewhere along the way I can ditch the pony.

"No way. I'll give you a ride."

My stomach plummets as my heart soars. I shouldn't want this so bad or dread this so much.

We make it out to his big Ford pickup, and he pulls out a tiny little ramp. It must be about eight inches wide, barely wider than his tires. He jumps on the bike and rides it up the ramp as if he does it every day. Which, come to think of it, he just might.

I stand there while he's tying down the bike, the pony standing next to me and watching him. I half expect it to bust out with a few sentences, like Mr. Ed.

"I'm thinking I can back my truck up over there," Ben says, pointing to a big mound of topsoil. "And maybe we can persuade the pony to climb in."

"But it's not really *my* pony. We could just leave it here."

Ben gives me a *yeah, right* kind of look. "It probably lives somewhere around your house, and it followed you here. The least you can do is bring it back." Enumclaw, as a whole, is a pretty rural area, so this is actually quite possible. I wonder which one of my psycho neighbors let loose their dyed pony.

I sigh and rub my hand over my eyes. I'm not sure when I opened my backyard up as a hostel for runaway ponies, but whatever. "Fine."

If the pony would just gallop off right now, all would be right in the world. But it doesn't. It waits patiently while Ben backs his truck up to a mound of dirt, and then, damn it all, the stupid thing climbs right in like it's spent its whole life riding around in jacked-up pickup trucks.

Ben closes the tailgate, and then, to my surprise, he rounds the passenger door and opens it for me. "Your carriage awaits," he says, a little smile on his perfectly full lips.

Somehow I doubt Cinderella's carriage included a motocross bike and a fluorescent pony.

I walk to the door and pass less than an inch away from him. I want to lean in, to rest my face against his jersey and just breathe him in.

I wonder how he would react if I did that.

I have to grab the handle on the inside of the door and use the running board in order to climb in, the truck is so high off the ground. Ben closes the door behind me and then rounds the front of the truck and jumps into his seat without using either. When he starts it up, the big diesel engine rumbles to life.

We pull out of the grounds and back onto the road. Thank God it's less than three miles to my house, because I think I might pass out and I'd hate for him to see me drooling all over myself.

"You looked awesome today," I say, when I can't stand staying silent any longer. "You know, before the equine intervention."

"Thanks," he says. "Did you see me almost bite it off the big one? I got a little cocky and almost didn't get my feet back on the pegs."

He grins and looks over at me, and I find myself grinning right back and looking him in the eyes.

Oh boy. Must not look him in the eyes. I turn toward the window. "They say overinflated ego is now the number-one killer of teenage boys."

I can feel Ben's eyes on me. "Oh yeah? And what's the treatment?"

"I hear electroshock therapy works nicely."

Ben snorts. "What, no water boarding?"

I shake my head. It's getting harder to stare out the window when I want to turn and look at Ben. Instead I pretend some black-and-white cows grazing in a nearby field are the most fascinating thing I've seen all day. "No, too messy."

"I tend to think an hour with Mrs. Vickers and about two-dozen trigonometry problems will wound anyone's ego."

I forget to stick with the window and turn to look at him. "I know, and it's still the first month of school. We're all doomed."

He smiles, flicking on his turn signal before glancing over at me. His lips look perfect, curled upward like they are. I turn back to the window.

"We should get together sometime and work on review," he says. The truck lurches for a second as he misses second gear.

I forget to breathe for a second, until my lungs burn and I take in the biggest breath I can without Ben noticing it. "Yeah, maybe. At Nicole's house. She has the same math class during sixth period."

"Right," he says, nodding. "At Nicole's house."

By the time we've pulled up in front of my house, my death grip on the door handle is making my fingers ache. He pulls the truck up to the curb, and just as he's reaching for the keys to turn the truck off, I shove the door open.

"Thanks, Ben, see ya tomorrow!"

And then I dash across the lawn. I'm only halfway there when I hear his truck switch off. He rolls down the window and shouts to me. "Uh, Kayla?"

I stop, clenching my teeth for a second, my back still to him, and then I turn around.

"The pony?" He gestures with his thumb to the latest bane of my existence. I seem to have a lot of those lately. Is it possible to have multiple banes of your existence?

"Oh. Right."

"How do you think we can get it out?"

"Um, there's a retaining wall on the other side of that fence. Back your truck over there and I'll go open the gate."

I resist the urge to smack a hand against my forehead as I hustle into the backyard. Since we have a corner lot, there's another gate in the back. The yard used to slope a bit, so my mom had the landscapers build this big retaining wall and level it out. It'll be perfect for unloading the pony.

Ben backs his truck up and then jumps out, walking around the back and dropping the tailgate. It's nearly perfect—just an inch or two above the top block of the wall. The pony backs up a little bit and then spins around and jumps out. She jogs over to the middle of the yard, then drops to her knees, then her side, and starts rolling around.

Ben laughs, and I realize, abruptly, how close he is. I take a less than subtle step away from him.

He tips his head to the side and regards me with his brows scrunched. "Do I make you uncomfortable?"

"What? No. What?" The saliva in my throat is choking me, I'm sure of it.

Ben sighs and shrugs. "Nothing. Never mind."

"Okay, well, I'll get the gate. Thanks for the ride."

He nods, but he looks at me a second longer than necessary and then turns and heads back to the truck.

He honks his horn once as he pulls out onto the street, and I swing the gate shut so hard and fast it rattles the hinges.

And then I inhale deeply and for the first time in half an hour, I no longer feel short of breath.

10

WHEN I WAKE up the next morning, I open just one eye, slowly, and look around the room. After that pony . . . and then the gumballs . . . I feel like I'm about to be ambushed.

But the gumballs have not reappeared. Thank the lucky stars for that. I don't know what he did with them, but my brother followed through on something for once in his life. And a glance out the window reveals that there is no pony eating our perfectly green grass. Life is blissfully normal.

As I head toward my bedroom door, I hear a noise.

Coming from my closet.

Seriously! If my brother has done one more thing . . . one teensy, tiny little thing, I am telling Mom. Life has been insane since he moved back and it's all his fault.

I march over to my closet and yank the door open.

My heart lurches to a stop as I stare into a pair of wide green eyes framed by long, curly lashes. There is a girl I have never met in my life sitting in my closet. For real. I scream and jump backward, dashing over to my computer chair and shoving it between us, as if it's going to double as a weapon.

Death by rolling chair.

I realize that the chair is going to do little to protect me, and I frantically reach toward my desk to produce . . .

A ruler. I stand there with it out like a sword, still hiding behind the chair. Maybe if I'm really lucky, I can make some throwing stars out of paper clips.

The strange girl is just chilling on the floor, cross-legged, wearing the most hideous outfit I've ever seen: red-and-white-striped tights, a blue cotton dress, and a white apron. Her strawberry hair is curly and loose, tumbling halfway down her back in big frizzy curls, pieces of it sticking out all over. She has a smattering of dark freckles across the bridge of her nose and lips so full they don't look natural.

She looks to be around my age. Except she doesn't look the least bit concerned to be caught in my closet.

If this is my brother's long-distance girlfriend, he has seriously bad taste. Then again, she *is* dating him, so maybe she's the one who needs help.

"Who the heck are *you*?" I ask, backing toward the door as if she's a rabid dog. I am filled with an irrational fear that she's going to spring to her feet and leap onto me, like a jumping spider or something.

"Ann," she says, her voice tentative, barely above a whisper.

"Okay, *Ann*, what are you doing in my closet?"

"Sitting," she says, as if it should be obvious. She blinks a few times and stares at me in the oddest way, as if it's me who shouldn't be standing in my own bedroom.

"Yes, but *why* are you sitting in my closet?"

"I'm your best friend. I live here!" she says, her voice sort of solidifying, becoming less of a whisper. She has an odd, proper sound to her words. It's not an accent per se. But it reminds me of the way someone pronounces a word they just learned five minutes ago. The cadence is slightly off.

"No you don't," I say, stepping forward. She needs to get out of my closet. Now. What does she think this is, Narnia?

"Yes I do."

"*No*, you don't."

"*Yes*, I do."

I clench my teeth. She is seriously annoying. "Right. And who are you?!"

"Ann," she says again.

"Ann who?"

"Just Ann."

"There is no *just* Ann."

She stares at me. I blink a few times, hoping she disappears. There's something oddly familiar about her. I step out from behind the chair to get a better look at her, still holding the ruler out.

If all else fails, I can measure her to death.

"Do I know you from somewhere?" My voice sounds more fearful than I'd like, and I clear my throat.

She laughs just a little bit, and for some reason it annoys me. Who is she to laugh when she's a trespasser? "Of course, Kayla. We have known each other for over eight years."

She knows my name. My stomach twists around. I don't understand this. She's freaking me out. Should I just run out and go find my brother? Maybe she's some escaped crazy person. Maybe she watches me through my window.

Note to self: Get new drapes.

"You need to get out of my closet," I say, my voice still shaky. I am not equipped to deal with trespassers before seven a.m.

"It is not my fault you shoved me in here."

Huh? "I did *not* put you in there. That's ludicrous. I'm not running a hostel."

Maybe a yardstick would suffice, but this ruler is feeling tinier and tinier in my hands.

"I've been in that box for five years," she says, pointing to a white box at the back of the closet. "It is not nearly as comfortable as your bed was."

Ann crawls forward, out of the closet, and unfolds her legs. As she's getting to her feet, she sort of trips and tumbles forward, crashing into my rolling chair and sending it slamming into the wall. I take a giant leap back.

The chair leaves a big indent in my perfect plum-colored drywall.

Great. At least my brother works at a hardware store.

She grabs ahold of the edge of my bed and draws herself to her feet, until she's standing at her full height, which looks to be quite close to my own five-foot five. She doesn't let go of the pole on my four-poster bed.

Actually, she looks kind of wobbly. Like those horses you see on Animal Planet just moments after they learn to walk.

As she's standing in front of me, one hand still gripping my bed, I get a good look at her. The whole room takes on a slow, tilted spin. Suddenly *I'm* the one who needs to hold on to a piece of furniture.

I know why she looks familiar.

She's dressed like my old Raggedy Ann doll. Is that why she was talking about that box? Did she dig through my things and see my old doll?

She looks like one big disaster. An outfit like that looks cute on a doll, but it looks atrocious on a teen girl. And with her hair sticking up all over the place and her pronounced freckles, she's gotta be the biggest loser I've ever seen in real life.

I cross my arms, annoyed. She thinks she can come in here and make fun of me for my onetime obsession with my Raggedy Ann doll? Is that what this is supposed to be? "Nice costume. A little early for Halloween, don't you think?" I ask.

Ann looks down at her dress, smoothing out the apron as she frowns. "You always liked it."

"Yeah, when I was seven!"

She shrugs and then finally lets go of my bed so that she can put her hands on her hips. She sways a little bit but stays upright. Jeez, was she pounding beers in my closet too? "I liked you better then."

Her voice has been morphing throughout our conversation, becoming more normal. The more she talks, the more she sounds like me and the more the worries multiply in my stomach. She must learn freakishly fast. All she had to do was hear me say a few words, and she's adjusting, changing to mimic me.

Why is she acting like she knows me? I'd remember someone who looked *that* goofy.

"You don't have to go home, but you can't stay here," I say, moving toward the door.

"I told you. I'm already home."

"You are not home. *I* am home. This is *my* room." My voice rises an octave. My brother would hear me if I started screaming, right?

But what if he's listening to his iPod?

"Our room," she says. She takes in my stance and then mimics me, crossing her arms and standing with her feet shoulder width apart.

Enough with this. I'm sufficiently creeped out. I take another step back and hold out the ruler again.

"Look, if you don't leave in the next thirty seconds, I'm calling the police."

"Why? Do you still have a crush on Officer Barrows?"

My eyes snap wide open. I never told anyone about that. When I was ten, I used to totally crush on the twenty-two-year-old cop who hung out in the crosswalk area at school. I would cross back and forth for no reason, probably driving him crazy.

I never even told Nicole about him; it was that embarrassing.

"How do you know about that?"

"You used to say you were going to marry him and live in a house with a white picket fence. And he would protect the—"

"I know what I said, but how do *you* know about it?"

She scrunches her eyebrows at me and gives me a *well, duh,* look. Why is it that I feel like the stupid one when she's dressed like a giant doll? "You *must* recognize me. I was pretty much your best friend for a few years. I know everything. Or did you forget about me once you stuffed me in that box?"

As her words sink in, I start laughing, spinning the desk chair around and plunking down on it.

This is rich. I wonder who put her up to this.

"You think you're *the* Raggedy Ann, don't you?"

Ann tries out a laugh, perfectly mirroring mine. It makes the hairs on my neck stand on end. It's like hearing myself laugh, played back on a recorder.

"I am not pretending, Kayla. It *is* me!"

"No, it's not! Raggedy Ann is a doll, dummy."

Ann sighs. "Aside from Officer Barrows, you also had a crush on the mailman, at least until they replaced him with the silvery-haired guy with the squeaky shoes. And you wanted to be a rodeo clown for about five minutes, until you saw a bull in real life. Also, your dad's middle name is Preston Lewis, which you always found ridiculous because it's two names, not one, and they both sound like surnames. Your favorite color is peach, even though you hate peaches because you find the fuzzy part totally unappetizing. In sixth grade, you discovered you started your period because—"

"Enough!" I say, covering my ears. No need to relive *that* memory.

With each revelation Ann had said, my heartbeat increased, and now it's galloping around my chest like a crazed animal.

She knows things I never told anyone, not even Nicole. And I'm not stupid enough to keep a diary or something. So either she's been living in that closet and eavesdropping on me for the last six years or . . .

No. That's completely, totally impossible. There is an explanation for this.

A logical one.

"Look, I have to go to school. So you can go back and sit in that closet and I'll go to class, and we can discuss this later."

Maybe if I can get her back into the closet and get the door shut, I can run from my room and get my brother to kick her out. Or maybe I really will call the cops. But I don't have time to figure out which option is better.

Ann shrugs, turns around, and heads back into the closet. When the door clicks shut and she's out of view, I nearly convince myself that I imagined the whole thing. But then I walk to the door and peek inside, and she's sitting on the floor amid my clothes, braiding her hair. I glance back behind her and see the white box where my doll had been, but it's empty.

I swallow and give her a weak smile and then shut the door again.

If only it were like a bank safe and I could spin it shut and lock her away forever.

Something tells me she won't be that easy to get rid of.

11

I'M NOT EVEN halfway to school by the time I should be walking up the front steps. I'm not so much walking as shuffling, dazed, deep in thought about the morning's odd developments.

Ever since my sweet sixteen, life has been turned upside down. It's like a clear before and after.

Before: normal.

After: insane clown posse.

I mean, Raggedy Ann? Gumballs? And a hot-pink pony? Maybe when I was little, I would have loved that stuff. I would have jumped for joy over the pony. Heck, if I'd known that ponies came in bright-pink colors, I would have begged for one. She even had the ice-cream cone on her hindquarters, like my very favorite My Little Pony.

I stop mid-stride then, my jaw so low it's nearly resting on the toe of my Chuck Taylors. It's as if all sounds have come to a screeching halt and the entire world has gone silent, except for the ringing in my ears. I can't see a single thing in front of me because it's all gone this sort of fuzzy gray.

I wish my birthday wishes actually came true. Because they never freakin' do.

No.

No, no, *no.*

Impossible.

I stand there, my eyes still out of focus, my breathing so hard that my chest starts heaving, like I just finished running the mile in PE.

I stare at nothing at all, trying to rewind the last few years and remember *exactly* what I might have wished for when I was nine years old, back when I was obsessed with that stupid Raggedy Ann doll. It was the year my dad left us. The year my mom was practically lost to the world, my brother was dealing with the divorce by staying out late with friends, and it was the year before Nicole moved to town.

I had no one.

I wish you were real, Ann. Then I would have a real friend.

Suddenly I need to sit, and there are no benches anywhere near me, so I simply plunk down in the middle of the sidewalk, cross my legs, and lean forward so my head is between my hands, my fingers on my temple, my damp, dark hair hanging in front of me. The chill of the dewy cement immediately seeps through my jeans, but I ignore it.

This is ludicrous. Wishes don't come true. And dolls don't come to life.

Ann *had* been acting weird, mimicking my posture and my

speech. It was like she still didn't know how to talk or walk and was figuring it out by watching me.

No, no, no. That's stupid. She's a human being, not a doll.

I blink a few times, though my vision doesn't come into focus. When I was seven, I was obsessed with blowing bubbles. Would I have wished for a lifetime supply of gum? I rack my brain, trying to remember what we did for my seventh birthday. It would have been the last time my dad and mom were together and we celebrated as a family.

I probably would have wanted something as trivial as bubble gum.

The pony. Ohmigod, the pony.

I definitely wished for that. I would have loved for my My Little Ponies to come to life.

I close my eyes for a long, silent moment, trying to clear the jumbled thoughts in my head. They're spinning around so fast I can hardly hear them.

I wish my birthday wishes actually came true. Because they never freakin' do.

This can't be real.

My party was three days ago. Every day, a new wish has appeared. First the pony, then the gum, now Raggedy Ann come to life.

This is not possible. No way.

I open my eyes and stare down at the wet concrete, taking deep, calming breaths. There is an ant crawling across the slab in front of me, but I'm so dazed I don't move away from it as it begins to climb over my Converse sneaker—yellow today, with Sharpie marker all over one of the toes from when I was bored in history class.

There could be a logical explanation to this, right? Like someone overheard what I said at the party and they're playing a joke. Maybe my brother and his friends all teamed up because they have very little else to do, and this joke is a real doozy.

But wait . . . did I say my wish out loud?

No, I only *thought* my wish.

Besides, even if I'm wrong and I said it out loud, how would they come up with all of this on such short notice? How could someone find a pony and dye it pink and get it in my backyard in less than twelve hours? Let alone have enough pink dye to change its color . . . So how does my brother, who has a brain the size of a pea, orchestrate something that insane?

Plus how did Ann know all those things about me?

And there's still the fact that Chase hasn't been hiding in the bushes to watch his tricks unfold. What's the point of a prank if you don't even witness the payoff?

And why would anyone spend that much money on gum?

Of course, the real kiss of death in my prank theory is that I've never told anyone my wishes. My brother—and anyone else, for that matter—couldn't possibly know that I wished that Ann could come to life and be my best friend.

I get up off the sidewalk and head back to my house.

I need to talk to Ann.

12

WHEN I YANK open the closet door, Ann is sitting on the floor, staring at the ceiling, her hair splayed out around her. She has a multi-colored string that has been tied in a loop and she's playing cat's cradle, or at least trying to, since it's meant for two people. Instead it looks more like a jumble of knots tied around her fingers.

"Oh good!" She sits up and holds out her hands. "I forgot all the good moves. You'll have to show me."

I just stare at her, totally ignoring her outstretched hands. "As if I remember! I haven't played that since fourth grade."

She scrunches her mouth together in a pout. It makes her look about twelve years old.

"I need to know if you're lying," I say, still standing in the doorway. I lean against the doorjamb and give her a good, long, serious look. She really is dressed exactly as I remember her. She's even missing her ugly white bonnet, the one I ripped off the doll because I hated it. At least she doesn't have a bald spot underneath, because the doll did.

"About?" She untangles her fingers from the string and then starts over again, trying to create a never-ending loop of *x*'s that once kept me entertained for hours.

"About being Raggedy Ann."

"Of course not. Why would I lie?" She looks up at me through her thick lashes, as if I'm the one being ridiculous.

"I don't know! A million reasons. Someone is paying you; you're really homeless; this is some kind of scam. I don't know. It just seems really, really unbelievable."

She shrugs. "Perhaps. I'm just happy to be out of that box. It's super-dark in there, you know. You could have at least left it cracked open."

I sigh and sink to the ground beside her, shoving the closet door open all the way. I lie back against the carpet and stare at the popcorn ceiling.

"Why are you here?"

Ann turns and lies down beside me, so that her strawberry tresses are nearly touching mine. "I've not a clue."

That makes two of us.

I should probably go to school, but I've already missed most of first period, and it's not like I could concentrate on cellular fusion when there's a life-sized doll hanging out in my closet. I'll just skip first and make it to second period once I get some of this figured out.

"I think you're one of my wishes," I say, a long moment of silence later. "I wanted you to be real when I was little."

"I don't follow." She turns her face toward me, and I can actually feel her breath on my cheek. So weird. Dolls are not supposed to breathe.

"A few days ago I said I wanted all of my birthday wishes to come true. And now they are. One every day."

"What were the others?"

"Gumballs. And a pony." I jerk upright. "Uh-oh."

"What?"

"That means I have twelve more to go."

"Wishes?" Ann asks. She seems a little slow. Or maybe I'm making no sense at all.

"Yes!"

I jump up and scurry over to my desk and rip out a sheet of paper from my magenta skull-and-crossbones notebook. I quickly scribble fifteen numbers in the left-hand column. I put a big *X* next to my first birthday, because I doubt I knew what a wish was then.

That means there are fourteen birthday wishes total.

I fill in *Raggedy Ann* next to my ninth birthday, *gumballs* next to the seventh, and I take a wild guess that My Little Pony was a sixth-year wish. That seems about right.

The rest of the list is left pathetically empty. Eleven blank spaces.

I stare at each number, trying to remember what I would have wanted most that year, but I have a hard time remembering that far back. What would I have cared about when I was four years old? Or ten, for that matter?

I draw a blank for each year until I get to the number fifteen, last year's birthday.

That was the year Nicole and I celebrated at Red Robin, and they brought me a big ice-cream sundae with a sparkler in it.

And Ben was there, several booths over, eating lunch with his friends. So I closed my eyes, made the wish, and blew out the sparkler.

I know what I wished for last year.

I wished Ben would kiss me.

13

SINCE GOING to trigonometry means sitting next to Ben, I decide to skip that one too. I'm *pretty* sure that only one wish comes true every day. But I'm not willing to test that theory. Not yet, anyway.

During gym, I get hit in the head with a volleyball and the teacher lets me sit out of class. It's not like I was doing anything other than standing there staring at the net anyway. I prefer to think of it as multi-tasking since I was deep in thought, trying to remember some of my childhood wishes *and* playing volleyball, even if I wasn't actually hitting the ball with anything but my head.

By the time I make it to lunch, I'm dying to talk to Nicole. The whole wish thing seems ridiculously unbelievable, but if there's anyone who will help me, it's her. If she doesn't take me seriously, I'll bring her over to my house and she can see Ann for herself. Also, we've been best friends for years, so she might have some ideas for the last few wishes on the list.

When I get to the lunchroom, she's in line for a salad, talking to Breanna Mills, one of the cheerleaders. Huh. I always thought Nicole hated Breanna, but they're laughing together about something, and she's clearly nowhere near scratching the girl's eyes out.

I guess if I can have a life-sized Raggedy Ann, it means anything can happen.

She catches me watching her and gives me the "one second!" pantomime, and I just nod and sit down at our usual table. She pays for her lunch, bids Breanna adieu, and heads over to me. She's a little bouncier than normal, or maybe it's just her hair. It looks like she curled it today, which I don't think she's *ever* done before. Nicole's hair is so straight and flat that it doesn't hold curls well.

Today, though, her hair looks like it belongs on a curling iron box, demonstrating how fabulous your hair *could* look if you bought their product. Perfect, spiral curls. Huh.

"Your hair looks . . . cute," I say. It does, too. But it's so different I can't stop staring at it as if it's freakish, which probably wasn't what Nicole is going for.

"Thanks! I had to get up at, like, five to curl it. I found this great new hair spray."

I nod and keep staring at her. It's not just her hair. Her skin is . . .

Flawless.

"Wow. You look . . . "

Nicole's grin widens. "We finally found a medication that totally works. Isn't it awesome?"

I nod. She looks radiant, positively glowing with happiness. "Yeah . . . I mean, wow . . . you look amazing."

Her grin widens and she gives a little spin, her curls tumbling over her shoulders.

I sense that something else is up, because Nicole doesn't sit down after her spin. She just stands there, holding her salad, grinning about her newfound beauty.

And then she finally drops the bomb. "Breanna says we can eat lunch at her table."

My jaw drops and I just stare at her. I can't believe she actually wants to eat at Breanna Mills's table. Or that we were actually invited to sit at Breanna's table.

I glance over at the alpha table, which is chock-full of jocks and cheerleaders. "There are no empty seats," I say, stating the obvious. I wouldn't sit over there even if there were several open seats and they were gold plated and heated and came with a personal assistant who would wipe my lips between bites.

Nicole's expression doesn't change as she glances back and sees that I'm right. She sets her salad down and sits across from me. She pops open the tab on her Diet Coke. "She's not that bad, you know. She's actually really funny."

I resist the urge to say, "Funny *looking*," because even I know that line got old in fourth grade. Instead I say, "Unless you're on the wrong end of her jokes. And just to remind you, we usually are."

Nicole just shrugs, but she obviously sees my point, because she nods too and then glances back over at them. It doesn't take much imagination to figure out what they're talking about. Probably planning their Stalin-like takeover of the cafeteria.

"I have a really, really crazy story to tell you," I say, once she's given up on being besties with the dictator.

"Yeah?" Nicole is chewing her salad and staring out the window.

"Yes. I feel like we've hardly talked since my birthday, so you have no idea what's been happening."

"Yeah, sorry, I've been crazy busy. . . . " Her voice kind of trails off and she stops chewing as she keeps staring out the window, the one that overlooks the courtyard where the seniors usually eat. "Are you seeing this?"

She uses her fork to point out to the windows. I follow her gaze, and when I see what she's pointing at, my mouth goes dry.

Uh-oh.

Code red.

Raggedy Ann has left my closet. Sound the alarm! Abandon ship!

She's standing outside playing hopscotch. She's still decked out in a blue-print dress, white apron, and neon-bright stockings. To make matters worse, she's added my black combat boots, so now she looks like Raggedy Ann on D-day.

I watch for a second, stunned, as a few of my classmates stop outside and talk to her. She stops playing hopscotch and puts her hands on her hips and starts a conversation with them.

Oh God, she's probably telling them she lives with me! This is the end of life as I know it.

"Uh, I think I ate a bad burrito or something," I say, getting up from the table. "Catch up with you later?"

Before she can respond, I ditch my hardly eaten lunch and rush outside. Raggedy Ann is so not on my happy list.

14

IT TAKES ME the full lunch period to stash Raggedy Ann back at my house, with a stern lecture about staying put. I make it back to class just as the late bell is ringing, my still-empty stomach gurgling in protest. Ann has moved up a notch on the list of people I am not digging right now.

During photography, Nicole and I make plans to go to a party-supply store in the nearby town of Puyallup, and I force her to stop at Wendy's along the way for fries and Frosties. Only after devouring both do I feel the world seems back to normal.

As Nicole parks her Cavalier in an empty space at the mall, my phone rings.

It's my mom. Weird. "Hello?" I answer as I climb out of the car. I pull the hood on my zip-up lime-colored hoodie, tucking my scraggly brown hair inside as it begins to sprinkle.

"Kayla?"

"Uh-huh."

"Did you skip school today?"

My eyes bug out and I look over at Nicole.

"What?" she mouths.

I shake my head, willing her not to talk. "Um, no. I was a little late, but I was there."

"I just got a call from your principal, and he begs to differ."

"I swear, Mom, I went to school today. I was late because I tripped and fell into a mud puddle right outside school, and then I ran home and changed. I missed a little class, but I went."

"I give you free rein because I trust you, Kayla."

Damn it, I actually snort, because what she's said is totally ludicrous. She gives me free rein because she'd rather work than hang out with me or Chase. I realize too late what I've done, and I can't undo it.

"What's that for?"

"What?"

"Do you have something to say?"

I roll my eyes. "Nothing, Mom."

"I give you everything, Kayla. I work hard for our family. Don't forget that."

"Mom, I gotta go. Talk to you later," I say, snapping my phone shut before I get myself in trouble.

Nicole is standing under the overhang near the mall entrance, waiting for me, and I jog across the parking lot to catch up. "What was that all about?"

"She found out I missed class today and wanted to lecture me about it."

"Lame."

"Yeah. She tries to act like she's mother of the year. So annoying. I could wear a giant chicken costume to school every day and she wouldn't even know unless someone told her."

Nicole nods. "Send a picture to her BlackBerry. Then she'd notice."

I grin. Nicole totally understands the dynamic in my family, and she always makes me feel better about how screwed up everything is despite the fact that life is perfect on her home front. She'll let me vent for an hour if I need to.

But today I don't want to think about it. I follow her into the mall, and we meander past all the little kiosks selling overpriced impulse buys and finally get to the costume store, our destination.

Although Halloween is still over a month away, the store is already fully stocked with choices. Scary hoods and scythes, presidential masks, skanky wench and witch options . . . the possibilities are endless.

"What if we do zombie queens?" I ask, picking up some green face paint. With my other hand, I grab some rubber teeth, ones that would make it look like your whole mouth was rotting out. I hold them up on either side of my face and give Nicole a cheesy smile as I model the costume options.

Nicole glances over her shoulder and then shrugs. "Hmm. I guess that could work."

I frown. Not the enthusiasm I'm looking for.

We've been planning since last year to crash homecoming dressed as something totally ridiculous. See, we went for the first time last year, as freshmen, and found the whole display of school spirit to be totally ridiculous. It starts with the pep rally, where the cheerleaders and football players parade around like kings and queens. And then later, at homecoming, they're actually *crowned* kings and queens, while the peons worship them.

Last year, just a month into our high school existence, Nicole and I were not yet wise to the archaic rite of passage. We thought we could show up without dates, have a good time, and get some fun pictures together.

But we apparently missed the memo that required that we show up in couture dresses on the arms of our dates in rented Calvin Klein tuxes. We were supposed to have corsages and salon-created updos. We were supposed to ride around in limos and eat hundred-dollar dinners.

We vowed that night that no matter what happened—even if we both got boyfriends—we'd come back this year in some silly costume and make fun of the whole thing. We knew if we *had* boyfriends that they'd be the cool type to go along with our goofy antics.

"I mean, if we wore tiaras and everything, we could mock both the dance and the homecoming queen. Dual purpose."

Nicole nods and picks up a tiara and gives it a close inspection. "I don't know, I'm not really feeling it." She puts it back on the hook. "We should check that costume place down the street."

"I doubt they have a better selection. This place is huge. I'm sure there's something here. What if we go as giant dolls?" I ask, turning to look at Nicole. She's staring at a his-and-hers costume of bacon and eggs.

"Huh?"

"Like, Raggedy Ann and Raggedy Andy. I have the perfect dress. You can go as Andy."

She curls her lip up and practically snarls. "No way."

"Fine, fine, you can be Ann, *I'll* be Andy."

"I meant the whole thing," she says. Her phone is vibrating, so she flips it open. It takes her about fifteen seconds to text something, and then she snaps it shut again.

I imagine the sort of text she's probably sending: *Oh, Benny boy, It's been a whole hour since I've run my fingers through your perfect, tousled blond spikes!*

I snicker, happy to have amused myself, because this whole afternoon is a bust.

Nicole is not into our costume idea anymore. I can tell. I'm just standing here, waiting for her to admit she's going to ditch me and the costumes and go to the dance with Ben, wearing a sparkly dress and heels. "Are you still into this, or are you having second thoughts?"

She snaps her phone shut. "Of course I am. We've talked about this for a year. There's no way I'm going to ditch you again, I swear. I promised I'd make amends for missing your birthday, remember? It's just that there's nothing here. Let's just go get smoothies. There's a salon next to Orange Julius that sells this awesome heat-activated curl spray."

That whole last sentence just makes me want to roll my eyes, but I don't, I just follow her out of the store, my heart sinking as we leave the costumes behind.

Maybe for my self-portrait photography project I'll just take a picture of a big empty hole, because that's how I feel.

15

THOUGH I DREAM that Ann and the pony run away to Mexico, I instead wake up early Friday morning to her leaning over my bed, staring me in the eyes, her nose touching mine.

She doesn't move when I open my eyes, either. She just smiles in this way that creeps me out because she's an inch from my face.

"I thought you'd never wake up!" she says, her green eyes flaring even wider so her thick lashes brush against her eyebrows.

"Uh, yeah, can you back up?" I'm surprised I haven't already knocked her over with my morning breath.

"Oh." She straightens up and takes a step back.

"Don't you need sleep?" I ask, sitting up in bed and pulling my blanket up around me. It's both creepy and weird to have a stranger watching you sleep. Even if said stranger was once a doll. Or maybe *especially* if said stranger was once a doll.

Ann shrugs and plunks down on the ground. "I've spent the last six years sleeping; I'm ready for adventure."

Great. Raggedy Ann wants to go Lewis and Clark on me. Somehow I don't think she's going to take kindly to me stuffing her back into the closet.

I cross my arms and scowl at her. "You and the pony are supposed to be in Mexico."

"That pony?" Ann asks, pointing out the window.

I hold my breath and then turn to look out my window. *Please be wrong.* I haven't seen the pony since Ben brought it back to my house, and I was crediting my strategically placed open gate. In the last twenty-four hours, I'd convinced myself that it was long gone.

But it is *so* not. I watch the pony graze on my mom's shrubbery. What am I supposed to do now? Does the Humane Society accept ponies? What about pink ones?

That's when I hear the washing machine start up.

My mom is home. And so is the pony. This is not good.

"You have to hide that thing!"

I leap to my feet and run toward the door. "Climb out my window, use the cherry tree to get to the ground, and then go get that pony into the garden shed, okay? I'll keep my mom distracted. Then climb back into my window and wait in here."

I start to step outside my room, but I trip on something and fly to the floor, skidding a couple of feet and totally skinning my chin.

A gumball bounces off the wall.

Stupid, *stupid* gumballs! I am going to . . .

Pony. Pony is the priority right now. I scramble back to my feet and am halfway out the door when I turn and give Ann another look. She's got one leg outside the window, on the roof, and the other on the carpeted floor of my bedroom. "I repeat, *come back in here.* She can't see you either or I'm totally screwed!"

I run down the stairs, taking them two by two. My mom is in the laundry room, which has no windows, but any second she'll walk into the kitchen, probably grabbing a cup of coffee along the way. She'll look out the window as she pours, and she'll see a bright-pink pony.

With an ice-cream cone on its butt.

I can fake like I have nothing to do with the pony, but unless I get the wishes to stop, crazy things are going to keep happening, and my mom is going to notice that there is only one thing they all have in common: me.

I slide around the corner in my socks just as my mom is walking out of the laundry room. "Mom! So good to see you," I say, walking toward her. I position myself so that in order to talk to me, she'll have her back to the window.

"Good morning," she says, one eyebrow raised. I think she already knows something is up. When does a sixteen-year-old race into the kitchen to talk to her mom? "What happened to your chin?"

"Huh? Oh, nothing." Suddenly it burns, like one big scarlet letter. Must act casual. I put a hand on my hip and lean against the countertop. "Um, so, I'm thinking of trying out for . . . " My voice trails off. Softball? No way she'd buy it. The school play? Probably not. "Captain of the debate team."

Great, that makes no sense either.

I let my gaze slip over my mom's shoulder. Raggedy Ann is racing toward the pony, who quickly spins on her haunches and starts trotting across the lawn, a giant chunk of our shrubs dangling out her mouth. The pony lets out a long, shrill whinny as it disappears out of sight, and I burst into a cough to cover it up.

My mom narrows her eyes and gives me an odd look. "Don't you have to be *on* the debate team to be the captain?"

"Oh. Um, yes. I mean, well, I *meant* that I was going to try out for the debate team *with* the captain. The captain . . . runs the tryouts."

Also, I'm going to set my hair on fire.

"Oh. I had no idea you were interested in debate," she says. I don't think she's buying my story. But she hasn't figured out what's wrong either, which is practically just as good.

"Yes. I'm . . . "

I narrow my eyes. The pony canters by with Ann's apron in her mouth. Ann appears, her arms flailing over her head, and the two disappear to the right.

"Do we have any carrots?" I blurt out.

"Carrots?"

"Yes. I would really love a good breakfast carrot." For some reason I flex my bicep as I say it, as if a carrot is going to give me huge muscles. Great. Maybe my mom wants tickets to the gun show while I'm at it.

My mom tips her head to the side. "Are you feeling okay?" She reaches out and touches my forehead.

"Yes! Fabulous. The carrot?"

My mom nods, still giving me a strange look, and heads toward the fridge. While she is leaning in, the door blocking me from view, I rush to the window and give Ann a "beheading" signal, as in, *knock it off and catch that stupid pony.*

She practically leaps into the air at my look and scurries after the pony. She has her apron back, and she's holding it up like it might double as a lasso.

Whoo boy, maybe I should have been the one to chase the

pony while Ann pretended she was a classmate. But she seems like she totally does not understand the art of acting cool, and I doubt she could pull off even thirty seconds of talking to my mom. This is evidenced by the fact that she's flapping her arms around like a chicken at this very moment.

I'm almost back to my mother when she triumphantly produces a carrot. She holds it up, but then her face scrunches a little as the carrot sort of leans to the side.

"That looks kind of rubbery," I say, reaching out and taking it from her. I can almost bend it in half. Ugh. I bet the last time my mom went grocery shopping and bought something other than frozen dinners was August.

Of 2006.

"Gross, let me toss that," she says, reaching out to take it back.

The garbage can is right by the window, with a full, unobscured view of the backyard and the circus act currently being performed by Ann and the MLP.

"No! It's fine, see?" I take a rubbery bite and then chew with a big smile and a rumbling, revolting stomach. This thing is disgusting, like carrot-flavored bubble gum.

My mom gives me another odd look. I glance to the left and am relieved to see Ann has the apron around the pony's neck and is leading it into the garden shed. Finally!

My mom just shrugs and then heads over to her coffeepot just as the garden-shed door swings shut. She pauses for a second and looks out the window. I wonder if she caught that last movement of the door.

She can't have. But I hold my breath anyway.

"Are you ready for your driving test this morning?" she asks, her back to me as she puts the coffeepot back on the hot plate.

I nod, my mouth still full of rubbery carrot. "Yep," I say, pieces of orange falling out of my mouth.

It's only a small stretch of the truth. If my mom had taken me driving even once in the last month, I'd be a little more confident. I've hardly been behind the wheel for a second since driver's ed ended last summer.

"Good. I have a quick errand to run and I'm going to drop Chase off at work, and then I'll come back and grab you. We should head out by seven thirty. That sound okay?"

I nod. It seems like my mom has been talking forever while I gag on the rubbery carrot. "Sure."

Then I dash out of the room, spitting the carrot into my hand as soon as I'm out of view. That was too close for comfort.

I need a plan.

I take the stairs to my bedroom two by two and am stepping through my door just as Ann falls through my bedroom window.

I stare at her for a second, realizing my life is about to get tossed in the toilet if I don't figure this out. "Okay. So, I have you . . . a pony . . . gumballs . . . "

I sigh and sink onto the floor. There's a fourth wish waiting for me. *Today.* Somewhere. I don't even want to *guess* what kind of havoc I'm going to encounter. They're getting worse every day.

"You're just going to have to stay here all day," I say, looking up at Ann. "With the pony."

Ann sits down across from me, carefully placing her legs until she mimics my way of sitting. On her it looks like a yoga pose. Any moment she's going to close her eyes and start saying, "Ooohhhhhhhmmmmm."

"I don't want to. Your school is more fun."

"Ann!" I say, my voice a little too loud. I lower it. "You don't get it. School only allows *students* on campus. Visitors have to register at the office and be escorted around. You can't just show up."

She pouts and crosses her arms.

"And that pony," I say, pointing out the window, "needs to be watched."

"But why do *I* have to watch it?"

"I can't! I have to be at school or I'll get in trouble."

"FINE!" She stands up and stomps her feet. "I'll watch the pony. But you owe me!"

Pft. I don't owe a doll and a My Little Pony anything. It's *them* ruining *my* life. But I don't say that aloud.

We wait until my mom leaves in her Lexus, my brother in the passenger seat, before we go downstairs and outside.

The shed is big, probably a dozen feet wide and fifteen or so feet deep. But I can tell from thirty feet away the pony doesn't like it. It's stomping its feet and kicking the walls.

Thank *God* my mom didn't hear this from the kitchen.

"Do you *see* why it can't be left alone?" I ask, shooting a pointed look in Ann's direction.

Ann just rolls her eyes. I narrow mine, because I know she had to have learned that from me, and I try to remember when I rolled my eyes in front of her.

I open the shed door and the pony tries to muscle past me. I yank Ann inside and shut the door. It takes a moment for my eyes to adjust.

I just found the gumballs. They are in trash bags, stacked up all over the place. I can't even see the lawn mower or the shovels in the back of the shed. One of the bags has been ripped—or maybe kicked—open, and gumballs have spewed out all over. No wonder the pony doesn't like it in here. The gumballs take up two thirds of the space.

"So just hang out in here. If you're careful, you can go inside and grab some snacks or something. But don't let anyone see you. I'll be back at two thirty, okay?"

Ann heaves a great big annoyed sigh and nods. "Okay, great. See ya later."

Then I dash out before she can stop me and hope she doesn't pop back up before my mom comes to pick me up.

☆ ☆ ☆

THANKS to this morning's ridiculous antics, I nearly blew my driving test. I started thinking about Ann's horrid clothing as I was parallel parking, and I got docked six points for bumping into one of the cones. Then I could have sworn I saw the pony wandering the sidewalk, but it was just a really overweight lady in a bright-pink T-shirt.

In the end, though, I received my hot-off-the-presses license. My photo is terrible and it's just a paper temporary until the real thing arrives in the mailbox, but *I have a driver's license.*

With all the other crap going on right now, it seems a little anti-climactic. But either way, I have a license, and I can't wait to show Nicole. It'll have to wait until photography because I missed bio. My mom drops me back off at school in time for the last twenty minutes of math class.

As I step through the door, the teacher is droning on up front. I pause and hand her my little pink slip of paper. She scans over it and nods, and then I head toward my seat.

Just mere feet away, I have a horrifying realization: If I don't know what today's wish is, it could be Ben. He could kiss me. Because near as I can tell, the wishes haven't occurred in order.

So who's to say my wish from my fifteenth birthday couldn't happen today?

My breath hitches in my throat, and my mind seems to slow down and nearly stop functioning completely. It's like every coherent thought I have just got stuck in the mud. I'm halfway to my desk, and my feet slow down, scrape along the carpet.

Ben wouldn't try to kiss me in class, would he?

I finally plop down in my seat, promptly sliding to the edge, trying not to be obvious, and lean against my left elbow, away from him. I'm barely balanced on the chair, but I try to look cool and casual as I jot down the day's math homework. I shift around, hoping to find a way to maintain this position, and something falls out of my jacket pocket.

A bright yellow gumball. It rolls down the aisle between the desks in my row, ultimately stopping when it hits a guy's faded black Adidas sneaker. I am so sick of those stupid things popping up all over the place. I swear it was *not* in my pocket ten minutes ago.

Ben gives me a look for a long moment, his eyes narrowed just a bit, taking in my odd posture. Great. I've been here two minutes and he can already tell something's up. I pretend not to notice, as if it takes every ounce of concentration to write down two sentences.

Ben finally just turns his attention back to the teacher. If he asks why I'm treating him as if he has bubonic plague, I'm not sure what I'll tell him. *Oh, I'm sorry, but according to my fairy godmother, you're totally going to kiss me today!*

My left leg is already burning from holding my weight up. There's no way I can make it through a whole class period while this far out of my chair.

I think of Nicole and what an awesome friend she is and force myself to keep sitting there, trying to breathe normally and not as if my legs are about to burn through my worn-out blue jeans.

I remember all the cool things Nicole has done for me over the years. One time while we were on a lame field trip, I split my jeans open because I thought it would be cool to try and climb up a welded metal sculpture. (It wasn't.) To make me feel better, she ripped a big hole in her jeans so that her polka-dot underwear was showing. If you knew how shy Nicole was—how totally mortified she gets over the simplest things—you'd realize that this was a really, really big deal.

Also, there was the time she told her parents she'd never go to Disneyland unless I could go with. And that time she helped me paint my brand-new room lime green and then repaint it plum purple when we decided that the lime green gave us headaches. We rode our bikes back and forth to the hardware store like a dozen times, collecting paint chips and checking them out in the natural light of my bedroom.

In other words, I cannot let her boyfriend kiss me because of some cursed wish, even though it sounds like total heaven. You do not betray a friend as awesome as Nicole. Even if she *did* miss most of my horrendous and fateful birthday party.

My leg starts to shake, in tiny little tremors at first until it starts to become more obvious.

"Are you okay?" Ben whispers as Mrs. Vickers continues to drone on and on up front.

I nod and hold my breath until he sits back again in his chair. This isn't working. I'm going to have to edge back into my seat a little bit, before I—

And that's when my muscles just give out and I crash down onto the floor, taking my chair with me. The class had been nearly silent up until this moment, and the sounds of my clattering seat echo across the room. Gumballs pour out of my pockets, ricocheting and bouncing across the dirty tiled floors.

It's like they're magically appearing. My pockets are the magician's hat, and the gumballs are a rabbit.

"Uh." I don't know what to say so I just leap to my feet and right my chair and plunk down so fast that the little feet on the chair sort of screech as I sit. "I'm okay," I add, for good measure.

The sound of the gumballs rolling across the floor seems to be the only thing I can hear. A few people pick them up and toss them in the garbage, but the others just ignore them, as if they don't exist. Or maybe they expect me to race around and collect all two dozen of them.

Ben is pursing his lips because he obviously doesn't want to laugh, like the rest of the class is. Mrs. Vickers mercifully gets everyone's attention and class resumes as my cheeks heat up and nearly burst into flames.

I can't live like this. I have to figure out how to end the wishes.

I spend the rest of the class scribbling mathematical notes

while leaning away from Ben. I feel really bad when he discreetly sniffs his armpits, because it's obvious that he thinks I'm repulsed by him.

He can never know the truth, which is the very opposite of repulsion.

By the time I make it to history, I feel like I need to take one deep breath after another to make up for math. I'm positively gleeful when I discover we're watching some kind of movie on Europe, because it means I can zone out and figure out a plan.

The film starts up and the lights go down, and I listen halfheartedly as the narrator talks about the storied history of Italy and how a lot of amazing painters and artists come from there.

The guy to my left, the one wearing a ridiculously fluffy sweater even though it's an unseasonable seventy-five degrees out, raises his hand. "Uh, Mr. Martin? The subtitles aren't working."

The teacher looks up from his desk and then nods. "Sorry, just one moment."

The teacher goes through some of the DVD menus and gets the subtitles turned on and then hits play again. As the narrator continues his monologue about the priceless works of art still found in Venice and Rome, I have a shocking realization: I don't need the subtitles.

I understand Italian.

I have never, not once, taken a course in Italian, unless that includes mispronouncing the menu at Olive Garden and listening to the waitress correct me.

Unbelievable. I listen for a few more minutes to the lilt of the narrator's accent, soaking in the words.

Elegante. Famoso. Rinomato. Museo.

Every word makes sense. As my classmates stare intently at the subtitles, I close my eyes and listen, and I know what is being said.

My father left us seven years ago. When the divorce was final, he wasted no time moving to Italy. His parents still live there, and he is a dual citizen. He attended a university here in the States, which was where he met my mother. I guess moving across town or across the state wasn't enough for him. He had to put a whole ocean between him and us, the family he apparently didn't want anymore.

When I was ten, a year after he left, I remember wishing I knew Italian so that I could visit him and prove that I could live in Italy with him. I figured if I knew the language, he'd let me stay, and everything would be good again. I could be a dual citizen just like him. I borrowed an Italian textbook from the library, but it was a hopeless cause and I gave up on the idea.

I remember sniffling as I pushed the book through the return slot. I was heartbroken watching it disappear into the hole, my hopes disappearing with it. Failing at Italian sealed my fate.

I was never going to see him again. I just knew it.

"This is not nap time, Miss McHenry. I do expect you to watch the film with the rest of the class."

"Oh!" I say, my eyes popping open to meet the stern gaze of Mr. Martin. "Sorry. It's, uh, just so rare for me to hear, uh, clear Italian. I was just listening."

"Do you speak Italian?" He gives me a skeptical look. Mr. Martin is the sort of teacher who probably keeps a secret blacklist of students he dislikes, adding to it each day. I mean, he's looking at me right now like I left the faucet running and flooded his house.

I nod and clear my throat. Either I *think* I speak Italian or I really do. Here goes nothing. *"Posso parlare bene nell'italiano. Non oh bisogno dei sottotitoli per capire il film."*

His expression changes. I can see that *he* doesn't understand Italian and is trying to decide if my words sound real or totally made up. Seeing as I'm not totally sure either, I tense, waiting for his answer.

Then he just shrugs. "I see. Carry on, then."

"Grazie," I say as my classmates turn to look at me. I just smile and rest my head on my desk and close my eyes.

Well, at least Ben isn't going to kiss me today.

Although that means I just totally humiliated myself in math for nothing.

16

BY THE TIME the day is done, I've made it through all my classes, I still haven't seen Nicole, and Ben gave me an odd look as we passed in the hall. All I want is to get home and pull my quilt over my head and pretend like nothing exists outside my bedroom door, even if that means locking Ann out.

I'm only halfway across the ball fields in the back of the school when I see Ann strolling down the sidewalk. She must have found some rope in the shed because she's made some kind of makeshift halter and she's leading the horse along with it, letting it stop for bites of grass here and there.

"*Mannaggia,*" I mutter to myself. Then I blink a few times. Great, now I'm even *thinking* Italian.

I jog across the rest of the baseball field, meeting up with her before she makes it all the way to the school. I glance back behind me and realize that several students are standing in the nearby parking lot, staring.

Great. If enough people didn't see Ann at school before, now they get to see her and the life-sized My Little Pony. Ann is bound and determined to ruin my life.

"I told you to stay in the shed!"

"It was boring in there. And the pony was hungry for more than old carrots. I wasn't going to go on campus, I swear. Just around it."

I glance back over my shoulder. People are pointing.

"Fine. I'll figure out what to feed that thing tonight. But you have to get it back to the shed."

Ann pouts. "I still don't see why you're punishing *me*. It's not my fault you had a magical birthday cake."

"Oh, don't be ridiculous. It wasn't—" The words die in my throat, and I blink a few times, staring at Ann but not really seeing her. Her frizzed-out red hair looks like a fuzzy blob of fire.

What if it *was* the cake?

I've made *lots* of birthday wishes. Every year, I made a wish. But none of them ever came true.

Until now.

And while my wish making was pretty consistent (close eyes, make wish, blow out candles), one thing changed: a gigantic pink mass of sugar.

I *knew* that stupid cake was trouble. With its four layers, big swirling icing, pink flowers, fancy candles . . .

"Ann, you're a genius," I finally say when my vision swims back into focus.

"I am?"

"Yes. Come with me. I have an idea."

We walk back to the house, the pony trotting merrily along to keep up with our longer strides. Its head bobs happily as its blue-streaked tail drags on the ground.

A car slows down, the driver leaning out the window to get a good look at my walking freak show. The pony is happy as can be, jogging along, occasionally nipping at pieces of grass.

I look back at her. Okay, so it *is* kind of cute. Especially when it wiggles its lips against my pocket, as if I have a treat in there and I'm holding out.

"Quit it," I say with a smile, knocking the pony's nose away. It seems to be annoyed, and it nips back at me.

"Ouch!" I jump ahead a few feet, out of the range of the pony's teeth. Freakin' thing just bit me.

"Where are we going?" Ann asks, quickening her steps to catch up.

"To the supermall. Well, not the mall, but a bakery nearby."

"Ooh, a bakery?"

"Yeah. I figure we can go to the same bakery where my mom got my sweet-sixteen cake and maybe I can buy a replica cake and make another wish to undo the one from my birthday."

Raggedy Ann yanks me to a stop and the pony smashes into us. "You're going to get rid of me?"

Her mouth is hanging open and she looks . . . horrified.

I cringe a little. I hadn't thought about her reaction to this plan. To be honest, I hadn't thought about her at all.

"Ann, there are wishes I made that just cannot come true. It'll ruin my life and my best friend's life and . . . it just can't happen. So I have to undo this."

"But I'll be stuck in that stupid box forever!"

"I won't make you sit in the box. You can hang out in my bed again," I say, even though the very sound of that idea seems too creepy to actually do.

"No way! I'm just starting to figure out this whole walking thing! You can't turn me back into a doll!"

Ann looks like she's going to either hyperventilate or run screaming down the street. I swear even her *freckles* are trembling.

"Okay, okay, calm down. I won't undo everything. I'll exclude you when I make my wish," I say.

Except I don't think I can actually do that, because I can't risk botching the unwish by trying to exclude her.

And also? Where is she going to live? Somehow I don't think my mom would buy that she has to live in my room because she's really my toy come to life. And I think you need birth certificates to go to school.

As Ann throws her arms around me in gratitude, I choke down the guilt in the back of my throat. She doesn't belong here, and she can't stay. It's totally not mean of me to send her back, because that's what any rational human being would do. Obviously.

She's a doll.

When I open the doors to the shed, I discover it's even messier than it was this morning. The pony has, ewww, totally pooped in here. And the gumball bags are in even worse shape, spilling everywhere.

There's hardly any room for the pony. But we have no choice, so we lock it up in the shed with a bucket of water and a pile of hand-picked grass and cross our fingers that it doesn't eat any of the gum and get sick because that would be *exactly* what I need to put the cherry on top of this whole mess. Then we jump in my brother's truck and head to the mall.

I'm a little nervous about driving that far the very same day I got my license, but I don't have to get onto the freeway, so I figure I can manage. We'll be back before my mom gets home, so hopefully no one will know about our little excursion.

Twenty minutes later, I'm driving around the parking lot near the mall, heading to Cassie's Confections, the place my mom always uses. I know, because I've seen the invoices sitting on her desk. Cassie has a *really* weird logo: It's a dancing fish. You ask me, you probably shouldn't associate a fish (and thus, that nasty fishy smell) with a bakery, but whatever. At least it's memorable. A quick call to 411, and I know exactly where to look.

I should have known based on the fact that my cake looked like it came from *The Wizard of Oz* that it was going to be trouble. I mean, the four tiers alone was ridiculous, let alone all those whimsical swirls and flowers.

I pull up at the bakery and Ann jumps out as soon as it's in park. Maybe she wants to be sure I don't race in, make a wish on the first cake I see, and ensure her disappearance.

We step inside the bakery, and I'm immediately assaulted by the smell of sweets. A display case is packed to overflowing with cookies, donuts, cupcakes, and a dozen or so sheet cakes with cartoon characters and golf clubs and wedding bells covering them.

A short, rotund woman is standing next to the display case, spraying it with Windex and wiping vigorously at its surface, her belly sort of shaking, like a bowl full of jelly.

"Hi," I say as I walk up to her. "My mom got me a sweet-sixteen cake a few weeks ago. Four layers, pink frosting? I was wondering if I could get another one. Maybe smaller, but almost identical."

The woman just keeps buffing away at the glass. "I haven't done a sweet sixteen in about a month. And I don't do layers."

I blink. That can't be right. "But my mom uses you all the time. Are you sure?"

The lady points to the cakes in the case and then picks up her Windex bottle again and sprays it, so that the desserts look blurry through the cleaner that drips down the glass. "Sheet cakes only. Like those."

"Do you have a worker here who might have made it?"

"Nope." She picks up the white rag and starts buffing again, big swirly round motions.

If only she could erase my wish as easily as the dirt on the glass.

"Okay," I say, my voice falling. "Thanks anyway."

Great. So now I have to figure out where my mom got my cake. And by the time she gets home tonight, it'll be too late to go on another expedition. I'm going to have to make it through at least one more wish.

I just have to pray that the wish is not Ben.

To console myself, we head to Mama Tortini's, an authentic Italian restaurant a few blocks away. Eating something deliciously cheesy is about the only thing I can think of that would cheer me up right now. The waiters are actually Italian there, with thick accents and dark hair. I might as well try out my newfound language skills, right?

When the hostess seats us, she stares at Raggedy Ann's clothing with an upturned brow. Whatever. It's not like the hostess's black nylons, black skirt, and white men's-style dress shirt with black tie is any better.

At least Ann's outfit has a little originality to it.

Though I guess I should probably loan Ann some of my wardrobe, huh? Then at least it wouldn't be so embarrassing to be seen with her. Guess we'll pick something out when we get home. I kind of thought she'd be gone before I had to worry about this.

I decide to go all out and I order fancy blended drinks for us, and it's all worth it when Ann's eyes practically bug out of her head. "This is so good!" She sucks so hard on the straw she looks like she's doing the sour-lemon face, and the glass quickly drops to half empty.

I forget to explain to her about brain freeze, and it soon becomes obvious she has one because she scrunches her face up and closes her eyes. It makes me laugh.

So maybe she's kind of annoying, but at least she's also sort of amusing. With Nicole constantly ditching me, I've been hanging out alone all the time, which just makes it too depressing to go out to eat or to a movie. I'd rather rip off my toenails with a pair of pliers or organize my closet than go to a movie theater alone.

The waitress comes back and pulls out her notepad. "Have you decided what you'll have?"

I smile at her. Here's to hoping my Italian is real and not something I made up. *"Ciao, cosa mi consiglierebbe?"*

I can see the slight change in the waitress. She obviously respects my mad skills at speaking Italian because she stands a little straighter, and her smile becomes a touch more genuine. *"Un piatto di gnochi con mozarela fresca è il risotto ai carciofi è ottimo."*

I purse my lips. Nicole had been bragging about her risotto a few days ago. Might as well try it. *"Mi sembra fantastico, allora prendo il risotto e per lei invece, gli gnocchi."*

Hopefully Ann will like the gnocchi.

"Qualunche l'antipasto?"

Ha. Appetizers. As if I'm trying to blow every dollar I ever made. *"Non grazie."*

She nods and takes the black-leather menus from us and then disappears in the direction of the kitchen.

"When did you learn Italian?" Ann asks.

"I've always known Italian," I say, picking up my fork and drawing circles on the white linen tablecloth.

"No you didn't. I would remember."

I sigh, resisting the urge to stab myself with my fork. "It was a wish."

"Why would you wish to know Italian?"

"Lots of people wish to know foreign languages."

"Why not just wish to go to Italy?"

I drop my fork and pick up my napkin. It's folded up to look like a weird little triangle. I concentrate on unwrapping it and laying it out on my lap, carefully smoothing out the wrinkles. "My dad moved there. I thought if I knew Italian, he'd let me come visit. I didn't just want to *go* there, I wanted him to *want* me there."

"Oh," she says, her voice quiet. I look up at her, half expecting to see a look of pity, but there is none. "I don't really remember him," she says.

"He left a year after my mom gave you to me." I pause. "Sorry, that sounds weird."

She shrugs. "No weirder than this," she says, gesturing to her body.

"True."

"So what was he like?"

I stare down at my napkin again. There's a piece of lint stuck to it, and I flick it off. It lands on the buttery-yellow tiles beneath my sneaker-clad foot. "Tall. Dark hair. Your typical Italian look and an accent to boot. I used to wish I had inherited his accent somehow. Sometimes my brother will say a word or two and it reminds me of him. He's brilliant, though. Really well educated, loved to read. He'd fall asleep in the den with a book propped up on his chest. Sometimes he'd read to me."

"Why'd he leave?"

I don't have a good answer, so I just twist my napkin around in my hands, waiting for something to come to mind, but nothing does. "I don't know. I mean, one minute he's there and the next he's just, *not*. I bet he never looked back, either. It didn't make sense then and it still doesn't. I don't see how he can just leave us and never see us again."

Ann doesn't say anything to fill the silence, so I do. "I don't think any of us has ever figured out how to fill the gap. It's like we're a table and one day someone cut off one of the legs, but none of us has moved to help hold things up, you know? Like we're waiting for him to come back and level it all out again. And nobody ever talks about him. Not my mom, and definitely not Chase. I feel like I'm the only person who even remembers he exists."

I feel myself getting a little choked up, so I take a long sip of ice water. The waitress walks up and sets down the bread sticks and salad, and Ann quickly rips into the warm, buttery bread. I feel sort of bad when I realize that I haven't even offered her any food until now. She's been alive for, like, a day and a half. I wonder if she ate any gumballs while sitting in the garden shed.

Then again, I'm not sure anyone else would have thought of feeding her either, right? Maybe that's because she's supposed to be a doll. Not a live girl sitting across the table from me, loudly smacking her lips as her cheeks bulge like a chipmunk's.

She realizes I'm staring and freezes, her mouth hanging open, a hunk of bread only halfway past her lips.

"It's impolite to chew with your mouth open," I say. "And your elbows shouldn't be on the table."

"What am I supposed to do with them?" she asks, still showing off the half-chewed food as she picks up her elbows and sticks them out at odd angles, like a chicken.

"Rest your forearm on the table. If you're not eating, put your hands in your lap. And also, don't chew and talk."

Okay, what am I, the etiquette Nazi?

She chews with gusto and as soon as she swallows the mouthful, she says, "Thanks!"

Like I've just offered to spit shine her shoes or something.

She picks up the tongs and puts a giant pile of salad on her plate and then chases a crouton around with her fork. "So, why don't you ever call him?"

"Who?"

"Your dad."

"Oh. Um, no thanks."

"Why not?"

I stuff a giant forkful of lettuce in my mouth to give myself some time to think. But even after I've swallowed it, I don't have a good excuse. "I shouldn't have to. He's the one who left."

"Yeah, but——"

A movement catches my eye and I lean out of the booth a little bit to get a better look.

Oh, snap.

Ben and Nicole have walked in and are being escorted to a booth in the corner. Nicole is wearing a dress I've never seen before, this pretty black halter top with a dusty-pink ribbon around the empire waistline, and a pair of matching pink heels.

Does she always do this? Dress like a girly-girl princess when I'm not around? Or at least when she's on dates?

Where'd her Converse and jeans go? Does Mama Tortini's really warrant getting *that* dressed up?

Ben, apparently, doesn't think so. He's wearing his usual loose-fitted jeans with sneakers and a bright-red shirt with some kind of blue graphic splashed across the shoulder. Even from thirty feet away, I can make out the line of his pecs and his shoulders. Boy fills out a T-shirt, that's for sure.

I shrink down into the smooth leather seat so I can just see the edge of their table, but I can't see them and they won't notice me.

"What's wrong?" Ann leans way outside the booth and cranes her neck to see what I'm staring at.

"Ann! Stop that!" I hiss.

She jerks back so fast the table jumps, and her water glass starts to tip back and forth. Her hand shoots out to catch it, but instead she knocks it over and it pours across the table and slides onto my lap, soaking through my jeans.

I clamp down on my lips to keep from crying out and snatch the napkins off the table and start blotting the water off of my jeans.

Ann is just sitting there, wide eyed, her frizzed-out red hair sticking out at odd angles, her horrible blue dress rumpled and askew.

Goose bumps are popping up all over my legs and arms as the

ice water seeps through the denim. Why did I think this was going to work?

I find the waitress and ask her to switch our dinners to takeout and then pay the bill as we wait. When the food arrives, I slide out of the booth and head for the back door. I'm only a few steps in the right direction when I realize that my shadow is no longer following me. She's heading toward the front door.

I cover the distance between us in seconds and grab her wrist and then yank so hard I think I must dislocate her shoulder. She cries out and nearly loses her balance, but I don't wait for her as I keep propelling her out the back entrance.

We make it outside before Ben and Nicole have a chance to see what the commotion is about.

"Sheesh," Ann says, rubbing her wrist. "What was that for?"

"Nicole was there with Ben."

She just gives me a blank look, her pretty green eyes staring straight at me.

Her eyes really are her best feature. Maybe with better clothes, non-frizzed hair, and about a thousand years of etiquette lessons, she'd be sort of pretty.

"Nicole is my best friend."

Ann looks back at the restaurant. "That's how you act around your best friend?"

"She was with Ben!"

"And?"

"And Ben is her boyfriend!"

"And?"

I throw up my hands and want to scream. "You don't get it. Ben is . . . he's . . . well, he's Ben."

"I fail to see the problem."

"I can't be around them at the same time. It makes me nauseous."

Ann shrugs. "You sure are weird."

"As if you're not. You're a doll!"

"Weren't you a doll once?"

I snicker. "Of course not!"

"Not an actual doll. But you dressed as one. In the *Nutcracker*."

My foggy memory slowly clears. "Oh . . . you mean ballet. I don't do that anymore."

"Why not? You love it. You spend hours upon hours practicing."

"*Spent*. I was ten. Of course I loved it."

"Does ballet not exist for sixteen-year-olds?" She looks at me wide eyed, completely serious. "That is so sad!"

I snicker. She's very dramatic. "No, it does."

"So why do you not participate?"

"I don't know! Ballet is stupid!"

Ann clucks her tongue. "My, you've changed."

"I would hope so. When I was ten, my most fervent wish was for you!"

She gives me a look that tells me in an instant I've hurt her feelings.

I swallow. "Look, it's not that I don't like you. It's just that I'm not that girl anymore. People grow up. They stop playing with Barbies and start . . . " My voice trails off. I'm not sure where I'd intended to go.

"Hiding from their best friend?"

She really is too clever for a doll.

We make it to my car, and Ann rounds the passenger side. I look at her over the roof, shielding my eyes from the setting autumn sun. "Look, there's nothing to talk about here. I'm not the ten-year-old you once knew. And you're not a doll, either. So let's just pretend *that*"—I point at the restaurant—"didn't happen. And stop asking so many questions, okay? Maybe I didn't live in a box for the last five years, but it doesn't mean I know any more than you do."

I climb into my seat and buckle my seat belt, then wait for Ann to do the same. She clicks it into place and then reclines her seat until it's practically flat, putting her feet on the dashboard and staring up at the sunroof. I try not to grimace at the dirt that she's grinding into the plastic dash. "So if you're not into ballet any-more . . . what are you into?"

I shrug and turn the key, backing carefully out of the parking stall. How do you explain to a doll that people don't like the same things for their whole life? That we grow out of Raggedy Ann and My Little Pony?

"Snow White?" she asks.

I shake my head.

"What about those black fuzzy-velvet posters? You used to get one of those every week and your whole room was covered in—"

"No," I say. God, I remember that. I had every poster they made, painstakingly colored with the markers they supplied. My rooms were practically wallpapered in unicorns and puppies and baseball scenes and meadows and rainbows.

"Karaoke?"

I snicker. I used to have epic dance parties in my bedroom, blasting ridiculous pop music, singing into my hairbrush. Ann and her plush friends served as my audience. "My musical tastes changed. They're not quite so suitable for . . . singing."

"Do you at least like ice cream?" she asks.

"Of course. *Some* things don't change."

"I don't see why so many things do."

"Ann, really. I was a kid then. A really stupid one. I'm much wiser now."

"But you smiled more then."

"Argh! This conversation is so over. You totally don't get it."

Ann turns her attention back to the clouds passing above. "No, I don't."

17

THAT NIGHT, I learn that Ann is a bed hog. I thought I would be nice and share my big queen-sized bed with her instead of making her sleep on the Berber. I've done that a time or two, and that carpet is *not* cushy at all. So I took a sleeping bag out of the hall closet for her and then folded my blankets in half for me, and when I fell asleep last night, she was near the wall, while I was comfortably snuggled up with my pillow. It's not yet dawn, but I can't sleep any longer. I am dangling off the edge of the bed, my pillow having been mercilessly shoved off, my blankets robbed by Ann.

I roll out of bed and move to my desk to dig through my bag, pulling out my binder.

I flip to the back, where I've stashed the picture of Ben. In the dim moonlight coming from the open curtains, I can just make out his face.

I lean over, my chin resting on my fist, and stare at the outline of his body, at the contrast between his dark hoodie and the sparkle coming off the water behind him.

He's achingly perfect.

There's no one in the world as amazing as he is.

I sigh, simultaneously wanting to toss the picture in the trash *and* laminate it for safekeeping. Then I shove it back into my binder. I could spend the next hour staring at him, but it's not going to change the facts.

I go to the bed and slide one of the blankets off Ann, and then I curl up on the floor and stare at the ceiling. I drift off a time or two but not for long, because I find myself watching as the room slowly gets lighter. When I can't tolerate it any longer, I sit up and look at her.

She looks rather comfortable, lying diagonally across the mattress, snuggled inside a sleeping bag, my quilt over the top. She has two pillows, one under her arm and the other under her head.

An errant gumball is under my calf, and I resist the urge to throw it at Ann. Instead I toss it in the garbage can.

I push my hair out of my face and glare at her, though she doesn't seem to notice because she's snoring loudly. *"Buon giorno,"* I mutter under my breath. The words are nice even if my tone isn't.

I kneel and pick up the ruler from the bookshelf next to me and poke her with it. Her snore turns into this weird gurgle for a minute, but then she resumes the sound of sawing wood.

Whatever.

I put a hand on the bed and stand up, but I feel oddly off balance, like I'm standing on gumballs.

I swear, if those things show up again . . .

A quick look, though, shows me there's nothing between my

feet and the brown Berber. Weird. It's like the ground is uneven. I keep leaning forward and have to force myself upright.

I walk to my closet, but I sway again and have to grab ahold of the doorknob to catch myself. I close my eyes for a minute, trying to find my balance.

My equilibrium is all messed up. It's like that stood-up-too-fast feeling you get when you've been vegging on the couch all day and then you jump to your feet. The world is a little crooked, and my legs are swaying underneath me to compensate. It would be one thing if I'd overloaded on sugar, but that's not the case this morning. Unless you count Ann's saccharine-sweet personality.

I glance at Ann one more time on my way to the bathroom. She's so not moving. I guess she only *thought* she didn't need sleep.

Just before I flip the shower on, I turn around and happen to glimpse myself in the mirror.

And let out a bloodcurdling scream.

Oh. Mio. Dio.

Boobs.

I have boobs.

I clamp my hand over my mouth and stare, my eyes wider than they've ever been, at my chest. I wore a tank top to bed, and I have enough cleavage to work at Hooters. And I'm not even wearing a bra.

Er, I don't think I even *own* a bra that would harness these things.

I swallow and step forward until I am directly in front of the mirror.

"Honey? You okay in there?" my mom calls through the door. The knob is turning.

Uh-oh.

"Don't come in!" I shout. "I'm, uh, naked. I'm okay, I just . . . um, stubbed my toe. I'm fine!"

I look over at the doorknob, willing my mom to let it go. If she walks in right now, there's no way I could explain away these babies.

The knob spins back into its normal resting position. "Okay. I've got a company-picnic thing today, so I'll be gone until at least six or seven tonight. I left a twenty on the counter so you and your brother can get some pizza."

I sigh, not moving my eyes from my reflection. Another pizza night. Of course. I wonder if she'll ever eat another meal with us again.

"Okay," I say when I realize I haven't answered. I'm still staring at myself in the mirror.

"Bye," she says, her footsteps retreating down the hall.

My heart is beating so loudly that it's making my chest heave, which makes me think of some horrible romance novel.

Because I have heaving bosoms. Or is it a bosom?

Whatever.

I pick my hands up, and they kind of hover over my chest. I don't think I can touch them. That's too . . . weird. Because they're not really *mine*, per se. They're . . .

Magic boobs.

Perfect.

I groan and drop my hands back to the counter. Steam is starting to fill the bathroom, and the top of the mirror is fogging over. I lean against the counter and get as close to the mirror as I can and then stare down my own shirt.

I feel like a perv right now. This is so creepy.

I bet I was twelve when I wished for these. I guess twelve-year-old boys and twelve-year-old girls think about the same thing, because I hated being flat chested. Nicole was an early bloomer, and I felt like such a dork next to her. All the boys stared at her boobs, completely ignoring me, like I didn't exist. I just stood there, her boy-shaped bestie.

That was the year we went roller skating for my birthday. My mom rented out this little room at the rink and brought in a cake and some of my relatives, and me and Nicole spent two hours straight skating. A group of boys was there. We talked about them all that night, eating candy and staying up late.

Eventually, the steam overtakes the window and I can't see my reflection anymore. It's just a shimmery silhouette.

A curvy, shimmery silhouette.

How am I going to hide this? Everyone is going to think I'm stuffing.

And not even in a subtle way, either. I went from an A cup to at least a C. Maybe a D.

EWWW, I'm going to have to raid my mom's bra drawer! At least, just until I get to the store. I'll just buy one bra that fits right to get me through until I get the wishes undone.

At least it's Saturday. Going to school like this is going to be a nightmare.

I have two days to figure out how to hide my ginormous new rack.

18

IT TAKES ME twenty minutes of digging through my closet to find an outfit that works on Ann, let alone one for me that will hide my chest.

I tend to like a lot of fluorescent colors with really bad designs on them, and the colors do *not* work well on Ann, being that she's a redhead. She does like trying it all on, though, throwing clothes all over my room in her excitement.

I bet there are a lot of ten-year-olds who would pay big money to have an actual life-sized doll who likes playing dress up. Maybe I should rent Ann out as a babysitter. Two birds, one stone.

She ends up in a baby-blue tank top I haven't worn since eighth grade and a pair of torn-up jeans. She seems to be a size smaller than I am, so I have to find a belt for her so they won't fall off.

Even with the ill-fitting jeans, though, she looks kind of hot.

Raggedy Ann has a banging body. Who knew.

While her hair is still wet from a shower, it looks kind of

normal—almost cute, because the water has tamed her curls. The strands look longer, straighter, and the darkened red is much prettier than the orangey red she normally sports.

But by the time we've been in the car for ten minutes with the windows down, her hair has gone insane, a little like Sideshow Bob on *The Simpsons*. Ann spends the whole ride giggling about the way it's whipping her in the face, halfheartedly trying to hold it down around the nape of her neck.

I have my mom's twenty in the pocket of my plaid cutoff shorts. They don't really match my hoodie, but I'm wearing it anyway to hide my honkers. It made sense at home, but now I feel really weird, like I shouldn't have left the house looking this freakish.

Ann follows me into Fred Meyer, and I grab a small cart.

I'm on a mission.

I was so distracted by my new boobs that I forgot to talk to my mom about the bakery. I don't want to wait another day, so we're moving to plan B: I'll bake my own cake, a perfect mini-replica of the sweet-sixteen monstrosity. I'll do four small layers and decorate them with frosting flowers and put four candles on each tier. If I'm careful, I bet I can get it to look quite similar to the birthday cake.

Then I'll make Ann sing me "Happy Birthday," I'll blow them out, and when I open my eyes, she'll be gone, my chest will shrink, I won't be spouting off in Italian every time I'm annoyed, the pony will be in her make-believe plastic barn, and the gumballs will be occupying gumball machines everywhere.

Let's be real here—if those are the first five wishes, do I really want to know what the others are?

Ann follows me across the store, her eyes roving all over the

place. She keeps stopping at various end caps and picking up bags
of chips and two-liter bottles of soda. She pokes the fresh loaves of
French bread and she knocks over a few boxes of crackers.

This is an amusement park to her.

"Ann! I don't have all day!"

Technically I guess I *do* have all day, but I'm on a mission here.
She groans and stomps after me to the baking aisle, and we stare
at the cake-mix boxes for a few moments in silence.

"This one looks yummy," she says, holding up a box of
German-chocolate mix.

"It needs to be white. Like this one."

I hold up a box with a picture of a white-frosted cake.

"Sprinkles!" she shouts, jumping up and down.

Just kill me now.

I toss two boxes into the cart and then ponder whether I'm
totally sure that it was white mix. It could have been yellow.

I crouch down and reach over to grab the yellow mix off the
bottom shelf. When I lean forward, my new chest knocks into the
shelf and a half-dozen cake-mix boxes make loud *smack* sounds as
they land on the floor.

I stare at them, contemplating just leaving them, then sigh and
scoop them up and place them back on the shelves. When I stand
up, I have to grab ahold of the cart to keep from tripping.

Next we pick out an assortment of frosting, including some
pink stuff in tubes that should work for making the flowers. I grab
a box of birthday candles and then drag Ann down to the refriger-
ated aisle to get some eggs and milk.

My back hurts a little already. I feel like I have mountains sticking straight out, and it's hard to reach for things because I knock into them. So not fun.

And also? It is so odd wearing your mom's bra. I took one straight out of the dryer so I know it's clean and all, but it totally gives me the willies.

I drag Ann over to the clothing section. If she was excited over the food, she's *ecstatic* over the clothing.

"You can buy *any* of this?"

I look over at her. She's holding up a pink V-neck with lacy arms and flowers all over it.

"Yep. And they'll give you the noose to hang yourself too."

Ann regards me with a skeptical look and then shrugs and puts the shirt back on the rack. I wonder how long it will take her to pick up sarcasm and wield it against me. I give her until tomorrow.

My mom's bra is a C cup. I think I'm probably supposed to be a D now, because I think I might bust right out of the top of it, but I refuse to buy anything with a D on it. I buy the most full-coverage C cup I can find and also a sports bra. Maybe if they don't have shape, they won't look so gigantic.

For good measure, I find the first aid supplies and grab some Ace bandages. Maybe I can bind them down and make them less . . .

Obtrusive.

By the time I've left, I've spent forty-four dollars' worth of my birthday money and all of the twenty my mom left on the counter. There goes the pizza dinner for my brother. Poor guy, he'll be eating Hot Pockets again.

I use the last six dollars I have in my pocket for a couple of dollar cheeseburgers, which Ann and I scarf down on the way back to the house.

This whole cake thing better work.

Because as it turns out, getting everything you ever wished for is really expensive.

19

ANN AND I get out the measuring cups and spoons and a few giant bowls. I flip on MTV, which, shockingly, is playing music videos. Katy Perry is just coming on-screen, introducing another poppy, bouncy song. She probably has a choreographed dance with a bowl of fruit later.

Ann is really excited about our baking experiment. "I've never baked a cake before!" she says, throwing her arms out. Her hands knock into one of the boxes of mix and it flies off the granite countertop and lands on the travertine-tiled floor with a loud *smack*.

At least it wasn't open yet.

"Chill," I say, picking up the box and ripping the top off.

She smiles and scrunches her shoulders up like a little kid who has been scolded. "But this is so cool! I saw your birthday cake when you turned eleven, you know. You put me on the counter, right next to it. It was this giant homemade thing. I think it was a turtle."

I scrunch up my brows. "I had a cake that looked like a turtle?"

She nods enthusiastically. "Green frosting and lots of sprinkles. It looked delicious."

"Oh. Um, right." I'm not sure what to say to that. Ann has a spectacular memory. I change the subject. "Uh, okay, we need to put the white mix in this bowl and the yellow in that bowl and get all the lumps out, because I don't know where my mom put the sifter."

My mom had this whole gourmet kitchen designed and stocked with fancy gadgets, because once upon a time she really liked cooking. I loved it too. We'd spend hours creating gourmet meals and then we'd make my brother and my dad sit at the table with blindfolds and we'd have them taste test it. They pretended to hate it, groaning and protesting, but they always sat right down and put the blindfolds on and then ate until they could barely move and we almost had to roll them into the living room.

My mom and I wouldn't tell them what the food was. We'd just make them open their mouths on cue and accept the spoonful of whatever we made. We'd giggle when their faces turned sour and then tell them all the ingredients.

It was amazing, the glow of my family when we were happy. Like we were one big clan from *Leave It to Beaver*.

But then he left and it's not the same with just my brother, and then my mom got too busy with her company and started leaving us cash for Chinese takeout or pizza delivery, and the gourmet tasting parties became just a memory.

I hand Ann a fork and the box of yellow mix, and she sets to work pouring it into the bowl and mashing down the lumps with her fork.

Then she eats a forkful of cake dust. It sticks to her lips.

"Ew! Don't do that."

"Oh! Sorry." Then she puts the licked fork back into the mix.

"Oh, gross." I grab the fork and toss it into the sink. "I'm not trying to get Raggedy Ann—ositis from you."

She just gives me a blank look. She never gets my lame jokes.

I crack the eggs since I'm not stupid enough to think Ann could handle *that*, and then we put in the vegetable oil and start stirring.

Ann holds the bowl in one arm and the spoon in the other, and then she spins around in circles and sings along to Katy Perry. A few glops of batter sort of spray out of the bowl, and then Ann loses her balance and knocks into the countertop. The motion makes her arm jerk and she sort of launches a big glop of batter at me.

It spatters across my apron. I freeze, my big wooden spoon still in the bowl, and stare at her.

"Seriously, Ann, take it down a notch."

That much bubbly energy should not be legal.

I set my bowl down and lean over to grab the two greased pans I've put out, and then Ann smacks a hand over her mouth and starts giggling.

"What?" I say, frozen, my hand still outstretched.

She points. I look down.

Oh God, my boobs are totally in the cake batter.

I slowly retreat, and the batter kind of plops back into the bowl, the rest streaking down my apron.

I sigh and rub my eyes. I slide my bowl to the side and then grab the cake pans and then we load them up with batter and put them in the oven.

"Now what?" Ann asks as she stoops over and stares into the

oven. After a moment passes, she opens the door and peers in to survey the results.

"It's not instant."

"Oh."

Ann stands upright again.

I'm half tempted to tell her we should see about taming her frizzed-out red hair, but then I remember that she's going to be gone in like an hour, tops. As soon as I make that wish, she'll be donezo, and I can go back to life as usual.

This better work.

★ ★ ★

BY THE TIME the kitchen timer dings, Ann has performed most of the dances on MTV, even the ones done by Shakira. Since the song lyrics happen to be *There's a she-wolf in the closet*, I suppose I should find it funny, or at least ironic, considering she *did* come from the closet. Instead there's something annoying about it. I can't help but be jealous because she's figured out that weird belly-dancing shimmy thing.

I wonder if Ann could be a world-class painter or a singer or something if she just had the right teacher.

I wonder what it would be like to have that kind of shimmering possibility, that kind of endless expanse of dreams. To just choose something and be good at it.

Whatever. Now I sound like I belong on the underside of a Snapple lid.

Ann stands back as I slide the cakes onto a cooling rack. We stir up the frosting as the cakes cool, and then I get out a big waxy sheet of paper and put the cakes onto it. I use toothpicks to try and secure them to each other, holding my breath like I'm playing a game of Jenga. They seem to stay.

Ann hovers over my shoulder and watches, so close I can feel her breath.

I trust her with the frosting, which believe me, is hard to let her do. I *do not* want this screwed up. She uses a butter knife and the results aren't pretty, but it does the job. Maybe I should have turned on some Martha Stewart instead of MTV.

She stands back as I do my best to replicate the fluffy pink-frosted flowers from my sweet sixteen. It might help if I had looked at the real deal for more than one incredulous second, but I didn't, so hopefully this is close enough.

I jam candles into the cake—four on each layer—and then stand back and admire my work.

It'll have to do.

"Okay, now sing the birthday song," I say to Ann.

She just gives me a blank look.

"You know, 'Happy birthday to you . . . '"

She just continues to stare.

It takes me ten minutes to teach her the song. You'd think as repetitive as it is that it would go more quickly, but she's really worried about getting it just right. I guess I should be too.

She's finally ready, and she sings me the song as I grip the edge of the countertop, my knuckles turning white.

As she sings the last "Happy birthday to you . . . " her voice going higher and carrying on longer than necessary, I close my eyes.

I wish every wish I'd ever made had never come true.

With a long intake of breath, I open my eyes and blow out every candle with one try.

Then I close them again for a quiet moment.

Wishing.

Hoping.

Maybe some kind of magical sense of peace is supposed to wash over me. Tranquility. Serenity. Something.

Finally, I open my eyes.

Ann is cutting into the cake with the butter knife she used for frosting. "This is going to be sooo good!"

I just groan and sink to the floor.

Maybe she'll disappear at midnight, like Cinderella.

Or maybe that's my life as I knew it.

20

I SPEND MOST of that night staring at the ceiling in my room, listening to Ann snore and trying to come up with more wishes to fill in on the list. If I can't stop them, it would be nice if I at least knew what was coming.

You'd think if I had used up a precious birthday wish—you only get one per year, after all—I'd at least remember what I wanted.

But I can't. I have some ideas, of course. I remember certain toys I was obsessed with. I remember when I wanted to be one of the voices in the Shrek movies. And when I wanted to fly an airplane.

But who knows if I actually wished those things?

So, as another day dawns, I sneak out of my room and throw on a sweatshirt. It's barely past nine o'clock, and Ann is still sleeping heavily.

I sit down on the last step at the bottom of the stairs and pull on my rattiest, most comfortable pair of Converse sneakers. I'm still lacing them up when I hear the stairs creak, and I turn around, expecting to see Ann's messy mop of red hair.

But it's my mom. Surprising, for nine a.m. Normally she'd be gone by now.

Sundays are usually huge event days—most often a wedding or a company retreat slash picnic—so she tends to leave in the wee hours to soothe the frazzled nerves of a bride-to-be or a hoity-toity CEO or any number of rich, spoiled people.

I mean if you can't plan your own party and would rather pay someone to do it, you probably have more money than necessary. And I've seen some of my mom's invoices. Her clients definitely have more money than necessary.

"Where are you off to?"

"The library."

"You're gone an awful lot these days," she says.

"*I* am gone a lot?"

Surely, I heard her wrong.

She nods. I narrow my eyes and give her a skeptical look.

"What's that for?"

I shrug and walk to the door to pick up my backpack. I should have kept my mouth shut. "I'm home way more than you, that's all."

My mom sighs. "Don't give me lip, Kayla."

My jaw drops. "I'm not! How is it lip if it's the truth?"

My mom crosses her arms. She's wearing a perfect, starched lavender blouse with pristine khaki pants. Her brown hair—a darker, much prettier shade than my own—is blow-dried into a perfect boardroom-worthy coif. "Why must you be so ungrateful?

I give you everything you want, and yet you insist on wearing the same old ratty clothes and complaining all the time."

I snap my jaw shut and clench my teeth. "Right, Mom. You give me everything I want. Got it."

"Kayla Louise! I threw you a beautiful party not a week ago."

"Did you, Mom? Did you throw *me* a party, or did you throw your company a party? Because it was kind of hard to tell the difference."

My mom glances at her watch, and I try hard not to roll my eyes. She'll never have time for me. "I have to go do bio home-work," I say, ripping at the handle of the door.

"Do you want a ride? I'm running late, but—"

"No thanks, I can walk."

And then I rush out the door. I don't need to hang around to know that she'll leave a twenty on the counter with a note about takeout, and I won't see her until sometime tomorrow.

Although, damn. Maybe before I mouthed off, I should have asked her about that bakery. I can't ask her now, after I stormed off. This is never going to get fixed if I don't focus on solving the problem.

The public library is a short walk from my house. It's open early on Sundays, which never made much sense, but I'm not com-plaining now, because it gives me somewhere to escape to.

Ann'll probably sleep for another hour or two and then won-der where I went. If I'm lucky, she'll try to find me and get hit by a Mack truck.

Okay, that's mean. I reach out and run my fingers along a chain-link fence as I walk, my mind wandering as I turn at the corner and head toward town. The Cascade Mountain range rises up in the distance. Even though most of the trees are evergreens, a few deciduous are mixed in, and the result is splashes of burnt orange and bright red, lighting up the hilltops. Further in the distance, the snowcapped peak of Mount Rainier juts into the skyline. Enumclaw is a big plateau about eight hundred feet above sea level, built on an old mudflow from when Rainier last erupted, a zillion years ago. Really reassuring, when you think about it.

But I'm not. Thinking about it, that is. I'm thinking about something far more urgent.

I wonder what today's wish is. I wonder if I'll figure out how to stop all this craziness before Ben tries to lay one on me. I'm still annoyed with myself for fighting with my mom when I should have faked a nice conversation and asked about the bakery. But *no*, I had to get all annoyed.

I wonder if it's really possible Ben would try to kiss me. Like, sure, something magical is at work here, but he's not a gumball. He has a mind of his own. Maybe he won't really try to kiss me at all. Maybe he'll just have the thought enter his brain and then he'll ignore it and kiss Nicole instead, and I've been silly to worry about it at all.

I sigh and kick a rock across the sidewalk. It skitters across the concrete and then bounces into the street.

Someone honks at me, as if I just tossed a boulder in front of their car and not a tiny pebble, and I just wave them away and hoist my backpack further up my shoulders. It's too early on a Sunday for people to be honking like that. They'll wake half the neighborhood.

The car honks again, and I turn to glare, but then just stumble to a stop instead.

Um, this has got to be the *weirdest* thing I've seen in Enumclaw in about, well, forever.

It's a guy in a bright-yellow convertible, never mind the fact that it's probably fifty-two degrees out and the dew in the grass hasn't even evaporated yet. If you live in the Pacific Northwest, you only get to utilize drop-tops for, like, a dozen days out of the year. Yet this guy hasn't put the top up.

But just as bizarre as the car is the driver: He's probably in his late teens, pushing twenty or so—which means his parents must be loaded if he's got his own sports car—and he has a tan so dark he must go to the tanning beds every day of the week. It's definitely not natural, not for this area anyway.

He's got on a tank top that shows off bulging muscles and a smile so big and sparkly he looks like he's posing for his actor's head shots, or maybe just a tooth-whitening commercial. I think I can actually *count* his teeth from right here on the sidewalk. He has that cheesy sort of look, like he's selling the Bowflex on a two a.m. infomercial.

His blue eyes are wide and bright and staring straight at me, framed by curly long lashes, and his gelled-within-an-inch-of-its-life blond hair looks more like a helmet. Even his eyebrows are sculpted.

And he looks like he oiled himself up, like one of those body-builder competitions where the people look like they're made of plastic because they're so freaking' shiny.

"Baby, where ya been?"

I think I throw up in my mouth a little. I glance over my shoulder and realize that yes, he's talking to me.

Ew.

I pick up a brisk walk. Maybe I should have told someone where I was going. He is kind of creepy, the way he's staring at me with that huge artificial smile.

I'm glad I don't have much further to go. The library is maybe a mile from my house, through nice residential neighborhoods, just across Cole Street, the quaint little main drag in town, with its little diners and antique shops. With this guy leering at me it makes me wish I'd driven, but I figured if I walked, it would give me more time away from home and Ann and everything else that's happening.

I ignore him as he shifts his car into gear and rolls along, paralleling the sidewalk.

"Sweetie, baby cakes, where's your car?"

"Uh, I don't have one," I yell, hoping that will get him off my back. "I think you have me confused with someone else."

"Sure you do, babe, it's a pink convertible. Did you leave it at your beach house?"

Despite my nerves, I snicker. "Okay, now I *know* you have me confused. I don't have a beach house."

I'm walking faster and faster, and this weirdo is just keeping pace, gliding along in his yellow convertible. Even idling, the engine is loud, rumbling, vibrating the air around us.

"Don't be silly, Barb. You don't have to walk. Jump in!"

I stop and spin toward him. "My name is *not* Barb. Just get lost!"

He rolls his eyes just a little. "Of course. Sorry, *Barbie*. I know you hate it when I call you Barb."

I open my mouth to fire back at him, but the words die in my throat. I snap it shut and step back, away from the curb. Suddenly the roar of that ugly sports car is deafening, ringing in my ears over and over. My hand feels a little shaky as I cover up my gaping mouth.

I pull it away so I can ask him a question. "What's your name?"

He laughs. "Oh, come on, honey pie, you know my name!"

"Tell me your name," I say, through gritted teeth.

"Ken."

Oh boy, my life just took a serious southward turn.

Ken. Freaking Ken. As in, Barbie and Ken.

And he thinks I'm his girlfriend.

He thinks I'm *Barbie*.

WTF, when did I wish for *this*?

★ ★ ★

I TRY *really, really* hard to get Ken to leave me alone, but he keeps coasting along near the sidewalk, calling me various pet names and trying to convince me that I am, in fact, Barbie.

Right.

It must be my cascading blonde hair that has him confused. Or my pink ruffled shorts and tank top . . . or the fact that I'm walking around on my tippy toes. At least I *do* have these great hooters. I'm like one for five at best.

I can barely deal with a real-life Raggedy Ann. What am I

going to do with Ken? At least he doesn't think we live together. And he *does* have a car.

"Come on, sugar, hop in!"

I stop and put a hand on my hip and glare at him. "If I let you drive me to the library, will you at least leave me alone to study and go . . . play beach volleyball or whatever it is that you do?"

His lips curl into an all-encompassing, all-American smile that shows off his dimples and artificially white teeth. Seriously, if we were in a room with a black light, I bet his whole mouth would glow.

I groan and roll my eyes but decide to give in. If that will get him off my back for the rest of the day, it'll buy me some time to figure out what to do about all this.

Ken jumps out of the car and runs around and holds the passenger door open for me. He stands there as I get in and then clicks the door shut as I buckle up.

So Ken is a gentleman. Go figure. I thought he'd be more of the football-meathead type, the sort who doesn't notice if he spends a whole afternoon talking about himself and crunching cans against his forehead.

"Go anywhere cool lately?" Ken asks, leaning on the center console and giving me a cocky eyebrow raise.

"Uh, no?"

"You always say that. I think you take your stewardess duties too seriously. You ought to have more fun."

Stewardess duties?

I rack my brains. There must have been a Barbie stewardess. Also, he must not know that *stewardess* is no longer PC, and you're supposed to call them flight attendants.

I turn to watch the trees dance in the autumn breeze, and a smile starts to play at the edges of my lips, until it becomes too much and I grin to myself.

There's no way I can miss messing with *the* Ken.

"Have you seen my zebra lately?" I ask, turning to Ken in all seriousness. One of my favorite Barbie play sets had been the safari one, where Barbie is wearing khaki shorts and hiking boots and she comes with a slew of animals. I imagined myself going on all kinds of African adventures. "She seems to have wandered off. With my . . . lion cub. And panda bear." I'm actually not entirely sure Barbie has a panda bear, but the zebra and the lion cub ring a bell. "Those three, I swear . . . "

I wag my finger like a stern librarian or something.

Ken wrinkles his brow. "That's terrible. Do you know where they went?"

I shake my head. It's getting harder and harder not to laugh. "Nope. One minute they were in my dream house, and the next . . . gone. I took out the Jeep to go find them, but no luck. Madge and I looked all day long."

Madge. Did I get that right? Or was it Midge? Hmm. My Barbie days were so long ago. For good measure, I blink my eyes, wide and innocent-like, and pout a little bit.

Ken furrows his brow even more, looking so entirely sympathetic to my plight that I have a hard time not losing it right then.

I decide to go for the gusto. "And since I decided to be a veterinarian instead of a pediatrician—you know, after I lost my bid for president and then my NASCAR career fell through—I've just really renewed my love of animals. Especially since I opened that pet shop."

I grab Ken's hand and really ham it up. "And poor Skipper, she's been so upset. She really loved that tiger. Er, lion, I mean."

I bat my eyes at him. "And I need to spend all day studying for . . . veterinarian finals. So would you mind looking for them for me?"

Perfect. Send him on a wild-goose chase and he'll forget to hang out with me. If only it was this easy to ditch Ann.

"You got it, babe," he says as we're pulling up at the library.

Before I can duck out of the car, he leans forward and kisses me, his gigantic lips—perfectly soft and moist, which seems gross for some reason—pressing into mine.

"Thanks!" I shout, even though he's like an inch from my face, and then I leap from the car. I slam the door to the yellow convert-ible and am halfway to the sidewalk when I see him.

Ben is standing on the sidewalk, near the glass doors, seem-ingly frozen with fascination as Ken backs out of the parking stall and heads out to the street. Presumably to find my lost zebra, panda, and lion cub.

"Ben," I say, surprised, as I sling my backpack over my shoul-der. "Uh, how are you?"

Why the heck is he at the library at nine a.m. on a Sunday? *He* can't be avoiding the life-sized doll hanging out in his bedroom.

"Good." He seems fixated on watching Ken pull out of the lot, the exhaust on his sports car revving up as the tires chirp on the asphalt. "Who's that?"

Ben turns to look at me, and I study his eyes, trying to gauge his emotions. Is he jealous?

I grit my teeth. I'm not supposed to *want* Ben to be jealous.

"Um, K—" I stop. I can't possibly admit that his name is Ken or it's going to be mega-obvious that the guy has some complex and thinks he's a doll. "Carson."

Carson was his last name, wasn't it? All the Barbie-details are pretty foggy.

I move toward the library door, and Ben steps to the side and sweeps his hands to the side, as if he's personally escorting me inside, even though the doors are automatic.

"Thanks," I say, staring at the ground as I rush past him so he won't see my cheeks warm.

So I'm a sucker for chivalry. Even with my pessimist nature, I can admit there's something charming about a simple gesture. Ben follows me as we step inside the library, where I inhale the scent of paper and books. Something about this place makes it feel like the outside world doesn't exist.

"Are you guys together?"

I look up, surprised, both at the question and at the slightly edgy tone in Ben's voice.

"Why?" I ask, before I can stop the word from slipping past my lips.

He follows me past the spinners with the paperback romance novels, past the children's section, past dozens of tall shelves of reference books to a couch in the back corner of the library, where a big window splashes the place with light. We plunk down on opposite ends of the sofa, a full cushion between us.

He shrugs. "Look, we're friends, right? I just thought the guy was a little odd. You can do much better."

I scrunch my brows and try to pretend like it takes all of my attention to dig through my backpack.

"So *was* he your boyfriend?"

"Yes, he's my boyfriend," I say, my annoyance growing. "He's totally awesome. Very . . . athletic. Awesome at volley-ball. And of course he has his own car and everything, which is awesome . . . "

Why, for the love of pizza, do I keep saying "awesome"?

That's something California Ken would probably say.

Even as the *awesome* words flood out, I want to hit reverse and reel them back in, but I can't stop it. It's like I need to convince Ben I have a boyfriend in order to make myself feel better about this whole thing.

"Sorry, sorry. I know it's none of my business," Ben says. "I was just surprised. You never mentioned a boyfriend, that's all."

"Oh." I deflate a little. "How are you and Nicole doing these days?"

Ben rubs his hands together and takes in a deep, slow breath. He looks . . . I don't know how he looks. But something is off.

"You guys aren't breaking up, are you?"

"What? No. Of course not."

"Oh. Okay."

"It's just—"

I stop fiddling with my backpack. "It's just what?"

"Never mind."

"Are you sure? Because if you want to—"

"No. Everything's fine," he says, with conviction.

"Okay. Well, anyway, I need to work on my bio homework, so . . . "

I pick up my biology book and wave it around, a little too enthusiastically.

"Oh. Right. Sorry."

Ben grabs his own book and yanks it open. A few sheets of paper fly out and flutter to the ground. One of them slides under my foot. I lean down to pick it up—recognizing Nicole's handwriting by the time my fingers are just gracing the page—but Ben grabs it before I can see what it says.

"Ow!" The paper slices my pointer finger as it slides out from under my hand, and a bright crimson drop of blood lands on the knee of my jeans.

"Oh, wow, sorry." Ben digs a tissue out of his backpack and hands it to me, and I hold it to my fingertip.

"Thanks."

I hold it to my finger as the throbbing eases.

But even when it stops bleeding, my heart still hurts.

21

WHEN NICOLE walks up to me the next day at school, all I can do is stare at her. Even from a few dozen feet away, I can tell she's wearing darker mascara than usual, and the edges of her eyes have an obvious smudge of eyeliner. Her hair is curled yet again, and today she's got on a—dare I say it—*cute* destroyed-denim mini, plus a black V-neck with a lacy blue camisole underneath. She's got on a pair of boots, too, different ones than she wore last week. They're black, with adorable little straps that zigzag all over the toe.

Last year she dressed more like me, in lots of hoodies and jeans, and she almost always wore Converse. I mean, it's not like I expected her to consult with me before she went back-to-school shopping, but it's just kind of . . . weird. To see her transform right in front of me and to have her not even say anything or make a big deal of it.

I've been sitting on one of the weird carpeted cube-like benches in the hall, flipping through my bio book. There's a quiz tomorrow and I can't seem to absorb anything in this chapter.

It probably has to do with the fact that I'm trying to hunch over and hide my giant boobs. Crossing my arms is out—it actually makes them look bigger. Smooshes them together. Not a good idea.

I spent fifteen minutes this morning with Ann, trying out the Ace bandage idea. It didn't really work. I mean, it basically added a few layers to my already-oversized chest, so it essentially just made them bigger. I gave up and went with the sports bra.

So now I just keep sitting cross-legged, kind of leaned over my book, hoping no one notices. I see Janae walking down the hall, and I hunch further. I'm hyper-aware of everyone around me, totally convinced every one of them have taken note of my magically enhanced assets.

"Hey," Nicole says, plunking down next to me. She has a new purse, too. It's gigantically oversized, sea-foam-green leather with a bunch of extra buckles. Who is this girl and what did she do with my totally untrendy BFF?

"Hi," I say, sighing as I snap the book shut. "I can't figure this out."

"Really? Do you need help?" Nicole is amazingly smart, probably because she spent her formative years indoors reading books thanks to a bevy of acne meds that caused sensitivity to sunlight.

I widen my eyes and throw myself at her feet. *"Sì. Sì. Sì . . ."*

I stop when I realize I'm answering her in Italian. "I mean, yes. Yes. Yes. Yes, a million times yes."

Nicole giggles and pulls me back onto the bench next to her. Her eyes dart around for a second.

Is she embarrassed by me?

She's never done that before. She's never cared about my out-rageous antics, never minded my dorkiness. It stings a little, but I push it aside. I'm probably being paranoid.

"Cool. When do you want to come over?" she says, digging through her bag and producing a pack of gum.

She hands me a stick and I shove it in my mouth. "Tonight? After school?"

"Oh, *tonight?*"

I nod. "Yes. *After school?*"

Nicole cringes, I'm sure of it, but then she resumes smacking her gum. "Ben and I have plans. What about at, like, seven?"

I shrug and shove my book into my backpack. "Okay. That's fine."

Nicole crosses her legs, her foot shaking like crazy.

I stare at her toe, thinking about that day she ditched me for my birthday, thinking that she's got something she's not telling me. What's with her and all the secrets lately?

"So . . . what's up?" I say, leaning back on my hands. Too late, I realize this position does nothing to hide my big ol' knockers. I'm wearing pin-striped pants today and a baggy faded vintage tee. A real vintage one, not a trendy American Eagle rip-off. I found it at Goodwill for seventy-five cents. I was hoping the baggy fac-tor would hide the boobs, but that seems to only work if I hunch forward.

I sit up, trying to reposition my chest.

"Not a whole lot," Nicole says. She doesn't even notice my

dilemma. She seems to be enraptured by watching the crowds of students walking by, jostling in the overcrowded hallway. The first bell will be ringing any minute.

She nods at someone, a bit of a smile on her lips, but I can't see who it is because Amazonian-sized Janae is blocking my view as she struts down the hall.

"Who are you—" I'm cut off by the shrill ring of the bell. Argh.

"See you tonight!" Nicole jumps off and bounds into the crowd.

It's as if she's forgotten we have first period together, that we normally walk to class side by side. That we'll see each other at lunch, because we always eat together. That we have photography together this afternoon. Just a *see you tonight*. What's with that?

Once she's disappeared into the crowds, I open my binder and slide my homework into the back.

I glance up, just to be sure she's really gone, and then look at the photo behind my homework.

The photo of Ben.

I stare at it for a long moment, the sounds of the students around me dimming.

He'll always be perfect.

And he'll always be hers.

★ ★ ★

BY THE TIME I get home from school, I'm a complete and utter mess. I have no idea what today's wish is, so I spent the whole time dodging Ben. He most definitely thinks I'm insane. At one point during math, I had unknowingly dropped my pencil, and he leaned over to hand it to me and I leapt up from my seat as if he was about to brand me with a hot iron.

The best part is that the teacher was up front lecturing and everyone was scribbling notes, so I looked totally bizarre leaping into the air, my book launching so far it hit someone's foot three rows up.

At least I'm completely ruining any future with Ben, which makes the whole *I'm crushing on you* thing a moot point.

All I want to do is stuff my face full of the ill-fated unwish cake, wash it down with Coke, and watch the most mindless television I can find.

Ann is sitting on the front porch when I get home.

"You can't just sit there," I say, not even bothering with the hello. "My mom can't see you."

Ann purses her lips and gives me a sideways look of annoyance. "Can't you just say I'm a friend from school? I'm bored of the shed and your bedroom."

I cross my arms, considering this. "Maybe. I guess."

"Good." She gets up and bounds up the steps after me. "Can we make another cake? That was fun."

I just sigh and find us a couple of Cokes and take a few slices of cake into the living room.

Ann lies down on one of the couches, balancing her plate on her stomach. "Whatever happened to that tutu you had?"

I furrow my brow. "What tutu?"

"The pink one, with glitter on it. You wore it to school on picture day."

I snort, and then it turns into a funny bark of laughter. "Oh God, I forgot about that. It's probably in a box somewhere. My mom keeps all that stuff."

"We should try to find it," Ann says.

"Why?"

"I don't know. I never got to interact with any of these things you did. I just had to sit still and watch or listen to the stories."

"Yeah, but it's too much work to find it."

"Let's paint your room, then."

"I just painted it a year ago."

"Yeah, but again, I didn't get to play a part in that. I think I would enjoy painting."

"Then why don't you paint on a canvas?"

"Why would I paint canvas?"

"That's what artists use." I wave my hand, like, *meh*, but it doesn't deter her.

"That sounds fun. Do you have canvas?"

"Oh. Um, no."

"Then why did you offer?"

"I don't know!"

"Do you have any coloring books?"

I laugh. "Why would I have coloring books? I'm sixteen!"

"So! Coloring looks like fun." She pouts then, crossing her arms.

"You think?"

"Sure. I want to try it."

I sit up and sigh. "Okay. I think I can find some old books and crayons or maybe just markers. I told you. My mom keeps *everything*."

Ann pops upright, her eyes blazing with excitement. "Really? Yay!"

I smile, amused. Was I ever that excited about coloring? Must have been, at some point. Seems like a silly thing to get excited about.

I dig through some of the cabinets where my mom stores board games and various tchotchkes, and I produce a couple of coloring books and a worn box of crayons, the kind with the sharpener in the back. They look like they were purchased in 1993, but they'll have to do.

Ann and I sit down on the living room floor, and I hand her a book, one of animals. My own is a Disney book, with various princesses flouncing around on the pages.

I flip through the book. I can't remember the last time I saw any of these movies. I forgot *Aladdin* even existed. "Do you want to watch *The Little Mermaid?*" I ask, surprising even myself.

"Yes! I never got to see it; you always blocked my view or knocked me over."

I hop up and dig through the old-movie collection. For once, I'm glad my mom never threw out the VCR. I load the tape, and it seems to take forever to fast-forward through the previews. I can't believe people used to have to wait for tapes to fast-forward or rewind. . . . It seems so archaic.

Once the movie gets going, I take my place beside Ann at the coffee table and flip open the book again. The pages are half filled, my meticulous coloring splashing across the pages. I loved outlining the images in dark lines, then filling in the images with lighter, pastel-like colors.

I settle on an image of Beauty with her horse and start on the grass, selecting a pretty green crayon and shading in the blades along the edges.

Ann is attacking her pages with gusto, scribbling furiously on the body of a puppy dog. It's blue, but she doesn't seem to care. "What else do you have?"

"What do you mean?"

"Does your brother still have Legos?"

"Hmm. I think so. I think they're in some big Rubbermaid containers somewhere." My mom makes us keep all of this stuff "for our children someday," which is totally annoying. By the time I have any kids, they'll probably be playing with holographic pets.

Ann puts down her crayon. "Let's play with them!"

I don't know why, but it actually sounds like fun. I go into the closet in the hallway and dig around, triumphantly producing two large tubs filled with Legos. I bring them into the living room and move the coffee table out of the way and overturn one of the tubs right onto the carpet. The blocks rain out in a torrent of primary colors.

The racket brings my brother out of his room. "Those are mine," he says. Like we're ten or something, and I just stole his prized possession.

I shrug. "You're not playing with them."

He stands there for a second, wearing just a baggy pair of jeans and no shirt. His eyes settle on Ann. "Who are *you*?"

I roll my eyes. He's totally checking her out. "Ann, this is my brother, Chase. Chase, Ann."

"You mean the freak has a new friend?"

I growl at him. My brother loves calling me the freak. As if he's normal or something. "Shut up," I say, not lifting my eyes from the Legos. I'm going to build a spaceship. I have no idea why.

He stands there for a long moment, not saying anything. "Where'd you get the cake?"

"There's this thing in the kitchen. Box shaped. It's cold inside, like a polar ice cap."

My brother grunts and rolls his eyes.

"Hey, it's been in there for twenty-four hours. I baked it yesterday."

"Can I have a slice?"

"I guess. But if you're going to eat it out here, then put a shirt on."

He surprises me by not protesting. He just moseys over to his room, throws on the same T-shirt he was wearing yesterday, and comes back. He grabs a slice of cake and soda and then sits down on the floor near us, a gigantic slice of unwish cake on his plate.

This may have been normal for us once, before he went away to college, but I haven't spent more than ten minutes in the same room as my brother for oh, *ever*. "How's work?" I ask.

He shrugs. "Same stuff every day. It's killing me."

I look up at him through my lashes. "You could go to community college, you know."

He shrugs again. "Maybe. But that seems a step backward. I'm supposed to be at WSU."

I look at him, one eyebrow raised. "That makes no sense. At least it's a step forward from retail."

He pauses, a big chunk of yellow cake on his fork. He seems to consider this. "I guess. Still sucks, though."

"They have campus housing at GRCC now, I heard."

He looks up at me. "Really?"

I nod. "Yeah. Nicole's sister lives over there and I think it's pretty cheap."

"Oh. Maybe I'll check it out."

I nod, noticing the slight lift in his voice at the prospect. I go back to digging through the Legos. My rocket ship begins to take shape. I can't tell what Ann is building. It's either a castle or a dog.

"Do you ever think about calling Dad?" I ask.

My brother's mouth is full of cake, so I have to sit there for a long moment until he swallows.

"Nope."

"Not at all?"

"Why should I? He knows where we are."

"That's what I say." I shoot Ann a pointed look.

"So why are you asking me?"

"I don't know. I just . . . I don't know." I concentrate on snapping three yellow Legos together.

"He was supposed to teach me to shoot," Chase says.

I look up at him. "Huh?"

"He promised when I turned thirteen, I could get a BB gun and he was going to teach me how to shoot."

Thirteen.

A month after my dad left, Chase would have turned thirteen.

"Oh, Chase, I'm—"

Chase stands up. "Like I said. I'm not calling him."

And then he takes his empty plate and puts it in the kitchen sink, downing the last of his soda and tossing it in the trash.

I guess I'm not the only one who's still ticked off at my dad.

I glare at Ann for making me think about him at all and then turn back to the Legos. I wonder if I could build a rocket ship big enough to blast me right out of here.

22

I PUT MY PLATE in the sink, on top of Chase's. *The Little Mermaid* is still playing on the television. She's singing about forks.

"I'll be right back," I say to Ann.

It hasn't occurred to me until now, but maybe there will be an invoice or a business card or something from that bakery. If my mom's not around to question, the least I can do is snoop for answers.

I still haven't received a wish today. I'm afraid to know what it's going to be. At any moment, Ben could show up trying to kiss me. Or maybe the president will call and ask me to become his military adviser.

It *has* to stop. Nicole doesn't deserve betrayal, and no matter what I do, kissing Ben is going to be seen as just that. It won't matter that I'll do everything I can to stop it. It won't matter that the only reason he's doing it is because of some ridiculous wish.

I take the carpeted stairs two by two and go into her office. It's pristine: white walls, beige carpet, big blond-maple desk. She has one of those hard plastic mats for her black-leather rolling chair, and little trays and organizers for all of her paperwork are lined up along the matching maple-wood hutch. The only thing next to her flat screen is a telephone and a cup of pencils, all perfectly sharpened to a point.

The bookshelf is filled with reference material and binders. The binders, I know, she uses for events. Each spine is carefully labeled: SMITH-GREENE WEDDING, HAPPY TIME PICNIC, RAINIER RETREAT. If I were to flip them open, I would see six dividers labeled with different elements: entertainment, catering, venue. . . . Back in the days when my mom was getting the company started, my brother and I would help her make a bunch of empty binders and think about what it would be like when she had so many events they were full of paperwork.

We would make sundaes with all kinds of candy mixed in and she'd tell us all about her plans while we organized the binders and stuffed brochures into envelopes. It was, quite possibly, the only happy family activity we've done since my dad left. If we helped her, she'd let us leave our messy rooms untouched. She'd relent on making the beds, on doing the dishes. She needed us to get things going.

I don't help her anymore.

I sit down on her office chair and stay still for a moment, listening for the sound of her car in case she comes home uncharacteristically early. I haven't been in this office in months, and I don't want to have to explain what I'm doing in here.

I pull open the first drawer I see; it's full of perfectly organized office supplies, each item with its own location. The next few drawers don't yield anything better. Files, blank paper, notebooks, a Rolodex.

I'm still sitting in her chair, tapping my feet against the plastic mat, when the doorbell rings.

I spring out of the chair and leave the office as if I was caught red handed in the middle of a jewel heist and bound down the stairs.

Maybe it's Hansen coming to serenade me or UPS with a special delivery of Everlasting Gobstoppers. This whole curse would be better if I had wished for cool things. A shiny new car, anybody?

Ann is grabbing the knob just as I arrive in the tiled foyer, and I shove her aside before she can answer it. The last thing I want to do is explain to someone why this virtual stranger is answering our door.

"Where's my brother?" I ask Ann.

Ann points down the hall, to his room.

I turn to the door, straining to figure out who is on the other side of the stained glass oval.

I can't tell who it is, so I just yank the door open. And that's when I come face-to-pectorals with Ken. I had hoped he didn't know where I lived. The fact that he does seems kind of creepy. Then again, there are no rules in this magic wishland. If gumballs can rain down and I can speak Italian, it seems nothing is out of the question.

He's wearing his standard-issue black tank top, the one that barely contains his bulging arms or his rippling abs. He's paired it with royal-blue basketball shorts, ones that have three stripes down the sides, and a pair of white sneakers. He basically looks like he just stepped off the NBA court, except he's not sweaty.

The movement of air as the door slides open makes his scent waft toward me, and he smells good, a little like pine needles or leather, something natural, outdoorsy. Something decidedly untrendy but still masculine.

I expected him to smell like plastic.

I look up and see his blinding white teeth as his thick lips curl into a smile. "Hey, sweet stuff," he says, leaning down to kiss me. I lean backward and he ends up sort of slathering my jawline with slobber.

Awesome.

"Uh, hi," I say. My eyes dart to Ann. She's positively beaming with glee, as if this new boyfriend of mine is the best news she's had since the day she came alive. Actually, she looks the most alive she's ever been. Her eyes are bright with excitement, and she's practically quivering as she watches Ken's arm slither around my waist.

I glance down the hallway. If my brother comes out and sees Ken, I'll never hear the end of it.

I turn back to the dolls in front of me.

"Um, Ken, meet Ann. My . . . friend."

Ann's beam brightens to a thousand kilowatts when I call her a friend.

Something weird swirls inside me. Guilt? I push it down.

"So . . . what's up?" I ask, unpeeling myself from Ken's grasp. It's a hard maneuver to manage while still acting casual because Ken is like a solid slab of muscle, and his arm doesn't slide off as easily as I'd hoped. I end up kind of wrestling my way out and almost tripping on Ann's feet.

Please let him be here for something quick.

"I've searched high and low, sweets, but I couldn't find them."

"And who is them?"

"The tiger, panda, and zebra."

He gives me another *well, duh* look.

Oh, right. "That's terrible." I glance over at Ann and she bobs her head up and down eagerly, agreeing with me even though she has no idea what we're talking about.

"I think it's possible someone picked them up. Maybe took them in," he says, giving me a sympathetic frown. "I'm sure they're in good hands now."

Right, because who do you know who *isn't* in the market for a panda, zebra, and lion cub?

"Well, that is just darn disappointing, don't you think?" Hmm. I wonder if that's how Barbie really talks. I feel like I should speak all formal and serious-like when I'm pretending to be her. Because, you know, she's been president and a pediatrician and probably homecoming queen. Jack-of-all-trades, that girl.

Ken nods. I walk to the door. "Well, thanks for letting me know!" I say, yanking the door open.

Ken doesn't move, just stands there like a perfect man sculpture, staring at me. His back is to Ann, and I catch her looking down, studying his back and then his butt.

"Ann!" I whisper, and her eyes pop up and widen, then her cheeks turn red.

OMG, she is totally crushing on Ken. If only there was a way to get them together and send them riding off into the sunset on their trusty My Little Pony, I'd have it made.

"I thought we could go out tonight," he says, his eyes flicking over to the open door. He knows I'm giving him the brush-off.

"Oh, well, you know. . . . " *No*, obviously he doesn't know, because I don't either. I scramble to come up with some kind of excuse. "I was hoping you'd . . . fix the roof on the beach house," I say.

He raises a brow. "I was just there last weekend. The roof is fine."

I swallow. Ken is more perceptive than Ann, more . . . human-like. Ann is one crayon short of a full box, but Ken is harder to trick.

"Oh, you know, I'm just really busy with those, um, nursing-degree finals."

"I thought you had decided on being a veterinarian?"

"Oh! Yeah, that's what I meant. You know, it's hard to keep it straight sometimes. So many careers, so little time." I wave my hand around and try to use my body language to get him to move toward the door.

"I'll go!" Ann says, bounding forward. "I *have* to get out of this house!" She throws her arms wide with a flourish, and her knuckles smack into the door. "Ow!" She shakes her hand and kind of jumps up and down as she howls a little.

"But won't you come too?" Ken asks. "I haven't seen much of you lately. And I thought I could go pick up some new tank tops . . . "

Ann gives me her puppy dog eyes. "Please? I want to go out."

And *I* want to smack my forehead. Ken and Ann just keep looking at me, waiting for me to relent.

Just then I hear my brother opening his bedroom door. I straighten and shove the two through the front door in front of me. Ann sort of bounces off of Ken.

"Okay, fine! We can all go to the mall. *One hour.* But after that, Ann has to help me study."

"Yay!" Ann says, jumping up and down.

Ken just gives me a gleaming smile and puts an arm around my shoulders. "Great!"

I can't stop the sinking sense of dread.

"Going to the mall, be back later," I shout at my brother, who by now is halfway down the hall, heading in my direction.

I slam the door shut and bound down the steps toward Ken and Ann.

This is going to be trouble. I just know it.

23

BY THE TIME we pull up at the South Hill Mall, my hair is a gargantuan mess, and my stomach has twisted in about ninety-nine painful knots. Ken drove a Jeep today—it probably matches *my* theoretical Jeep—and he took the soft top off. Ken really should go back to California, where cars like this make sense. It's almost October, not nearly warm enough for this kind of vehicle, and I think there are now some orange leaves on the floorboard from some of the trees we passed.

The only thing that makes me feel better is that Ken's hair has blown out of the helmet look he had, so at least the windblown look works for one of us. Maybe it will be slightly less embarrassing to be seen with him now. If he would just throw on a normal-looking T-shirt and stop smiling so often, he'd seem kind of normal.

Ann, sadly, looks quite a bit worse for the wear. Her hair is positively insane. Maybe I should get her some hair products or something.

I take the rubber band off my wrist as we walk toward the food court entrance, smoothing out the flyaways and winding the band around my hair. While my hands are occupied, Ken takes the chance to wrap his arms around my waist and yank me up against his rock-hard body. Seriously, it's like being shoved into a wall.

I force a tiny smile in his direction and then weasel out of his arms.

"Where do you want to go?" I ask, of no one in particular.

When Ann doesn't pipe up, I turn to my left, and then to my right, and then over my shoulder. What the?

I stop and spin around. The mall isn't very busy, as it's a Monday night. I don't see her.

I backtrack a few dozen feet, and then I spot her: She's standing in front of Deb, her nose pushed to the glass so that it's totally smashed.

"*So* pretty!" she exclaims when she sees me. She jabs a finger into the glass. "I love that."

She's pointing to a pale-pink scoop-necked top. Someone has put a wide white belt around the waist and paired it with jeans and heels.

In other words, it's something a cheerleader would wear.

"Pink would clash with your hair," I say.

"But they have it in blue too!" She scoots over to the next mannequin and taps on the glass.

I sigh and study the display. Deb is one of the least expensive stores in this place. The top is probably ten dollars.

"If I buy it for you, you have to watch the pony all day again tomorrow. No complaints."

Her head bobs up and down and she claps. "Deal!"

I can't help it. I smile just a little as she bounds into the store.

At least . . . until she starts trying to rip the shirt off the mannequin.

★ ★ ★

THIRTY MINUTES LATER, I'm drowning my sorrows in a Cinnabon, a practically bottomless Diet Coke next to me. I've picked a nondescript round table in the corner of the brightly lit food court. I can hear the squeals and laughter of the shoppers around me, and my vantage point is perfect for people watching. A mound of sticky napkins sits next to me, and the treat is half eaten.

Ken said he needed more Muscle Milk. Ew. So Ann went with him to go pick up a jug of it. I'd been skeptical that he could pay for anything, but turns out Ken comes equipped with his own credit cards. Go figure.

I'm staring at the birthday wish list, trying to think outside the box on the things I would have wished for. It's half full now, thanks to the wishes I've already received. But I'm no closer to filling in the remaining blanks than I was a few days ago.

"Kayla?"

I hear the one voice that can make my heart spasm in my chest.

Ben.

"We have *got* to stop meeting like this," he says, smiling at me.

"Hey," I say, smiling back at him, though I know my smile is more tense than pleased. My eyes dart around. No sign of Ken or Ann.

"Mind if I sit?"

Ben is holding a big red tray with a plate of Chinese food piled high in the middle. He's wearing faded blue jeans and a loose-fitting, faded-black Kawasaki T-shirt. It makes his body look lean, muscular.

He's staring at me and I realize I haven't answered him.

"Oh, um, sure, go ahead." I pick up the wish list and jam it into my pocket.

Maybe I should shovel the Cinnabon into my mouth as quickly as possible and leave before my troupe of deranged dolls shows up. I hadn't planned on letting them out of my sight, but keeping up with Ann and staying out of Ken's arms was too hard. I wanted a break. And some sugar.

"Come alone?" he asks.

I shrug. "Not really." He just looks at me, waiting for me to fill him in, but I don't. "How about you?"

He nods as he finishes chewing the first mouthful of his dinner. "Just me. Nicole says I don't own anything *fancy* enough to wear to the Philharmonic."

Huh? "Philharmonic?"

He nods. "Yeah, we're going with some other couples in like two weeks. I think she's convinced I'm going to be horribly under-dressed. So I'm trying to find something to wear that won't be, like, physically painful. Do you think jeans are *ever* okay at a concert? Like if I buy new ones or something?"

I seem to be just staring into the distance, and I have to blink several times to bring him back into focus. "Oh. Um, no. Nicole probably plans on wearing a dress."

His face falls. "Figures. I got the button-down she wanted, but I was hoping to ditch the slacks."

I swallow uncomfortably and nod. I can't really picture Ben dressed up. He's more of a rugged, outdoorsy type. It would be easier to picture that guy from *Survivorman*—the one that drinks his own pee to survive—wearing a tux than Ben in slacks. "That's nice of you. To get dressed up for her, that is."

He takes a big bite of his food and chews for a long moment. "You think?"

I nod, but I don't say any more. I feel left out, just picturing them going to Seattle for something special while I'm sitting in my room, alone.

They're going to some fancy orchestra concert with a bunch of people.

And I'm not invited.

Because I'm not a couple.

I didn't even know they were friends with other couples.

I scrunch my eyebrows. "Wait, who are you—"

"Sugar!" Ken calls as he mounts the steps of the food court and joins me and Ben at the table. "Sorry it took so long."

He leans down and kisses me on the temple, then on the cheek. My skin crawls where his slobber is left behind. But I don't wipe it away. I just smile.

It must be fake, my smile. It must be *beyond* fake because inside I'm cringing and panicking as Ken pulls up a chair on one side of me and Ann grabs the other.

We have reached terror-level yellow.

Ben looks at me. Obviously, he is awaiting introductions.

"Um, Ben. This is . . . Carson," I say, waving my hand in Ken's direction, "and my friend Ann."

I hope Ken doesn't correct me, doesn't tell Ben his name is Ken.

Great. They rhyme. That's how awesome this is. Gah, how

come every time Ken is around all I can think is *awesome* this and *awesome* that?

Ann does her puppy dog smile and shoves her hand out to shake with Ben, somehow smacking his plastic fork and sending a chunk of General Tso's chicken launching through the air. Ben ducks just in time, and it lands behind him, on the white tiles. I half expect an overplayed *splat* sound effect when it hits, but it's nearly silent.

He doesn't look fazed, just reaches out and shakes Ann's hand. She grips it and shakes too enthusiastically, so Ben's whole arm is like a ripple of a wave.

Ken shakes his hand too, much more reserved and under control. He doesn't correct Ben when he says, "Nice to meet you, Carson."

Maybe his beach ball buds call him by his last name too.

Then Ken turns to me. "They had a killer sale at the vitamin store. Muscle Milk was two for one," he says, holding up the biggest shopping bag I've ever seen.

My eyes dart to Ben. His eyes are bright with repressed laughter, and I watch as he discreetly glances at Ken's bulging muscles.

"Gotta keep these babies fed," Ken says, setting down the bags.

And then, dear God, he flexes a few times and actually *kisses* his bicep.

Terror level: orange.

"What is that?" Ann asks, leaning toward me.

"Um, a Cinnabon?"

"I want some!" And then she yanks the whole plate off my tray and plops it down in front of her. She reaches over and takes the fork right out of my hand and jams it into the remaining Cinnabon, lifting it up as one big bite and sort of folding it into her mouth.

While she chews, her cheeks are swollen and puffy, like a chip-munk with an entire mouthful of nuts.

Ken leans back and looks a little bored, crossing his arms at his chest so that his pecs and biceps swell even bigger. Ken seems to take notice of his bulging muscles and looks down at his chest.

And then it gets even better. He uncrosses his arms and looks at his pecs and then makes *them dance*. One, then the other, pops up and down and up and down, while Ken looks inordinately pleased.

I, on the other hand, am horrified.

Terror level: red. We have reached meltdown, abort mission.

Ben stares straight at me, his lips quivering the tiniest bit as he takes another bite of his Chinese food. His eyes dart back over to Ann, whose mouth is crammed full of Cinnabon, and then back to Ken, who is still admiring his own chest.

I want to kick him under the table. We stare straight into each other's eyes for a long moment.

And then it happens.

It's a tiny muffled laugh at first. He tries to hide it with his fist, turn it into a cough. But it doesn't work. The laughter builds and rumbles in his chest, and then it breaks loose, and he bursts out laughing.

I glance from Ann's bewildered expression to Ken's bored one, and then I can't stop myself either. . . . The laughter bubbles out of me until I'm consumed by it, until I'm doubled over, laughing hysterically.

Ben looks up at me, his eyes taking me in as he keeps laughing, like he can't understand why *I'm* laughing too.

But he doesn't know the half of what has happened so far this week. It's like everything has overwhelmed me in one big wave, and something has broken loose and all I can do is laugh at myself.

It takes us several minutes to regain control of ourselves. By the time we do, there are tears at the edges of my eyes, and my sides are burning. Ben takes a long, slow drink of his soda to calm himself.

Ken and Ann are just watching us, a little bewildered and confused.

"So, Carson," Ben asks. "Do you know where I can find a good gym?"

I try to kick Ben, but my foot only connects with the leg of the table. He hears the loud bang my shoe makes as it connects with metal, and his grin widens.

Ben's not a gym sort of guy. His muscles are from working for his dad's landscaping business and from riding bikes, nothing more. They're thick and well defined, but he doesn't have the artificial bulk like Ken has.

"If you need some pointers, dude, I'd be happy to help."

"Oh yeah, that would be totally awesome, dude," Ben says, with a thick surfer accent. Then he actually flexes under his shirt, pointing to his arms.

I want to be angry with him or at least annoyed, but all I can think about is all the silly things I've said to Ken while pretending I was Barbie, and I can't help but think we have the same sense of humor.

It doesn't mean I want to sit around and see if this goes somewhere, though.

"Um, I think we should get going," I say. "Right . . . sweetie?"

I can barely grind out the last word. I'm not sure I should be claiming Ken as a boyfriend anymore. Maybe I should stage a breakup with him. Maybe he'd stay away then.

Why didn't I think of that sooner? If I break up with him, problem is solved.

He looks up. "Sure, honeydew."

Ben's lips quiver again with barely contained laughter.

"Come on, Ann," I say, pulling out her chair. She has Cinnabon and frosting all over her chin and has only managed to actually swallow half of what she crammed in her mouth.

"Nice seeing you, Ben."

"Yep. See ya in math," he says. He doesn't take his eyes off me. They're still bright, sparkling with amusement.

"Okay, then," I say, backing away from the table. I jam my hands into the pockets of my jeans. "Nice seeing you," I repeat, and then cringe.

I can't get out of here fast enough.

Ken is *so* getting locked in the shed with that stupid pony.

We're only halfway out of the food court when I finally realize that Nicole told me we couldn't study directly after school because she'd be with Ben.

But Ben was at the mall.

So Nicole was . . . where?

We walk back toward the entrance we came in at, down by Sears. The mall has been undergoing renovations for a while, with all new tiles and skylights and pretty rock facades around the support beams. Now it looks like they've added a big fountain.

Huh. Maybe I should try making a wish in the fountain. I mean, it can't hurt at this point.

I stop and dig into my pockets, staring at the copper pennies and silver nickels that glimmer beneath the surface of the water. I produce a handful of change and decide to use it all in one swoop.

I lean against the edge of the rocks and close my eyes.

I wish every wish—

My stomach drops into my knees as I feel Ann's body against mine, like she's tripped right into me, and my eyes pop open just in time to see the water rushing up toward my face.

I go under, the icy water completely covering me, and I flounder around until I feel a strong arm grab my shoulder and yank me upright. I cough, gasping for air, my hair flopping over my face as the water runs in rivulets down my skin.

Ken is leaned over the edge, a hand gripping my arm, his eyes wide with alarm. "Are you okay, honey?"

I sputter and spit out the water left in my mouth. Just as I'm nodding, my legs start to tingle, a tiny bit at first, until it multiplies and spreads. It's like both legs fell asleep at once. I wiggle my toes, trying to rid myself of the feeling, but it doesn't feel right. It's like my toes are stuck together with superglue.

I haul myself up onto the ledge of the fountain and pull my sneaker off so that I can dump the water out, but then my heart nearly stops and I try to shove it back on.

Oh. Mio. Dio.

I scramble out of the fountain as fast as I can, but it's difficult and my legs aren't cooperating.

Because I'm not totally sure they're legs anymore.

My skin is bluish, kind of iridescent. And a little scaly.

It looks like fish scales.

Ewww, what the heck was in that water?

The tingling turns to a weird needling, like when your foot is *really* asleep. My eyes dart around. Is anyone else seeing this?

My toes feel like they're trying to stick together. Like they're webbed.

Like instead of feet, I have fins. Frantically, I squeeze the water out of my socks and my legs and try to shake off the water that's still dripping down my back and limbs. The tingling gets worse, and I don't know if that's a good thing or a bad thing.

I blink several times and watch as my toes becomes toes again and the sliminess on my skin dissipates.

And that's when I realize what this is.

I think I'm turning into a mermaid.

This has gone way. Too. Far.

"Uh, I hurt my ankle, can you carry me to the car?" I say. I can't be here. Not if I go full-on fishy.

"Sure thing, doll!" Ken scoops me up as if I'm lighter than air and we head to the car. I will him to move faster, to get me out of here while I'm still normal.

Normalish.

We make it to the Jeep and now I'm pretty thankful that the top is off so that the wind can blow around and dry out my pants. I sneak a peek, and my skin still looks a little blue, but it's going back to normal.

Awesome. Apparently I can't get wet anymore, at least not as long as the wishes are still around.

I want to kill my seven-year-old self.

Because apparently, once upon a time, I wished to be a mermaid.

And now I am one.

24

ON TUESDAY, I spend twenty minutes gathering grass by hand for the stupid pony. I think if I don't start feeding it more, it's going to bust out of the shed. I rip out as much grass as I possibly can, then dump the pile in the shed. We're all out of rubbery carrots.

Ann helps, but she keeps getting distracted, yakking about an episode of *The Real World*.

By the time I'm sliding into my seat in bio, my jeans have grass stains on the knees and the bell is ringing, so I have no time to talk to Nicole and get the scoop on yesterday and the fact that she was so totally trying to ditch me for reasons yet unestablished. I skipped a shower this morning because I haven't figured out what I'm going to do about the whole problem with water and, well, me morphing into Ariel. At least I washed my face and slathered on half a stick of deodorant. But my hair looks terrible.

To make matters worse, we have a pop quiz. If a quiz can be fifty questions long, that is. It takes the whole class period and I'm positive I completely, totally flunk it.

Nicole doesn't seem to have my troubles, though, because she skates out of class the second the bell rings, her quiz already nestled among all the others on Mr. Gordon's desk. I leave the last ten questions blank and reluctantly hand it over.

By the time I make it to lunch, I'm in a horrid mood. I had to spend all of trigonometry leaning away from Ben again, and he most definitely thinks I hate him. I guess I should be relieved. Maybe he'll stay away. But instead it makes my heart twist around in my chest.

I empty my pockets of gumballs in a trash can and then head to the cafeteria. As I pass a couple classmates, I can't help but notice that one elbows the other and nods in my direction.

The other one clearly mouths, *Oh my God*, and then, even worse, she grabs the front of her shirt and holds it way out, mimicking the size of my chest.

I walk faster in the direction of the cafeteria, holding my binder in front of my chest in a feeble attempt to conceal the fact that it's half the size of the state of Rhode Island.

Right now I want nothing more than to bury my worries with a giant cafeteria burrito and about three cans of Mountain Dew.

My hand is on the cafeteria door, and I'm about to swing it open, when I see Nicole through the glass.

She's at their table.

The cheerleaders' table, that is. She's already eating her salad and nodding at something Breanna Mills is saying.

I just stand there, watching her, as the other students jostle by me to get through the doors. They stream past me, happily oblivious to the unease raging in my empty stomach.

I retreat a few steps, sit down on a bench outside.

I don't even know who she is anymore. She's dressing differently, she's become outgoing, she's laughing and having the time of her life.

Without me.

There was a time she would have waited outside the cafeteria doors because she was too timid to go in and run the social gauntlet alone. She would have sat on this very bench until I arrived and we'd go in together.

I mean, I'm kind of happy for her. I always knew people would like her if she would give them a chance, talked to them, got outside her shell. But she was afraid to do that, hiding behind her hair, hoping no one gave her a good look because she knew her skin wasn't perfect.

And now it's like . . . a complete 180. She's Little Miss Popular.

She hasn't even noticed that I'm missing. There's not even an empty seat next to her. What would she do if I walked up? Would she move to our table and eat with me, or would she just shrug and stay put?

Would *I* end up eating alone, watching her from across the room? Would she do that to me?

My stomach twists around, feels like it's hollowing out.

I thought my only worry was that I was losing her to Ben.

But turns out I have far more competition than that.

This is lame. Why can't I just do that? Find some friends? Stop putting everything into Nicole?

But I'm not like Nicole. Not this version of Nicole, anyway.

People don't get me, don't get my warped sense of humor. They won't want to be seen with me, would be embarrassed by my clothes and demeanor.

Nicole was different.

Was being the operative word.

☆ ☆ ☆

IN PHOTOGRAPHY, my portrait hasn't changed. I've taken two rolls of pictures of my Converse shoes, especially the yellow ones I drew all over, but it's one boring shot after another. Artistic? Most definitely not. It looks like a pair of shoes sitting on some carpet, not like art.

I turn toward Nicole, who has hardly spoken to me since we got into the darkroom. I thought maybe she'd say something about lunch. Something that would let me know she noticed I was in bio and photography but not sitting next to her in the cafeteria.

But so far, nada. I glance over at her. Her face is scrunched up as she works on her photos. She's wearing some designer-looking jeans and a flowered, flowing peasant blouse. "Why aren't you working on your assignment?" I ask.

Nicole looks up at me. She's working on pictures of road signs. There is no way a Yield sign is supposed to be her self-portrait. "I already turned it in. I thought I'd make some cool photos for my room."

"You turned it in already?" It's due on Friday. I still have not a clue what I'll do. "What did you take a picture of?"

Nicole shrugs and waves her arm around, making the bracelet jingle on her wrist. "Oh, you know, just some random stuff at my house."

She's not looking at me, just staring right at her enlarger, trying to find a good focus. Her toe starts tapping.

I'm beginning to hate her toes. It's hard to tell in the darkroom, but it looks like they're painted a bright shade of pink. She's wearing heels, too. Nothing extreme, but still, high heels with a peep toe.

Her hair is curled, too, and swept back in a messy twist. But it's messy in a stylish way, not messy in an "I don't care how I look" kind of way. And she's *accessorized*. With bangle bracelets and a string of pink plastic pearls.

Everyone is changing. Everything is changing, spinning out of control. I want to be nine again. I want to wish for Raggedy Ann and gumballs and stupid things, things that prove I have almost nothing of real concern in my life.

I don't want to have to wonder if I should make a transatlantic call just to talk to my dad.

And I don't want my best friend to keep ignoring me.

How come, if I'm getting everything I ever wished for, I feel so confused and empty?

"Why are you acting so weird these days?" I ask, unable to stop myself.

She looks up at me. But it's not surprise. More like worry.

"What do you mean?"

"I don't know. It's like all of a sudden you're trying really hard to fit in. I don't even recognize you. You're changing." My voice comes out sort of tentative at first, then gains steam as I let out what I've been worried about ever since school started.

She crosses her arms. "What makes you think I'm the one who changed?"

I snort. "Of course you have."

She shakes her head. "What, there's something wrong with dressing better? With being pretty, for once in my life?"

I stare at her as she turns back to her enlarger, as if the conversation is over. My mouth is parted slightly, but I can't seem to get any words to form. Not the right ones, anyway. "You didn't want this last year," I say, my voice lower.

Nicole pulls away from the enlarger. "Are you kidding me? Of course I did. But being popular is out of the question when your face is one big zit, don't you think?"

I'm surprised at how angry she sounds. "Nicole, if you wanted to be popular last year, you could have been—"

"That's a lie, and you know it."

Her voice is so sharp I can't help but step back a few feet and lean against the table in the center of the room, the one covered in shallow pans and chemicals for developing the photos. "So what, now that you're pretty I'm not good enough?"

Nicole rolls her eyes. "Oh, come on, that's not what I'm saying!"

"Are you sure?"

My heart hammers a little faster in my chest. Nicole and I have never gotten into a fight. Not like this.

"Yes. It's just really hard to get them to like me when you're standing around and—"

"Ohh, I get it." My stomach twists. "I'm an embarrassment, right? Maybe you'll hang out with me at home but not at school?" I lean in, my eyes narrowed, and lower my voice. "Do you want me to be your *secret* friend?"

I move away from the table and grab my things and start shoving them into my backpack. My backpack unzips as I try to jam my binder into it and I end up dropping everything. The binder skids across the floor and a bunch of papers fall out, and at least a dozen gumballs skitter across the floor.

Nicole sighs and then looks at the ground. "Kayla, stop freaking out. You're not understanding—"

Her voice stops abruptly when she sees what has fluttered to the ground in front of her toes.

And my heart stops at the same time.

It's the picture of Ben.

The picture I have of *her* boyfriend just fell out of my backpack and is sitting at her feet.

Oh God, this is so not good.

She starts to reach down to pick it up. "Why do you—"

No, *no, no, no*. Something needs to happen in the next half second. An earthquake. A fire drill. Anything.

She can't know, she can't see this, she can't—

But it's too late. I feel our years-long friendship ripping down the middle, tearing apart, as she bends over.

She stops short of touching it and just stares at it. She blinks a few times and then looks up at me and just keeps blinking faster and faster, as if she can blink away the truth.

"It's not what it looks like," I say.

I'm not sure why I said that. Because it's exactly what it looks like. My cheeks begin to burn. The feeling in my stomach is horrible. The dread, the embarrassment, the hysteria, just keeps building inside me.

Everything is ruined. It's over. She's going to hate me now.

I know what she's thinking of as she stands there, blinking and blinking and blinking, like she has a gnat stuck in her eye. I know what she's picturing, remembering. She's thinking of those times I asked her for every detail of their date, of those times I agreed a little too wholeheartedly how perfect Ben is.

And I know she knows. Maybe this picture finally confirmed my secret crush on him, but everything I've done until now has been sketchy enough to support the theory.

It feels like my insides are emptying out as I stand here, waiting for her to tell me what I already know: I have no friends in this world.

"Wow. I mean, wow." Her voice isn't bitter now, it's pure anger. And it's directed at me.

"Nicole, I'm so sorry. I—"

The sharp look in her eyes makes the words evaporate.

She leans down again, her eyes never leaving mine, and picks up the picture and grips it so slightly in her hand it crumples and folds, and I can't see his face anymore but I know it's ruined, and I try not to flinch.

She laughs, the anger melting together again with the bitter undertones. "Well, then, I bet you'll be just ecstatic to hear that he dumped me. Is that what you've been waiting for?"

My jaw drops. "You broke up? Why?"

She laughs at me as she crumples the picture into a ball. A few of the students in the darkroom turn and look at us. "How could you do this to me?"

"I didn't *do* anything, I swear, I—"

"What? Lusted after my boyfriend behind my back?" She's spitting the words now, and they're getting louder.

I can't seem to close my jaw. It weighs a thousand pounds.

"I can't believe you," she says, slinging her bag over her shoulder. She gives me one last disgusted look and then leaves the darkroom.

I think I just lost my best friend.

25

BY THE TIME I make it home that afternoon, I feel like I've been spun around in circles and no longer know which way is up. I don't know what to do about Nicole, about the wishes, about anything.

My only condolence is that I don't run into Ann or the pony as I'm walking home. I'm not sure I could deal if I encountered them.

I slow as my house comes into view. The right bay in the garage is open, and my mom's Lexus is parked inside. This is weird. I can't remember the last time I came home from school and she was there.

I stop and just stand there, staring at it. Somehow I know this is not a good thing, that her being home can only lead to disaster, at least as long as the wishes are still hanging around. My mom is never home, not in the middle of the day.

I shake my head and pick up a walk again. Whatever it is, it's not like I can stand out on the sidewalk all day.

I slip my key into the doorknob, but before I can turn it, the whole thing swings away from me, my keys still jangling from the lock.

My mom is on the other side, giving me a hard look.

This is not good. After the blowout with Nicole, the last thing I want is another showdown.

"Is there something you'd like to tell me?" She doesn't step aside, doesn't move so that I can enter the house.

Whatever it is, she's seriously mad.

I stare at her, blinking.

I don't know what she's asking. Did she find out about my *boyfriend*, Ken? Has she discovered Ann, my new bestie, has been staying the night every night for the last week? Or is it the garden shed filled with gumballs and a pink pony?

"Um . . . no?"

She narrows her eyes. She's unimpressed by my lack of honesty. But it's not like she'd believe me on, oh, *anything* that has happened in the last two weeks. No way.

So my lips are sealed.

"Nothing . . . in the garage?"

I swallow. It's hard not to fidget. I'm just standing on our front porch like I'm an unwanted houseguest. But my mom is so mad she doesn't seem to notice that she hasn't let me inside.

I don't know what's in the garage. But whatever it is . . . it can't be good.

"What's in the garage?"

My mom rolls her eyes, slowly, and then shakes her head. She seems to have lost her patience altogether. But I'm not playing games with her. Not really.

"Don't play dumb."

"But I am! I mean, not dumb, but I don't know what you're talking about."

"Come." She steps aside and opens the door, and I realize she's not wearing her heels. She never takes her shoes off unless she's going to be home for a long time.

So either she's been stewing about something for hours or I'm in *really, really* big trouble, and she's canceled whatever she has going for the evening. I'm not sure which scenario is more favorable.

I follow her to the garage, my feet feeling heavier with every step, until it's like my limbs are filled with sand.

At this point, nothing would surprise me. Maybe there's an elephant with a red bow in the garage. Maybe the entire cast of *Twilight* is sitting in some director's chairs, ready for my one-of-a-kind interview. Maybe my brother is dressed up as a giant pickle.

My mom opens the heavy door leading into the garage and steps into the space. It's dim for a moment as she reaches over and flips on the fluorescent overhead lights.

They blink and flicker to life, revealing my mom's silver Lexus.

And a lime-colored dirt bike.

Holy crap, there is a fluorescent green dirt bike in the garage, sitting innocently next to my mom's shiny car.

My mom turns to look at me, shooting me a look that must wither anyone who stiffs her on a bill.

"That's not mine," I say, crossing my arms, hoping it's true, knowing it's probably not.

I knew I'd really wanted a dirt bike for a while. I guess if I think about it, it still sounds like fun.

I just didn't know I ever wished for one.

For about two years, I asked for a dirt bike for every birthday and every Christmas. My dad always said I could have one once I got a little older, and my mom always shot him death glares when he said it, but I figured he would sway her to the dark side sooner or later.

That's part of what sealed the deal with Ben. I wanted a bike, he had one.

Fate. Kismet. Back in seventh grade, my fantasies with him involved me dreaming of him showing me how to ride. He'd take me out, and I'd hang on to his waist and rest my cheek against his back, and life would be perfect.

My mom reaches into the pocket of her khaki slacks and produces a key ring.

A key ring with a big black plastic-encased key and a string of beads.

Beads that perfectly spell out *Kayla*.

"Where did you get that?" I ask. For some reason I reach out to grab the key, which makes me seem completely guilty. She snatches them away, continuing to dangle them as if they are the key piece of DNA evidence in a murder trial.

"Your room. I forgot a file and stopped in to get it. Once I saw the bike, I checked your room. Chase has been at work all day, so I knew it wasn't his. Do you care to explain yourself?"

I just stare, because it's not like there's a way to explain away a lime-green dirt bike, especially not one with a custom key ring.

"I throw you an enormous sweet-sixteen party and this is how you repay me?"

Pft. I can't stop the escape of breath, the one that sounds like bitter laughter.

"What's that for?"

I look up at her. If she hadn't thrown that stupid party, if she hadn't insisted I make a wish, I wouldn't be in this mess in the first place. It's *her* fault there's a motorcycle in the garage. "I didn't want that party and you know it. You know it because I told you over and over. *You* wanted the party so you could impress your clients."

She narrows her eyes. "I can't believe you're being so ungrateful! A hundred girls would kill for a party that expensive and nice!"

"Maybe! But maybe if you paid one *ounce* of attention to me, you'd notice that I am not one of those girls!"

She crosses her arms. "What do you mean, if I paid attention? I work my butt off for this family!"

I laugh, shaking my head. "Don't pretend your job is for us. I know it's because you want to impress Dad. News flash, he doesn't care about you or me or any of us."

"Kayla!"

"What? You know it's true. You're obsessed with your stupid company. Nobody in this family even talks anymore! You don't eat dinner with us, you don't watch TV with us. Dad might as well have taken you with him when he went to Italy!"

My anger blazes and I look her in the eyes, but what I see wrenches straight through me.

Because I see something there that I'm not sure I've ever seen.

Hurt. She masks it well, but for one, *tiny* fraction of a second, I saw it.

And then, with sad clarity, I realize: He left my mom, too. Her husband, the man that swore to love her until death do them part, reneged on his promise, just like he did on all the others—the BB gun, the dirt bike, everything.

Maybe her company isn't all about impressing him. Maybe it's about forgetting him.

My mom grinds her teeth, the mask back. "I don't have time for this conversation. I've got a retreat in Eastern Washington for the rest of the week. Chase in is charge." She's looking for her shoes and jamming her toes into the crème leather pumps. "We'll discuss this when I get back. Until then, you're grounded."

"But—"

"We will finish this later." She glares at me and the look on her face makes the words die in my throat. I can see being grounded is the least of my concerns.

"Okay," I manage.

I'm frozen in the doorway as she backs the car out, and I'm still standing there when the garage door shuts, staring at the lime-colored bike in the second bay.

Is it wrong if I want to take it for a test spin?

I'M ON MY WAY to my room, fuming about this whole stupid, mess of a day, when I see something sitting on the counter.

My mom's planner.

I glance out the front window to be sure she hasn't come back right away for it and then scurry across the tiles and unsnap the button holding it together.

It's pristine, perfectly organized, nothing out of place. The total opposite of my life right now.

The front is a series of plastic pages that hold one business card after another. She must have a hundred cards.

I scan the first couple of pages. They're DJs, banquet halls, caterers. My fingers glide over the surface as I scan the business names. A bakery isn't among the first few pages.

A low humming noise outside catches my attention. I turn to see my mom parking in the driveway.

She's realized that she forgot her planner.

I start flipping the pages faster, whipping through them. I have to find the card. I *must* find the card.

To undo the wishes, to undo this mess I'm in.

More rental halls, an inflatable-bouncy-house company, a few florists. My heart climbs into my throat as I hear her car door slam.

If I don't find it, I'll never get to the bakery. After today, my mom's not going to be doing me any favors, even if it's just looking up the address for a bakery. And she's definitely not letting me out of the house to go buy a cake.

And then on the last page, I see it.

A big blue cake, carefully designed and imprinted on the card. It looks fancy, Dr. Seuss–like. Definitely in the style of my sweet-sixteen cake.

Betty's Bakery is embossed in burgundy swirly print across the top.

My fingers scramble to find the opening, figure out what side the card slides in on so that I can yank it out.

I hear my mom's heels clacking across the slate stoop. She's going to catch me digging through her planner.

My fingers find a gap in the plastic and I yank the card out and then flip the planner shut and dive behind the island just as the door is opening.

I count her steps as she crosses the foyer and walks across the tile. I hold my breath and listen as she re-buttons the planner.

Then silence. I don't know what she's doing. I think she might be listening for me. Wondering if I'm up in my room or in the garage. *Please don't look for me.* I don't need The Big Lecture: Part II.

I close my eyes and try not to sigh aloud as she turns around and heads back to the door. I don't breathe until I hear her car door slam and hear her back out of the drive.

The business card is smashed in my palm, but it's still in one piece.

★ ★ ★

IF MY LIFE were a natural disaster, the president would now declare it a federal emergency and call in aid. The Red Cross would try to revive my social status and repair my relationships with my mom and best friend.

Since that's not happening, it's time to kick this plan into high gear. Ann and I are heading to Betty's Bakery, which turns out to be outside a completely different mall than the one we went to last time. At least now I have the card tucked into my pocket and I know where I'm going.

I'm pinning all my hopes on reversing everything.

Unfortunately, it's pouring rain now, covering the freeway, making it a little tough to speed, which I really want to do. My fingers grip the steering wheel and I glance down at the speedometer, wishing it said ninety-nine miles per hour. The faster this is over, the better. Everything's changing, crashing down, and I'm afraid I'm going to fall apart just like the rest of it.

Ann clears her throat. She can tell I'm worked up over something. "Ken and I bought you something. Well, Ken bought it. I just came up with the idea."

I look sideways at Ann. I'm almost afraid to hear what she's going to say next. The wipers are hardly keeping up with the torrential downpour. I turn my attention back to the road. "What?"

Ann digs into her pockets. She found a pair of my jeans from junior high, when I was a size or two smaller. She's also wearing a Hello Kitty T-shirt, the one I bought to pair with combat boots. She hands me something, a piece of paper.

When I see what it is, my eyes widen and I shake my head and toss it back at her. "No way."

"But you like ballet!"

"*Liked* ballet. Past tense, remember?"

"You don't have to dance in it, silly. We're going to go and watch."

"Pretty sure I'm grounded."

"Forever?"

I snort. "No, but probably for at least two weeks. Longer if I get in trouble again."

She frowns. "But the ballet is on Saturday. And we bought four tickets in case you want to bring a date."

I whip around to look at her. "What do you mean, if *I* want a date? Isn't Ken my date? Or doesn't he *think* he's my date?"

Ann gives me this, *I don't know how to tell you this but . . .* look.

My eyes flare wide. "Oh my God! I'm the third wheel!"

I smack my forehead and then spread my fingers so I can see the road through them. "You and Ken are, like, totally into each other, aren't you?"

I don't have to look at her to know the truth.

"Unbelievable. First Nicole and now you . . . Why does everyone around me hook up?"

Ann kind of shrugs and crinkles her nose, because she knows it's a rhetorical question. Or maybe it's not. I don't know.

"Won't you come, though? It'll be fun!"

I switch the wipers up to the highest notch as the downpour increases. I should have worn a jacket. Ann should have too. "I told you I'm grounded. And besides, I might be sticking hot needles under my toenails that day. I'll have to check my schedule and get back to you."

"Oh, come on, you have to come. If you don't, Ken probably won't go."

I look at her sideways. "What do you mean? I thought he was into you."

She kind of squirms in the seat. "Well . . . I was kind of hoping he could be. Because you're not into him. So maybe if you brought a date, he'd turn his attention to me . . . "

Maybe if Ann had asked me this yesterday, I would have considered it. But today? When so much is going wrong?

"Please? I really want to go. Ken showed me YouTube videos, and—"

"You watched YouTube videos with Ken?"

She nods.

"How? When?"

"We used your computer earlier today."

"*Ken* was in my room?"

She nods and then looks out the window, as if what she just said is no big deal at all.

"Ann! You can't just let people into my room like that. My mom could see you!"

"I wasn't even there when your mom was home. Besides, it's *our* room," she says. "He was *my* guest. And you have no idea how bored I get when you're not around."

My hand tightens on the wheel. I stare, unblinking, out at the sheets of rain pouring down over the freeway, blurring the red tail-lights in front of me. The dynamic between Ann and me is getting increasingly complicated. It's like she's Pinocchio, and she's ready to assert her independence. I don't know how to deal with it, how to keep her under wraps. "He didn't, um, like dig through my stuff, did he?"

She shakes her head. "Of course not."

Silence falls between us. Just the muted sounds of the radio and the pounding of the rain. I flip my blinker on and take my exit. A big semi-truck roars by us to our left, and Ann jumps.

"So, will you go? Pretty please?"

I sigh and pull to a stop at the light just off the ramp. I feel like a tiny little ant lined up with all the other cars, ready to go marching two by two to get out of the rain. "I told you, I can't. But maybe we can figure out how to get Ken to go with you."

If I'm lucky, this cake thing will work and there will be nothing left to figure out.

The light finally turns and I hang a left and follow traffic for a few blocks to get to the mall. I feel tingly and nervous as I pull into the lot, my eyes scanning the nearby buildings for the bakery, aka, the reason for this entire disaster. Or at least, what I'm hoping is the reason.

It's the only thing that makes sense. Because I've had a birth-day every year for sixteen years, and I've never had my wishes come true. Then my mom buys this ridiculous frosted masterpiece and presto, magic. Maybe this bakery's recipes include hair of witch and slime of a toad or something. I don't know, but it's my last resort, so it better work.

I circle around to the back, and my stomach seems to trip

all over itself when I see the swirling letters spelling out *Betty's Bakery*. Ann shrieks and points to the sign and bounces around in her seat.

I still haven't told her that she's going to be part of the unwish. How would I start? "Oh, by the way, have fun today because it might be your last"? That'll go over well.

She doesn't understand that real life means school and jobs and paying bills, and there's no way she can function like that. So she has to go back . . . to wherever she came from.

I park the car as butterflies swarm my stomach. This is my one shot at fixing everything. I *have* to make this work. Because if it doesn't?

Well, there is no *if*. There's just a *when* it works, life will be back to normal. I can apologize to Nicole and forever stay away from Ben.

Ann and I cross the blacktopped lot, my sneakers feeling sticky, like I'm melting into the pavement, even though it's probably forty-eight degrees out and still pouring rain. The rain starts soaking through my jeans, and my skin begins to tingle.

I realize with a jolt that I *must* get out of the rain, and I pick up a dead sprint and dash through the sparkling glass door. I take a deep calming breath as I step inside the well-lit place.

The glass display case parallels the long wall to my right, and it's filled with a colorful array of cupcakes, cookies, and cakes. There are big portraits on the wall, giant posters of frosted, mountainous treats: wedding cake towers, cartoon-themed birthday cakes, giant cookies placed in a pyramid of mouthwatering sugary sweets.

I follow the pastel-colored tiles to the counter, where a petite gray-haired woman is leaned over, a phone propped up between her shoulder and her ear, scribbling down an order.

"Uh-huh. Lemon filling. Strawberry filling? I suppose we could do half and half. Right. Well, no, you probably wouldn't want them mixed together. One side lemon, one side strawberry. Right. Okay. The twenty-fifth? Yeah, it'll be tight, but we can do that. Okay. I'll call you when it's ready. Thank you."

She sets the phone in the cradle on the wall and turns back to her order form, scribbling down more directions for the filling-challenged customer. I wait quietly for her to notice me, but when she doesn't, I clear my throat.

She jumps back from the counter and looks up at me, her brown eyes widening to the size of the cupcakes.

"Sorry," I say, grimacing. Whoops, didn't mean to scare her.

"We need a cake," Ann says, peering into the display case. "That one."

"No, not *that one*." I look over at Ann, wondering why she's trying to take charge of this expedition. "I think you made a cake for my sweet sixteen last week. Pink, lots of flowers, four tiers. I'd like to get another one. Identical."

The woman leans back against the counter behind her, crossing her arms over her flour-dusted black apron. She has a smudge of frosting on her chin, and I swear, she has sprinkles in her curly gray hair. "I require two weeks notice for custom cakes."

My heart seems to stop beating altogether. "This is an emergency. I really, *really* need that cake, *today*."

She puts her wrinkled hands into the pockets of her apron. "You do realize that cake cost three hundred dollars?"

I practically choke on my spit. I can't afford that, not by a long shot. Thanks to all my Ann-related expenses, I have maybe forty bucks to my name. "Can you make a mini-version?" I say, feebly. I'm not even sure a mini-cake would do the job, since my homemade one didn't. Then again maybe it's the ingredients, not the size.

"I still need a couple weeks notice. I'm backed up as it is, working late every night, seven days a week. No time for an extra order."

I look down at my feet, fighting the urge to scream. This is not good. Not good at all. "Please, I need that cake," I say, shoving my hands deep into my pockets. I'm wearing a pair of jeans my mom bought me. It's a little weird to feel so . . . normal. They fit well, with no rips or tears or ink to be seen.

"Look, the only thing I sell out of the case is cookies," she says, pointing to the display case, "or you can place an order and come back for it in two weeks."

I grind my teeth and stare at the case. "I can't even take a cupcake?"

At least those are made of cake batter, and maybe if I got one white and one pink . . .

"Those are sold by the dozen. Sixty dollars."

Holy crud, this lady really overcharges. I dig through my purse. All I have on me is thirty dollars and a metric ton of pennies and nickels.

"Okay. Um, one cookie," I say, my stomach sinking. This probably won't work. I'm doomed to live my life with Ann and Ken and the rest of my twisted troupe.

The woman stuffs a cookie into a paper sack and then hands it to me. "On the house. You look like you could use it."

Okay, so suddenly she's feeling all generous?

"Um, thanks."

I head to the door, dragging my feet, while Ann bounces around behind me. The door is half open when I hear the old lady speak again.

"It'll be over by Monday."

I freeze. My hand on the door tightens until my knuckles turn white. I turn around and face her.

"What does that mean? Everything goes away after the last wish?"

The woman looks up from the cake she is frosting. "Pardon me?"

"You just said it'll be over by Monday. Does that mean as soon as I receive the fourteenth wish? They'll all just *poof* into oblivion?" I ask, stepping toward her.

Her eyes dart back and forth and she steps back. It's like she's looking for a freaking silent alarm, like I've gone mad. "I said no such thing."

"You did! You know what's going on!" My voice gets higher, frantic. The woman backs up until she's pressed against the countertop behind her. "Tell me how to fix this!"

She puts her hands out, as if she's been cornered by a pack of wild dogs. Like I'm crazed or something. "I'm going to have to ask you to leave."

I take in a ragged breath, trying to calm myself. I can't freak her out. "No, please, it's okay. I just need help. One of these wishes can't come true or my life will be over."

"Miss, I have no idea what you're talking about. You need to go or I'll have you removed."

So this is how she's going to play it. Feign innocence. Make me deal with it on my own. Stupid lady and her magical cakes. I think the sprinkles have gone to her head.

I stomp to the door and shove it open, Ann trailing after me. By the time we get to the car, I'm positively fuming.

Maybe I should be happy. Now I know that Ann and Ken and the pony won't be lurking in my life forever. But all I can think about is kissing Ben and betraying my best friend.

That lady is responsible. I don't know what she puts in those cakes. . . .

I can't believe this! What a disaster! If she's right, there's no way to undo it. Not until I get the last wish.

Not until I kiss Ben.

I hate my life.

Ann gets into the car and buckles her seat belt. I just stand there next to the driver's-side door, the rain soaking through my T-shirt. My legs begin to tingle, but I still don't move.

I'm screwed. Totally, completely screwed. I have six more wishes to survive, and I don't know what any of them are.

No, I know what the last one was. So what are the others?

Could I have wished for anything worse than what's already happened?

27

BY THE TIME I get home from the bakery, I'm so frustrated by everything that I want to scream and rip out my hair.

I tell Ann to check on the pony and then go inside. She pouts, but I'm so furious I don't even care.

I take the stairs two by two, tripping over the last one and landing hard on my knees. I scramble to my feet and then make it down the hall and fling my door open. I head straight into my closet. I want to find everything from my childhood. Every stupid, cursed thing and destroy it, before it comes to life too. I stand on my tippy toes to find the boxes that have been occupying one corner of my closet for years.

I yank so hard on the first one that it topples over and the lid flies off and everything inside the box scatters across the floor.

A couple dozen My Little Ponies land in a heap, their pink, blue, purple, and white manes tangling together. I kick the one nearest me and then reach up for the next box and take a big swipe at it and it falls off the shelf.

Children's books. *If You Give a Mouse a Cookie. The Little Ballerina. Cinderella.* All those stupid books meant to teach kids they can be anything and everything. That life is one big happy cookie.

They don't make books called *Soon, Your Best Friend Will Abandon You.* They don't make one called *Too Bad You'll Grow Up and Become Such a Loser!* And they definitely don't make one called *It Doesn't Matter if You Speak Italian Because Your Dad Doesn't Care.*

I rip another box down and a few dozen Barbie dolls fly out, littering the closet floor with their perfect waists and long legs and luxurious blonde hair, hair that looks nothing like mine.

I don't feel any better. In fact, I feel more balled up inside, just as angry as ever. I turn around and yank a bunch of pink flirty shirts and dresses off the hangers. This section of the closet is reserved for the clothes my mom buys me, the stuff I'll never wear, not in a million years. The hangers swing around as the clothes rip and tear off, landing on the floor in a big heap.

By the time the whirlwind is complete, my closet is trashed, a huge mountain of junk overflowing and spilling into my room.

I slide to the floor and stare at the pile of junk as my heartbeat slows, as the rage starts to disappear, replaced by sad, bitter dejection.

It's going to happen. I'm going to kiss Ben, and I'll never be friends with Nicole again.

I pick up an errant Barbie and toss it onto the stack of junk next to me. I let my eyes wander over the stuff I haven't looked at in years. It seems like it was never even mine, like it belongs to someone else entirely.

But it *is* mine. Maybe I'm someone else now, but once, all this stuff was me. I just decided not to be that person anymore.

And maybe that's why I'm not handling this well.

Because for the first time, I've finally realized something: I chose this.

I chose to have a single friend and to block out everyone else.

I chose to dress like a freak and make fun of everyone else, ensuring my total social-leper status.

I chose to quit ballet.

I chose to be more angry with my mom than with my dad, when at least she's trying.

I chose to put all this stuff in boxes and pretend I was never anything but what I am right now.

I chose this.

I look down at my Converse for a minute and then back into the closet.

It's like a big time-warp piled up next to me. A visual representation of who I once was.

I blink a few times and look closer at the stack.

Suddenly I have an idea. I jump up and go to my desk, where my 35mm camera is sitting, and pop the lens off.

I take a series of pictures: a few of the outfits my mom has bought me but I've never worn, a couple of my old ballet slippers, a few of my report cards, a couple of the school pennant, and a series of pictures of the birthday gifts that other people bought me.

I don't know if anything comes out, if it's just going to look like one big uninspired mess, but I take enough pictures that I'm hopeful. Maybe tomorrow I can develop something. The project is due soon, so this is my only chance.

28

WEDNESDAY turns out to be an unmitigated disaster.
Nicole doesn't even look my way, let alone talk to me. And I don't
even know if I *want* to talk to her. Do I owe her an apology for our
fight? Or does she owe me one?

My light, goofy friendship with Ben has transformed into an
odd, uncomfortable acquaintance. I don't blame him for not knowing how to act. I'm the one who keeps acting like he's some highly
contagious leper. Every day, if I haven't received my wish yet, I go
out of my way to avoid him. Sometimes he'll be heading my way
down the hall, and I'll abruptly veer out a side door.

Maybe it's stupid and I won't be able to avoid kissing him, but
I keep doing it anyway.

He'd have to be a complete idiot not to notice. On top of
all that, I keep yammering on and on about Ken, hoping somehow that's going to be enough to keep him at arm's length. I'm
still thinking it's possible Ben will use his own common sense and

choose not to kiss me. So if he remembers I have a boyfriend, well, that's a good thing.

My mom is still out of town, and she'll be away until Friday. We haven't talked since our blowout.

My back hurts all of the time because of my huge chest, the gumballs are everywhere, the pony is getting crankier every day, and I'm still talking in Italian.

I'm absolutely *dying* for a long, hot shower to relax, but for the last couple days I've had to settle for a sponge bath and washing my hair in the sink, because there's no way I want to find out what happens if I submerge my legs for more than two-point-five seconds.

By the time I'm walking up the stairs to my room, I'm muttering Italian curses under my breath.

When I walk into my room, Ann looks suspiciously happy, the polar opposite of my mood. She's spinning around and around in my rolly computer chair, the very chair I once foisted between us to keep her away from me on the day she appeared.

Too bad I didn't succeed.

I glare at her and throw myself onto my bed, resting my cheek against the cool lime-and-orange-plaid quilt.

If I can't be happy, she shouldn't be either.

She stops spinning and nearly falls out of the chair. Her eyes look sort of loopy and crossed, so I know she's dizzy and hasn't noticed my scowl.

"What's got you all hyped up?" I say, not even attempting to cover my hostility.

"I'm going to a party!" she says, her voice so chipper it's practically filled with rainbows and ponies. If, you know, that were possible.

I want to throw things at her. Rocks, maybe.

I sit up on my elbows and give her a closer look. "Who invited you to a party?"

"I don't know! Some girl named Janae. I wrote down the address," she says, waving it around in the air.

I leap off the bed like a puma on attack and snatch the paper out of her hand.

3322 Weatherby Lane.

Janae's house.

Unbelievable.

"Where did you get this?"

"From your notebook," she says, pointing to where she ripped out the sheet of paper.

"Not the paper! The address!"

"From Janae. Duh."

"Ann!" I screech, totally exasperated. "How do you know Janae?"

"I don't."

My eyes flare and I want to throttle Ann. Instead I take a deep, calming breath, unclenching my fists.

"Start at the beginning. How do you know about this party and why did she give you her address?"

Ann shrugs and gives me a look like, *Sheesh, why are you so annoyed?* "She called. A half hour ago."

Ann points across the room to where my cell phone is still sitting on my nightstand, where I put it last night to charge and forgot it when I went to school.

"You've got to be kidding me," I say, rushing over to my phone. I flip it open and find the call log. Sure enough, Ann answered a

call thirty-six minutes ago. I punch the call button and listen as
it rings.

"Hello?"

I blink and yank the phone away and slap it shut.

That was definitely Janae.

"That was rude!" Ann says. "She's very nice."

"Janae is *not* nice. Far from it."

"She said it wouldn't be a party without me."

I'm gripping the phone so tightly in my hand that it makes my
fingers hurt. "Did she know it was you?"

"What do you mean?"

"Did you say, 'I'm not Kayla,' or maybe, 'Hello, this is
Ann'?"

Ann blinks a few times and tips her head to the side as she
stares up at the ceiling. "I guess not."

"So now Janae thinks I'm coming to her party?"

Ann twists a frizzy strand of hair around her finger. "Yeah. I
suppose. But I can still go, right?"

"No, you cannot go!"

Ann pouts and crosses her arms. "You sure are grumpy a lot.
What'd I ever do to you?"

I so don't have time for this.

"Don't you get it? These stupid wishes are destroying my life!"

The playful pout turns into a real one. "Everything is always
about you."

I fall onto my bed, exasperated. "What do you want me to say,
Ann? Everything is a wreck."

Ann spins the chair toward the wall. "I heard that lady at the
bakery, you know."

"What?"

"I'm not stupid. I have a few days left, tops. So whether you like it or not, I'm going to this party."

There's a strange pressure inside me, like an elephant is perched on my chest. I don't know if I feel guilty about Ann or panicked about my life, but it's like the whole world is sitting on me.

"Why would Janae invite me to a party?" I ask, though I don't expect Ann to have the answers.

"I don't know. Maybe she secretly wishes you two were best friends."

I snort and give her a skeptical look, but the look melts away as Ann's statement rings in my ears. Realization dawns, slow and clear.

"She didn't," I say quietly. "I did."

I stare at the ceiling in my bedroom, trying to find shapes in the popcorn texture. It's so quiet except for the rain pounding outside. "Not to be best friends. But that she'd invite me to her birthdays and pool parties."

I sigh, long and drawn out. At least it's another wish down, right? I pinch the bridge of my nose and close my eyes, trying to figure out what I should do next.

"If I rent movies and we make sundaes and stuff, will you skip the party and hang with me?"

"No," Ann says. "I'm not wasting any more time sitting inside these four walls. I'm going insane."

Fair enough, I think, but I don't say it aloud. I feel myself slowly resigning to the idea of showing up at Janae's, being completely humiliated, and going home. It's not like my life can get any worse, and at least Ann has tried to be a good sport.

Can I really deny her any more? And would it matter if I did? It's not like I can wrestle her to the ground and tie her up and put her in the closet. She's probably got the address memorized and she'll go whether or not I go with her. If I accompany her, at least I can do damage control.

"Whatever. If we're back by ten, when Chase gets home, my mom will never know the difference."

Ann's whole face transforms into a glowing smile, and despite the nagging worries in the pit of my stomach, I find myself unable to resist smiling back at her.

She better be worth it.

Because if my instincts prove correct, tonight will be an utter disaster.

29

"THIS IS CRAZY. Let's just go home," I say, grabbing Ann's hand and trying to pull her off of Janae's stately front porch. I nearly knock into one of the big white pillars.

"No way," Ann says, yanking her hand out of my grasp.

Before I can stop her, she smacks the doorbell, and I hear elegant chimes ringing down the hall behind the double front doors with their fancy leaded glass and oversized, overly polished doorknobs. My heart leaps into my throat, and briefly, I consider sprinting across her perfectly manicured green lawn and diving into the bushes.

But before I can get my feet off the porch, the door swings open.

Janae, wearing red skinny jeans and knee-high black-leather boots, along with a cream-colored turtleneck sweater, smiles at us. "Hey guys! Come on in!"

It's a weird smile. Slightly vacant, a little plastic. It hasn't yet occurred to her that I'm not one of them, that I don't belong here.

And that's not good. Because it throws my theory about Ben just *choosing* not to kiss me right out the window. If Janae invites me to a party and doesn't even realize I don't belong here, Ben is going to kiss me.

Ben is going to kiss me.

And there's nothing I can do about it.

I don't even realize I'm just standing here, totally mute, until Ann gives me a little shove toward the door. I glare back at her. It took us the better part of an hour, but we figured out how to use a curling iron to loosen up her kinky curls. She used bobby pins to sweep a few of them away from her face, and the rest of them tumble down her back. She tried out six different eye shadows, finally settling on an icy blue that complements her green eyes and makes her freckles look exotic.

She's wearing the blue scoop-neck top I bought her at the mall when we were with Ken and a pair of jeans I didn't even know I owned. They're boot cut and fit her like a dream. The shoes don't really go all that well—just some basic black-clog-type things from junior high, but she slips them off at the door, so it doesn't matter anyway.

Ann refused to let me wear my normal clothes. She absolutely insisted that I could not "ruin this for her."

Apparently she's figured out that my style isn't exactly in, well, style. She's so eager to have a real teen experience that she turned me into her dress-up doll and forced me to look . . . cute.

The jeans I can live with, but the crimson V-necked sweater freaks me out. Because I have *way* too much cleavage to wear a V-neck. Ann swears that I look great, but now that I can't change, it's starting to feel like the worst choice in the world.

I follow Janae toward the back of the house, where the heavy sounds of a base beat steadily intensify and begin to mix with the hum of conversation.

The hall opens up to an enormous, cavernous space with twenty-foot ceilings and the biggest flat screen I've ever seen. The Old Navy dress clique is perched on the couches. Shiny hair, pearly smiles, manicured hands, and gleaming jewelry don't even *begin* to describe how perfect they all look.

Though the music continues to blare, the conversations stop.

Maybe Janae hasn't realized it yet, but the rest of these people *know* I don't belong.

"Food and drinks are in there," Janae says, waving her hand in the vague direction of the kitchen. "And the bathroom is the second door on the right."

"Okay."

I try to be discreet as I take deep, calming breaths and head to the kitchen to occupy myself as everyone stares. I'm pouring some root beer into a cup, knowing it's not the same thing the others are probably drinking, when I realize Ann is not beside me.

She's standing next to two guys in the living room. One of them is slipping a strap over her wrist so that she can play with the Nintendo Wii. Another one is *totally* checking out her butt.

Conversations slowly pick up again, though I still catch people watching me and whispering.

Janae is queen, and they know it. There's no way they'll say anything to her, or me. Will they?

"Kayla," Ann calls, waving me over. "We need one more player."

"Oh. Uh, no thanks."

Ann puts a hand on her hip and cocks an eyebrow. "Not acceptable. Get your booty over here."

She did *not* just say "booty." I shuffle across the room because with Ann shouting at me and hollering across the room it's drawing attention, and that's the last thing I want.

"He's your partner," she says, nodding at a junior I recognize from school. He gives me the faintest of smiles. I wonder if he realizes he just drew the short straw.

I hold out my hand, and he slips the strap over my wrist, his fingers brushing along my skin. I look at him, unable to resist smiling as our eyes meet.

Damn. He's cute. Dark hair, dark eyes.

Of course, those eyes are *totally* staring down my cleavage right now.

I resist the urge to inhale deeply, as it'll make my chest rise, and turn toward Ann.

"What are we playing?"

"Tennis. Doubles, of course," Ann's partner says. His hair is shaggy and blond, and he reminds me of, well, Shaggy. From Scooby-Doo. I think he's going for the artsy, deep look. And he does have killer hazel eyes, when you can see them past the hair that flops over his forehead. I'm pretty sure he has a name that rhymes with Mill. Phil . . . Bill . . . Will.

I think I met him in freshman PE.

Ann customizes her own Mii, one with red, funky hair. I can't help but laugh at her excitement. I choose one named Tim, which I think is Janae's brother's name, instead of making one to look like myself.

The tennis match starts, and I miss the first serve. I laugh nervously and try again, this time smacking it so fast Ann's not ready, and she swipes at it but misses.

"OH!" I holler triumphantly, throwing my hands in the air. My partner high-fives me. I feel like I'm five years old, high fiving, but I'm grinning just the same.

"Look at the audience," Will or Brill or Frill says, pointing at the way the cartoon people bob up and down maniacally whenever we get a good play.

I'm so distracted by them I miss the ball flying toward my character and my partner sort of leaps into the air, his hand and controller flying dangerously close to my face, but he manages to hit it.

Ann screeches and tries to smack it back, but she wasn't ready, and the ball sails right past her digital image.

"Nice save," I say to my partner. "Uh, my name is Kayla, by the way."

"Todd," he says, with another one of those nods. His dark hair is a little over-gelled. Not Ken-style over-gelled, but like he could have done without that last glob of hair product. "Nice to meet you," he says, lobbing the on-screen ball back across the net.

Thrill, Pill, or Grill knocks it back across, straight at my Mii, and I barely manage to return it in time. The cartoon heads bobble excitedly when Ann hits it back and it skims across the net, ultimately landing in bounds, and neither me nor Todd manages to hit it back.

"We suck at this," I say, grinning at Todd.

"I would have to agree," he says, missing another ball.

We play for another twenty minutes, and I'm shocked to realize

I'm enjoying myself. And even though it's stupid, I do feel a little flush of excitement whenever Todd checks me out. He's no Ben, but it's still flattering.

Someone on the couch asks me about the history assignment we just turned in today, and as I start venting about the Revolutionary War and all the dates and battles, I miss the ball twice more.

Maybe I was wrong to avoid these people. I mean, I don't have to be their best friends, but it's not killing me to let my guard down a little and have some fun. It's not like the whole universe imploded. I mean, no one's jumping down my throat or anything. Given that I'm not always nice to them, it's pretty cool that they aren't being rude.

I hear the doorbells chime again, and Janae gets up from the couch where she was holding court and goes to answer it.

Todd and I are losing miserably. Once again, Ann's learning curve was shockingly short, and she rocks at Wii tennis.

Todd and I hand our controllers off to the next people in line, and I'm heading to go find my discarded root beer when I come face-to-face with the new arrival.

"What are you doing here?" I ask, staring at Nicole, hoping my shock isn't evident. She looks just as perfect as ever in a ribbed pink sweater and a pair of relaxed, wide-legged jeans. Her blonde hair is styled in that new look of hers, big loose curls that bounce perkily when she walks. She fits right in with Janae's crowd.

I guess she *is* one of Janae's crowd.

"I was going to ask you the same thing." She tips her head to the side and gives me a cocky, annoyed look.

I don't give her an answer, and she doesn't give me one. She goes to sit next to Janae—*right next to her*—and I retreat to a stool in the kitchen.

I feel like the room is filled with electricity, popping and siz-
zling. People are whispering again. It's hard to keep pretending I
don't notice, hard to keep staring into my fizzy drink as if it holds
the secret to life or at least the SAT answers. That familiar discom-
fort starts to rise again.

Someone crosses the tile floors—which at this point feels like
she's just crossed the border between two cities: Perfection Town
and Loserville.

The girl, Kelsey, I think is her name, picks up a plate and
scoops some tortilla chips out of the bowl in the middle of the
island.

"People say you got implants, you know."

I blink a few times. She's not looking at me, but it's not like
she's talking to anyone else. I nibble on my lip and resist the urge
to look down at my chest. "I didn't."

"I know, that's what I said."

I look up at her, surprised.

"I mean, it's pretty stupid to even think that, you know?"
she says.

I nod. "Definitely."

I didn't expect this girl, someone I barely know, to be an ally.

"I mean, duh. You would have had to miss school for a few
days, at least, to recover. I've wanted to do the supplement thing for
a while, but I don't know which ones work. What'd you use?"

Oh.

Definitely not where I thought she was going. "Steroids."

She straightens. I think she's actually contemplating the merits
of my answer. "Really?"

I nod, my eyes wide and genuine. "Oh yeah. I mean, the

mustache is a total hassle, and I accidentally ripped the refrigerator door right off its handles, but man, aren't these suckers worth it?"

I use both hands to emphasize my rack, and the girl gets a horrified look on her face and backs away, slowly, like I'm about to launch an attack. She keeps one wary eye on me as she retreats into the living room.

I watch as she whispers into the ear of the girl next to her and nods in my general direction.

I shift on the stool as I watch Ann laugh, and Bill or Will or Phil slings an arm around her. I don't know where they come from, but gumballs start dropping, hitting the floor with loud cracking noises. There must be a dozen, rolling in different directions.

The doorbell rings and Janae gets up. "You better pick those up," she says, flouncing out of the room. She stops for a second and backs up and stares at me, her eyes narrowed. The wheels, they are a-turning. I can tell she's starting to realize I don't belong here. She blinks a few times and then shakes her head and continues toward the entry.

I get off the stool and chase down the gumballs, and I hear a few girls snicker when I lean over to fish one out from under a houseplant. Somewhere in the last twenty minutes, things have shifted, and I'm getting progressively more uncomfortable.

The sound of Janae's boots clicking along the tile makes me look up. She's standing in front of me, her arms crossed, staring down with a look of spite.

Oh, crap. She's figured out that I'm not one of them.

"Some dude is at the door, saying he's with you. You know this party isn't some open-invite thing, right?"

"Uh, who?"

She shrugs. "Some freak with really bad hair."

I close my eyes and take a deep, steadying breath.

Ken.

"I don't know what made you think you belonged here, but you don't. So the sooner you and your bizzarro boyfriend get out of my sight, the better."

Okay, well, my almost-bonding moment with Janae is officially over, and it's time to bail.

I stand up, wishing I was Janae's perfect five-ten height, and look her square in the eyes. "Don't get that designer floss you call underwear in a bunch," I say.

"Just go," she says.

"Baaaaah," I say, staring her dead in the eyes. Bleating is my fall-back, the old standby if I can't come up with something better.

That same confused look crosses her face.

I turn to the living room. "Ann, we're leaving."

She turns around. "No."

I blink a few times. "Um, yeah. We *are*."

"Then go. I'm staying." She turns back to the screen in time to smash a ball back across the net.

"Sweetie?" Ken's voice carries down the hall.

And that's when I hear it.

The clattering of hooves on expensive Italian marble. The shrill, happy little whinny. The gumballs, once again, tumbling out of my pocket.

The sound of the last bit of my reputation shattering.

The pony trots into the kitchen. For about a second and a half I harbor the fantasy that the pony won't notice me, but I'd never be that lucky. It lets out a another whinny and runs right up to me, shoving its nose into me so hard I fall backward and knock into the granite countertop. My elbow hits the two-liter bottle of root beer I'd been pouring earlier, and it flies off the counter, rolling toward the sink.

I swallow, watching my life go up in flames as the soda spills out onto a beautiful, pristine white rug, one that probably came from Europe and cost as much as an exotic island.

"If someone doesn't get that *thing* out of the house in the next half a second, heads are gonna roll!" Janae screams, and even though she says it like she wants *anyone* to take care of it, she's staring straight at me.

"Ann, *we are leaving*," I say, with absolute conviction.

The scene with the pony and Janae's screaming seems to have changed Ann's mind, and she flings the controller at her partner and scurries after me. I push the pony toward her, and it merrily runs after her, as if it didn't just single-handedly etch my name in stone on the D-list.

The last thing I see as I glance back to the living room is Nicole, staring in shock, surrounded by the mocking faces of the rest of the A-list.

30

ANN AND I ditch Ken and walk the pony home. As she heads into the backyard to put the pony away, I don't say a word to her. I go straight to the garage and open the big door and roll the bike out.

She comes back out front as I'm pushing it across the driveway. "Where are you going?"

I regard her for a moment with narrowed eyes and then turn away. If I speak, even one word, I'm going to blow up.

I push the bike into the backyard, near the retaining wall, and then jog inside and swipe my brother's truck keys off the counter.

Ten minutes later, I'm pulling into the field near the motocross track. It's almost nine and the night sky is filled with clouds, which means it's pitch black out, but the whole place is lit up with the yellow glow of a dozen big stadium lights.

There's someone on the track. I let my foot off the gas and the truck rolls to a stop.

Ben.

My breath hitches in my throat and I just sit there, watching him fly into the air, again and again. Watch him pop a wheelie that lasts a hundred feet.

Watch him nail a perfect backflip.

My jaw drops and I just stare.

How long has he been doing backflips?

I sigh. I thought maybe I could sneak over here and ride a little, but I can't, not in front of Ben. I'll make a fool of myself.

I'm about to shift into reverse when Ben stops his bike and turns to look toward me.

Oh, dang. My headlights are on, but at this angle, he can definitely recognize the truck.

I close my eyes and rest my forehead on the steering wheel. I contemplate leaving anyway, pretending I never saw him, hoping he'll pretend he never saw me.

But I don't want to. And I already got my wish today, so I know he won't kiss me. At least not tonight. And maybe he deserves an apology for the weird way I've been acting.

I know I can't explain why I'm acting so strange, but I *can* apologize. And then I'll go home, crawl into bed, and never leave the house again.

I shift back into drive and bump along across the rutted grass, ultimately killing the engine when I pull up next to his truck. Ben leans his bike up against the fence, then pulls his goggles off and slides his helmet over his head. He slips his gloves off and sets them on the seat and then runs his fingers through his spiky blond hair.

My heart seems to be pounding in every direction, thump-thump-thumping against my rib cage. I wonder if he can hear it.

Ben climbs over the railing and jumps to the ground, the

buckles on his boots rattling. I slide out of the truck and try to smooth the wrinkles from my V-necked sweater.

I forgot to change.

Dang.

Ben walks up to me, and I notice the subtle way his eyes dip lower, just for a heartbeat, before he meets my eyes. He was totally checking me out. I try not to grin or blush or give away that I noticed.

"You look g—" His eyes shift over to the bed of the truck, and a look of surprise settles over his features. "You have a bike."

I try not to be disappointed that he didn't finish his sentence. The next word started with a g. I look . . . good? Great? Goofy? Gargantuously horrid?

I nod. "Yeah, for my birthday," I say. It's sort of the truth.

"Wow. That's awesome."

I nod.

"Are you going to ride?"

"Oh, um, no. I don't know how to ride, actually."

I really should have thought out this apology thing a little better. Obviously Ben was going to notice the motorcycle.

"So you came to the track with a bike and you were just planning on hanging out? And what? Bonding with it?"

I snort and feel myself relax at the playful tone in Ben's voice. "Um, well, no, but then I saw you and I don't want to interrupt."

"Don't be silly. I'll grab my ramp, and I can teach you a few things."

And then before I can protest, he's untying the ropes I used to secure the bike and unloading it.

It looks a little small next to him. His is definitely bigger.

I follow him over to the gate, my nerves multiplying and

intensifying. There is no way I can do this without making a complete tool of myself.

"Do you have a helmet?" he asks.

I shake my head. "No. I guess I can't ride. I'll just forget it and go home," I say, grabbing the handlebars from him.

"You can wear mine."

"Oh."

He walks over to his bike and grabs his gear as I stand there, holding the bike, wondering if it's totally crazy to actually give it a shot.

Maybe just a teeny bit. Two minutes. A hundred feet. The bike's gonna disappear in a few days, so I may never have another chance. And I really have wanted to try riding a dirt bike. Every time I watched Ben, I imagined myself as him, soaring into the air.

What's the harm?

"Hop on and sit down," he says, "and then you can put the helmet on."

He's standing so close to me, taking the handlebars out of my grasp. He seems extra tall right now. I face the bike and swallow, slowly, resisting the urge to just lean back into him. I feel weird and shaky, being so close. I tell myself I'm nervous about riding the bike.

I swing a leg over and sit down on the bike, one black-Converse-clad foot firmly planted in the dirt on each side. Ben hands me his helmet, and I pull the goggles and gloves out of it. I start to slip my fingers into the gloves, but Ben places his hand over mine.

My heart flops all over.

"It's hard to buckle the helmet if you have gloves on. Save them for last."

All I can feel is his palm over my knuckles, warm, soft, perfect.

I nod and slip my fingers out of the glove as he lets go of my hand.

I sweep my hair back over my shoulders and tuck a few strands behind my ear, then slide the helmet over my head.

I'm wearing Ben Mackenzie's helmet. I can't get over it. It's a little too big for me, but I want to keep it on forever anyway.

I fumble around with the strap, but I can't figure out how it works.

"Here, let me help you," he says, leaning closer to me.

His fingers brush against my chin as he slips the nylon strap through a couple of silver loops. Each time his skin touches mine, my nerves jump and twist. How many times has he touched me today?

For the first time, I've lost count.

My stomach has a whole line of cancan dancers in it.

Once the strap is secured, he leans further over so that he can look me in the eyes. The visor sticks out, so he's at least a foot away, but he seems so close. He puts a hand on each side of the helmet and tips it back a little bit to get a better look at my eyes. I can't breathe.

He picks up the goggles and slips them over the helmet and tightens the elastic strap.

Then he steps back, and I fumble with the gloves. When they're on my hands, I nod, as if I'm ready to just go for it.

"Do you know how to start it?"

I look up. "Uh, turn the key?"

I feel muffled inside this helmet, miles away from reality.

Ben laughs. "Sure, but then you have to kick-start it."

"Oh. That sounds hard."

I turn the key, but of course nothing happens, because Ben

knows what he's talking about. Ben pulls out the metal bar that I hadn't even noticed, and I try four times to kick-start it, but the fourth time my foot slips off and the big metal kicker thing slaps my shin. It stings.

"Here, let me get it going for you."

I hop off the bike, and Ben brushes against me as he climbs on it. Is that the tenth time he's touched me? The fifteenth?

The bike looks so small when he's sitting on it. It fires up on the second try, and then he holds the clutch in for me and gets off the bike. I sit down and grip the handles with an über–death grip.

"Okay. This is the front brake, and that goes to the back one. This is the clutch, and that's the gas. It works just like the transmission in your truck. Let slowly off the clutch and ease on the gas. Not too abrupt on either."

I nod, the too-big helmet sort of bobbing into my eyes. I don't tell Ben that my brother's truck *isn't* a stick, it's an automatic.

I concentrate on Ben's instructions, hoping not to make a fool of myself.

And then everything goes horribly wrong. The clutch pops free of my fingertips and the bike jerks forward, and I lose my grip on the right handlebar while the bike revs, and suddenly the world is streaming by so fast the colors bleed together and I can't see anything.

I feel arms around my waist, and the bike disappears from under me and I'm crashing to the ground.

No, not the ground.

I'm falling onto Ben.

We tumble into the dirt, and I feel the way he's bracing himself, absorbing the impact with his shoulders and arms, making it so that it's almost like I'm falling into a pillow. If, that is, pillows were wrapped in pounds of perfectly sculpted muscle.

Vaguely, I hear the bike crashing in the background. I take in a few deep breaths to calm my racing heart. It's revving higher than the bike was just seconds ago.

Our legs are sort of tangled, one of mine settled between his, and I can feel the buckle on his boot digging into my calf. My hips must be just an inch below his, pressing into him. One of his arms is slung around me, so that I can feel the weight of his hand on my lower back.

I shove at the helmet, trying it get it out of my eyes. The goggles have a thin, sheer layer of dust on it, making everything look a little hazy.

Yet even through the tint of the dirt, I see Ben's eyes, crystal blue, staring straight into mine.

Neither of us says anything, we just keep blinking and staring.

And all I can think is, *I wonder if he'd kiss me if I wasn't wearing this stupid helmet.*

I hate myself for cursing the helmet, with its giant plastic visor and big plastic thing that sticks out in front of my jaw, keeping Ben at a distance. It would be impossible to kiss wearing it.

I should be thanking the stars I'm wearing it, because it's the only thing stopping me from bridging the gap and forever ending my friendship with Nicole.

"Are you . . . okay?" he finally says, after we've stared at each other too long. I'm surprised I can even hear him over the pounding of my heart.

I nod, and the helmet bobs loosely on my head.

His beautiful, full, completely kissable lips curl into a smile. "Didn't I tell you not to pop the clutch?"

"I don't even know what that means," I say, my voice husky and hoarse. I clear my throat.

I know I should get up, put some distance, some air between us, but I can't get myself to move.

I'll never be this close to him again and I don't want it to end.

He shifts underneath me, and I realize I need to get up. As I peel myself away from him, I feel like I'm losing something, giving up something I will never have again even though I've only just discovered what it could be.

I'm glad Ben can't see my face when I turn a little, using the helmet to obscure my expression. I don't even know what my expression *is*, because there are too many emotions raging inside me: longing, hurt, confusion, fear, and utter, complete infatuation.

He climbs to his feet and brushes the dirt off his riding pants. His shoulders and chest seem to be rising more rapidly than normal. Is he breathing as hard as I am? Is his heart racing like mine?

I unbuckle the strap and then slip the goggles and helmet over my head, hoping as I run my fingers through my hair that I don't look like a total wreck. "Maybe I'll save the motocross lessons for another day," I say, grinning at him, trying to obscure the feelings raging inside me.

"And maybe next time I'll wear full body padding."

I laugh and try not to wonder if Ben is really edging closer to me or if I'm imagining it. I step back. My bike is about twenty-five feet away, on its side. Even knowing it's going to vanish in a few days doesn't stop me from cringing at the sight of it in a heap.

"Why'd you and Nicole break up?" I ask abruptly, staring at the bike instead of Ben.

Ben blows out a long breath and runs his fingers through his hair. "Honestly? It wasn't any one thing. I mean, we did everything we were supposed to do. We went to dinners and movies, and we celebrated our anniversary, and we introduced each other to our parents. But it just wasn't there."

"So you dumped her?"

The bark of laughter is enough to make me turn and look at him. He looks beautiful and irresistible in the shadows of the stadium-style lighting "No. *She* dumped *me*. I mean, it caught me off guard, but she was right. There was nothing real between us."

"Oh," I say, wondering if there would be something real between *us*. Does he ever feel what I feel? Does he count the times we touch?

"I should go," I say, walking over to my bike. "I'm grounded and my mom will kill me if she calls the house and realizes I'm not home."

I walk over to the bike, but before I can pick it up, Ben is jogging up to me. He grabs my arm. "What's up with you these days? You're all over the place."

I keep staring at the place where his fingers touch the crimson sweater. He notices and slowly releases my arm.

Even though I lost count, I'm positive we've never touched this much. I'll never forget this night. I'll be playing it over and over again in my mind tonight.

"I'm sorry if I've made you feel bad," I say, still not looking at him. "But you're Nicole's boyfriend, or ex-boyfriend, or whatever, and that's that."

Ben doesn't say anything and somehow I doubt what I just said made any sense to him.

"I don't understand you," he says.

"And you won't. I have a boyfriend. An awesome boyfriend," I say. I'm grasping at straws now. I walk away from him and pick up the bike. "I have to go."

I feel lower than low right now as I push the bike off the track, Ben trailing me. One second I'm laughing and staring at him like I want to kiss him and the next I'm shoving him away and running.

I have to sort things out with Nicole before I can talk to Ben about anything. And the wishes need to get out of the way.

Everything is much too complicated to throw this . . . *thing* with Ben into the middle of it all.

Ben loads the bike for me, and I stand aside as he ties it down, quickly and easily, his skilled hands working much quicker than mine had when I loaded it up.

When he shuts the tailgate, silence settles around us like a veil.

"Thanks for the lesson," I say, stepping backward, away from him.

"Sure." He takes a few strides toward the track, then stops and looks up at me. "Are things ever going to be normal with us again?"

"I don't know what normal is," I say, yanking the truck door open. "I really don't."

And then before I can say anything else, I climb in, fire it up, and drive out of the fields, blinking hard against the tears that seem to come from nowhere.

31

THROUGHOUT the next day at school, Nicole still doesn't speak to me. I spend my lunch in the darkroom, trying to develop photos for the project, but I'm too distracted to come up with anything good. When the bell rings, I head to the big bathroom down the hall, my backpack haphazardly crammed full of my stuff and slung over my shoulder.

I shove the door open, hard, and when it bounces off the wall, the girl near the sink jumps up into the air and turns to glare at me.

I stop.

It's Janae.

But it's . . . not.

Her face is . . . completely broken out. Like, totally covered in acne. Pimples litter her forehead, go down her nose, sprinkle her chin and cheeks. What did she do—cover her face in chocolate and then sleep in it?

She sees me staring and her eyes narrow into angry little slits, but the effect is ruined because there are tears streaming down her face, so I know her wrath is tempered.

It's so weird to see her . . . well . . . ugly. I've never seen so much as one pimple on her face, *ever*. I mean, Nicole has battled acne for years, but Janae?

O. M. G.

I freeze halfway to the bathroom stall and give her another long look.

This is a wish! Finally, a cool freakin' wish.

I take in the array of pimples covering her face, obscuring her perfect beauty, and one half of me wants to jump for joy as the other half feels torn and sad, which I don't understand. Because Janae is mean, deserves everything she has coming to her.

I remember wishing for this now. When we were twelve, Nicole's acne really kicked into gear. Guess if she got boobs early, she got the acne to go with it. Janae was perfecting her mean-girl tactics by then, and for the next few years, she'd make Nicole burst into tears a time or seven.

And Janae had really dished it out on one of my birthdays, because by the time Nicole made it to my house to have cake and go out with my family, her eyes were red and swollen. Janae had ripped into Nicole so hard that Nicole spent the first hour of my birthday celebration sniffling.

So I'd wished that Janae would know what it was like to be suffering from something she couldn't control, to have everyone see it and judge her and laugh at her.

"Oh," I say. The word seems too big, echoing on the bathroom walls. "Um, sorry."

She can't know what I'm sorry for, why I'm apologizing, but I can't stop the word from escaping anyway. Because some part of me really is sorry. The pain in her eyes is just as real as the pain in Nicole's had been. *Has* been, for years.

"Yeah, right," Janae says as she turns back to her reflection.

"No, seriously, I mean, that *really* sucks."

Okay, foot, meet mouth.

Janae blinks a few times to clear the tears from her eyes. "Thanks, freak. It's this awful new lotion, I think." She sniffles and stands up straighter, as if to pull herself together. She runs a finger under her tear-streaked eyes, but it smears the mascara even worse, leaving black winged smudges around the edges of her eyes.

"Whatever. Your melodramatic hysterics are a bit over the top," I say.

She turns to look at me, really look. I want to shrink away, because even a tear-streaked, snot-filled, acne-covered mess, she's still the same person. "You're just saying that because if *you* looked like this, you'd probably get out a Magic Marker and connect the dots and tell everyone they're constellations."

Is that a compliment or an insult?

I shrug. "Your face will be back to normal by Monday. Chill." I *know* it will be back to normal by Monday because the wishes end then.

Janae turns toward me and crosses her arms. "Don't you have a lamb to sacrifice or something? Another body part to enhance, perhaps?"

Oh. Okay, well, that answers that. She was definitely trying to insult me.

I guess some people just never change, even with wish intervention.

I head to the bathroom stall and listen as Janae turns the sink off and leaves, the door swinging back and forth a few times. Before it stills, however, a new group of girls enter.

"I didn't know steroids did that, though. Are you sure?" The voice is nasally, annoying. I don't recognize it.

"I don't know, but Miranda saw her changing in PE and said her boobs were really that big, that it didn't look like she was stuffing. How else do you get that big overnight? That is totally *not* normal."

"As if that girl has ever been normal."

I freeze. I suddenly want to pick my feet up off the ground so they won't see me, but I am afraid to move, afraid to alert them to my presence.

"Actually, she was totally different in junior high. She was in my computer science class."

"Really? 'Cuz these days she's totally weird. I heard she has a purple goat at home."

"Why?"

"I don't know, she probably milks it and makes goat cheese."

The girls' laughter rings out, filling the room. I fume. I want to leave the stall, but every moment I wait makes it seem harder to reveal myself.

There are about a thousand things I could say to them right now. I could offer them some goat cheese, wiggle my boobs, say something snide.

But instead I just sit quietly and listen until they've left the room, and then I get up and go wash my hands.

I make my way to my locker to ditch a few of my books. I'm just swinging the door shut when someone taps me on the shoulder, and I jump.

Uh-oh.

It's Ken.

"Hey, sweetie," he says. "I want to apologize for last night. I didn't realize it was a school kind of thing."

I glance around. So far no one has noticed him.

"Um, yeah, this is too. A school thing. This *is* school, actually."

"I know, but Ann said she's been here before, so I thought maybe it wouldn't be a big deal if I just dropped by."

"Oh?" I'm going to kill her. Was I not clear enough about the visitor policy here?

My heart stops altogether when he plants one hand on either side of my shoulders, so I'm trapped between him and the locker.

PDA alert! PDA alert!

I try to turn away, but it doesn't work, because Ken just leans a little bit to the right, and before I can take another breath, his lips press into mine. My fingers tighten around the straps of my backpack.

Ken pulls away, enough so that I can speak.

"I think we should see other people," I blurt out.

He doesn't move. He's leaning in close, like he could kiss me again at any moment.

"What?" I can feel his breath on my cheek, warm. It smells like cinnamon or Red Hots or something.

"Look, you're, um, awesome, but I just don't feel sparks anymore. I think we need to break up."

His eyes search mine as his face remains expressionless.

"Is that really what you want?"

"Yes. It is."

He nods, but he doesn't move away from me. I feel like he's staring at my lips, like he wants to kiss me again to convince me to change my mind. "I can't say I'm surprised. You've been acting weird for days."

I clear my throat because it's like he doesn't realize he's still so close to me. "And also, Ann . . . she likes you. You should give her a shot."

One eyebrow goes up. It's hard to see because his face is so close to mine. "Ann? Really?"

I nod. I wish he'd back up.

"Maybe."

Huh. That was entirely too simple. He stands up, and I feel like I can breathe for the first time in ten minutes. "I guess I'll catch you later," he says, and then walks away.

I watch him leave, feeling a little bit bad but also suddenly, gloriously free, and then I turn around.

Ben is standing there, in the middle of the hall, watching me. His expression makes guilt tear through me.

He looks betrayed, his blue eyes staring right at me, accusing me. His shoulders, behind that perfect, ribbed navy sweater, are slumped.

I don't understand it, but he looks hurt. Like I hurt him. Stuck a knife in and twisted.

And now I know.

I know that during the moment at the track, when I stared at him and he stared back, he wanted to kiss me as much as I wanted to kiss him. That he cursed that helmet just as I did.

That maybe he *does* count each time we touch.

He shakes his head, slowly, and then spins around and walks the other way.

And as I watch him disappear around the corner, I can't help but wonder if this is the exact moment where I officially lost everything.

32

I DON'T SLEEP at all that night. Not a single, solitary moment. I listen to the rain outside my open window, listen to the snores coming from Ann, and try not to toss and turn, because I know I'll never be comfortable no matter how I lie.

As soon as the sun rises over the Cascade mountaintops, I climb out of bed and throw on jeans, an old T-shirt with a rabid-looking unicorn, and a plain black hoodie. I sweep my boring brown hair back into a ponytail as I head out into the backyard to get the pony.

She'll be gone in a couple of days, and I've spent this whole time wishing she'd disappear. So I might as well give her one nice morning. I'll take her to the park down the street and let her eat all the grass she can for the next hour or so, until I have to drag my weary butt to school.

I swing open the door to the shed, and the pony bursts out.

I crinkle my nose as I step into the shed to find the rope halter Ann made for her.

I sure hope that the poop magically disappears at the same time as the pony. So gross.

I slip the rope onto the pony and wrestle around with it until it vaguely resembles something that will keep her from running away. I guess that's ironic since I've spent this whole time wishing she *would* run away.

I let her take little snatches and bites of grass as we drift to the gate and cross in front of the house.

We don't get anywhere near the park, though, because there's a car in the driveway.

A voice drifts over me. Someone is standing on the front porch. "Kayla."

Even after all these years, all this time, I know exactly who it is. I don't have to turn and look.

I stand there, one hand gripping the rope, twisting it around, as I stare at the dew-covered grass.

I take in a few slow, calming breaths and then turn to face him. His dark hair has started to gray, so that it's salt-and-pepper, which catches me off guard so much I can't stop staring at it, thinking that he's old now, that he's aged. It's been seven years, and yet he seems so much older.

He's wearing dark, crisp blue jeans with a light sweater and a sports jacket and some kind of fancy leather loafers with tassels. He looks like a total yuppie.

"Hi, sweetheart," he says, his Italian accent more pronounced than ever. He smiles at me. It makes a few crow's-feet appear around his eyes. Laugh lines. I want to know who he's been laughing with.

"Dad," I say, my voice shaky, unsure. I hate it. I want to be nonchalant, confident, unaffected by him being here. Instead I feel myself spinning around and around inside. Am I happy he's here? Excited to see him? Or do I want him to leave? And why is it so hard for me to know which one I want?

I study his steel-gray eyes. I don't know what I want to see there. Answers, maybe. Yes, I want answers. But I'm not sure there's an answer in the world that would ever make it okay to do what he did.

"I realized I missed your sixteenth birthday."

I nod.

"And I know I've always said I'd get you a car when you got your license."

I guess he did say that. Maybe. But I don't like the way he says *always said*, as if he's always around to say something at all, let alone that he'd get me my own car. I only talk to him on special occasions, and the last one was almost a year ago.

I feel anger build a little bit, somewhere deep inside me. "Why are you here?"

He shifts his weight, looks a little bit uncomfortable. I feel oddly triumphant. "I told you. To get you a car."

"No."

"What?"

"No. I don't want your stupid car."

"Oh," he says, shrugging, looking a little confused and lost.

That's it? *Oh?*

I expected something more. I expected apologies, guilt, some kind of speech.

And even though I already expected it, his lack of true, deep emotion is a confirmation that he is a wish, that he's not here entirely of his own volition. Because if you go to all that effort because you have the idea to make some grandiose gesture, wouldn't you have a thing or two to say about it?

I wonder how long it took him to get here, how much time he spent driven by something he didn't understand. Hours sitting on planes, hundreds of dollars, thousands of miles.

And here he is, staring at me, the one thing I wanted more than anything else, and it only makes me feel empty.

I remember all those birthdays I stared at the phone, all those times I would be apprehensive of opening the Christmas card, because I was afraid it would simply say *Dad*, when I wanted so much for it to say *Love, Dad*.

I think of all those stupid times I'd watch other people's dads. All those times Nicole rolled her eyes about her dad, and I secretly wished I could do that, but I had no reason to. For my dad to be annoying he had to be around, and he wasn't.

His absence seemed so much bigger than anyone else's presence. He missed everything. He never bought Chase the BB gun like he promised, never taught me to ride a motorcycle, never helped me study for a test or watched me get ready for a school dance. Not that I've gone to many.

But the point is, he never got to be part of anything, and he doesn't even care.

I guess I knew I must have wished for this at some point. Must have closed my eyes as tight as I could and wished he would come back, then blew out the candles, hoping it would really happen. I must have believed that if I wanted it bad enough, he'd appear, just like in all my dreams and fantasies.

And here he is and yet it means nothing. Because I didn't want him here physically, I wanted him here emotionally, and that's one thing I'll never have. He's never going to be that kind of dad.

And I don't need to be that kind of daughter.

Not anymore.

"Did you want something?" I pull on the pony's lead rope, and she steps forward.

"Um, no." He pauses, chews on his lips. "I love you," he says, the words sounding like a question.

The moment is awkward. I breathe slowly, listening to the silence as the words die around me.

And then I look up at him and shake my head. "No."

I pull harder on the rope and start across the yard, the pony following me. I stop at the edge and give him another look. It might resemble pity. Maybe disgust. I don't know what I look like, because I can't put a finger on what I feel. But it's not regret, and it's not pain, and I can't ask for anything other than that. "No, you don't. If you love me—if you loved *any* of us, you would've showed it by now." He just stands there on the porch, staring at me. "And you know what? It doesn't matter anymore. I don't need you."

"Kayla—"

"No. You don't deserve my time, and I won't let you buy it with a car."

I step onto the sidewalk and head down the street, the pony happily trotting after me.

It starts to sprinkle as the house disappears from my view. Maybe I didn't wish for him to show up and say "I love you." Maybe I wished for me to not need him, to not care about him anymore. I can't be sure, I can't go back and listen to myself make that wish, but the truth is, it doesn't matter.

Because not needing him is the best thing that's come of this, the best realization of all. It doesn't matter if Ann and the pony and Ken and everything else disappears on Monday, after I receive the last wish.

Because this feeling of independence, of total freedom, won't vanish. That much I'm sure of.

My happiness doesn't rely on other people. It doesn't depend on them needing me, wanting me, approving of me.

It's inside me, just where it was when I was little and My Little Pony reigned supreme, before life got twisted and turned upside down, before everyone else moved on and left me behind. Somehow I lost the power to be happy, but I'm taking it back.

Starting today. Today, I choose me.

33

IN PHOTOGRAPHY later that day, I spend the hour trying to get my photo flurry to become a self-portrait. I set the enlarger up and expose one of the negatives to the photo paper for just a few seconds. Not long enough for a clear picture . . . that would take several seconds longer. Then I swap out the negative for a new one and expose that one for a few seconds. I find one of the better photos of my Converse and I expose that one too.

After I've run what must be a dozen negatives through the enlarger, I move over to the table and put the paper through the development chemicals, a series of pans that will turn the paper into a picture.

I've overexposed the photo, so I try again, this time running each negative for half as long.

And that's when I get the desired effect: The photo looks a bit like a blob at first glance. But on closer inspection, the details start to pop out—the laces of the Converse shoes form the squiggly border along the bottom of the photo. The frayed ends of a friend-ship bracelet peek out on the two sides. Directly in the middle of the photo is the face of a Barbie doll, partially obscured by the bow on a shirt I've never worn.

But in between all that, it's a mass of overexposed black. It looks a little like a mess, which is what I expected. By exposing so many pictures on top of each other, the photo paper has had too much light on it, turning it dark.

I stare at the photo for a while. I wonder if Mr. Edwards will like this or think it's just a big disaster.

Because the fact of the matter is, it *does* represent me. I let everyone else's opinions of me turn me into something else entirely. I became dark, negative, cynical. The big blob on the paper staring back at me, no identity at all.

This photo is me, in all of its ugly, messy glory. If Mr. Edwards doesn't like it, well, there's not much I can do about that.

I take out a sheet of photo paper, but I don't expose anything on it. I want it to be a plain, glossy white sheet of paper.

My clean slate. Because I'm starting over.

I rip out a sheet of notebook paper and scribble down a quick explanation and then paper clip it to my photo and the blank white page and drop it in his box.

And now, my clean slate begins.

34

AFTER PHOTOGRAPHY, I trudge up the polished wooden bleachers in the gym. There's a mandatory pre-homecoming pep rally. I really hate these things and everything they represent, but I'm forcing myself to remain neutral.

Clean slate, clean slate, clean slate.

Kayla McHenry is not going to sit in the stands and bleat at the cheerleaders. Not today. Today, I'm going to sit up here like every other student at EHS, happy that I'm not stuck in class, enjoying a nice Friday afternoon. No matter how many "go team!" cheers I have to shout, I'm going to be just like everyone else.

Maybe I should have saved my clean slate for Monday, done the whole baby-steps thing. This is more than one giant leap for mankind. This is epic.

Plus, on Monday, all the wishes will be over.

No, *no*, I refuse to put this off.

Clean slate starts now. I swear.

I'm just glad the last two wishes will happen over the week-end. With a little luck they'll be discreet and I can just hide out in my room, waiting for it all to end. Once they're gone, I'm going to have to seriously figure out how to get my life back on track and undo the damage they've done to everyone around me.

The wooden bleachers creak beneath my feet. Some of my classmates are very clearly avoiding meeting my eyes, because they don't want me to sit near them. They're probably hoping I don't bleat at them. I guess they're not aware of my clean slate.

I've never been so aware of how people see me. Of the fact that I created this image. It's like a clown painting on their face.

Except a clown can wipe it right off, and people can see the difference. For me, well, I'm going to have to prove it.

If I don't want to be a spectator in my own life, then I've got to change things. And as soon as school is over, I'll have to find Nicole and maybe we'll patch up what we have left of a friend-ship. Or maybe we'll discover we're going different ways. But I can't just *not* talk to her. I have to know what's going on with her, why she's become someone else in such a short time. And if in the end, we're not able to see eye to eye, then fine. But at least I have to clear the air.

I find a seat in the middle somewhere, far enough up that I have a decent view of the shiny wooden gym floor, of the championship-sports banners that flutter along the tall, cinder block walls. Most of the school is here now, the sounds of their laughter and conversations building and swelling, filling the room. Teachers flit about, maintaining order, smiling politely at the students.

My mouth goes dry when I see Ben walking up the bleach-ers. He's so busy picking his way around the crowded stands that he doesn't see me, so I hunch over and kind of lean on my elbow, one hand over the side of my face, my hair sweeping forward and masking me. My breathing gets a little shallow as he gets closer.

I don't know what to say anymore, and I can't handle another conversation that resolves nothing.

Unfortunately, I'm only quasi-lucky. He sits down behind me. I don't think he has realized it's me in front of him so I stay still, praying that this is the sort of assembly conducted with the lights turned down low, although that seems pretty out of the question given that this is a pre-homecoming pep rally.

Across the gym, the athletes are assembling onto a smaller set of bleachers. The maroon-and-gold jerseys on the broad-shouldered football players quickly fill one end of the stands. The less-obtrusive swim team and girls' basketball teams make up the other half.

Finally, the principal, a tall gray-haired man who looks completely overdressed in a slate-gray pair of slacks, white button-up, and somber tie, walks to the center of the gym, holding a cordless microphone.

He asks the gym to quiet down, his monotonous voice amplified by the speakers mounted in the corners of the gym, and then moves to stand off to the side of the bleachers just as a long, low base beat rumbles through the gym. The students around me recognize their cue and begin stomping on the wooden bleachers, until the entire room is one echo of rumbling, grumbling bass.

Reluctantly, I follow along, stomping my feet, feeling the bass rumble through me. I feel dorky, but I keep it up anyway, determined to step outside my norm.

The sounds of a synthesized guitar and keyboard—some kind

of generic top-forty pop song—blast through the speakers, and the cheerleaders bound through the double doors at the opposite end of the gym. The girls in front throw in a few cartwheels as the rest of the squad fans out around them, waving their metallic gold pom-poms.

I'm watching, totally overdosing on how saccharine they are and repressing the need to grimace, when a particular face comes into focus.

And then I can't see anything else.

Nicole. She's grinning so wide that I have to wonder how many Crest Whitestrips she went through to get a smile that sparkly.

I whirl around to look at Ben. "She's a *cheerleader*?"

But Ben looks just as shocked as I do. He glances down at me for a second—he obviously had no idea how close to me he sat—and then back at Nicole again. His mouth is slack, his entire body is still, motionless. He's not even blinking.

I turn to look at her again.

She really is a freakin' cheerleader. My best friend, Nicole, the cheerleader. That twilight zone portal I stepped into in the bathroom with Janae has expanded to swallow the whole school. She even looks like them: Her slim waist and long legs look great in the maroon-and-gold uniform.

"Did you even know she was trying out?" Ben asks, leaning forward and shouting into my ear to be heard over the song.

I shake my head. My ponytail must brush his cheek.

"It all makes so much sense now," he says, his voice a little lower.

"What makes sense?" I ask, still watching Nicole. I'm

mesmerized by the girl on the floor, the one exuding happiness and confidence. It's like watching someone with Nicole's body and an entirely different personality.

"Why she dumped me."

"What do you mean?" I ask.

The music behind us dies down as the cheerleaders start into some kind of yay-team-style shouting match, jumping up and down and waving enthusiastically. Nicole is kicking so high it's a wonder her whole leg doesn't dislocate at the hip and go flying into the crowd.

He kind of snorts. "Well I mean, I'm . . . me," he gestures to his worn-out jeans, his sneakers, his spiked-out blond hair, "and she's . . . that."

I glance over at the cheerleaders again. Nicole is still jumping up and down, clapping her pom-poms together as her ribbon-clad ponytail bounces. It's hard to believe it's her. Last year she was hiding from everyone, embarrassed by her acne. Now she seems to have highlighted her hair, put on makeup . . . . And she's standing there, the most confident girl in the room.

Even as it hurts, I feel a little proud of her.

"I can't believe she didn't tell us," I say.

Ben nods.

I turn back to watch Nicole again. It's hard to look at anything else, the sight of her down there is *that* unbelievable.

The cheerleaders pick up a bunch of boards with letters, spelling out *Enumclaw*, and they step forward one at a time to get the crowd to spell it out with them. Nicole has the *M*, and when she steps forward, her cute little pleated skirt flutters around her perfectly tanned legs.

When it's over, they cheer and bounce over to the front of the athletes' bleachers, where they line up along the ground, sitting in identical positions, as if they've practiced even that.

I glance back at Ben. "She was always busy after school, wasn't she? Like that day I ran into you at the mall?"

He nods.

"It was practice. And tryouts were the last two weeks of August. She wasn't ditching me for you; it was cheerleading."

He shrugs.

I laugh, though it's only half in amusement and half because I want to whack myself with a clue stick.

This whole time, it wasn't Ben stealing her away at all, but cheerleading. I can't believe she did this and didn't even tell me—or him—about it.

I don't know whether to be infuriated or relieved, so instead I just keep laughing, rubbing my face, trying to hide my giggles from the quieting gym. I'm delirious, confused, lost.

I don't even know what happens for the rest of the assembly, because all I can see is Nicole, seated among the other cheerleaders, whispering and giggling. From across the gym, I can still see that she's glowing, happy, more alive than I've seen her in months. She leans in to hear something another cheerleader said, nodding.

I wonder what kind of secrets she's telling, secrets she obviously won't ever share with me.

They're her friends now.

And I am not.

Why didn't she tell me? Why would she go out for the squad and then join it and not even say a word? It's not something that's kept a secret . . . they wear their gear to school on game days. They're in the yearbook.

Did she even care at all what I would say? Did it bother her, keeping this secret, or could she care less?

Because by the looks of her big pearly-white smile, I'm betting on the latter.

35

AFTER THE CHEERS from the pep rally have died down and most kids have headed home, I sit on the hood of Nicole's car for what feels like forever. And I don't even know why. I don't know if I want to tell her off or beg forgiveness. All I know is that I want answers.

The days of October have officially melted into fall, and there's a brisk feeling in the air. I should have worn a jacket today. Something other than my usual jeans and hoodie. Even my toes inside my red Converse are getting a little tingly and cold. But it's not like I started this day planning to sit on the cold hood of Nicole's red Cavalier.

The cheerleaders must be having some super-secret meeting to discuss the dry cleaning of their spandex underwear or maybe they want to color coordinate the ribbon in their ponytails. I don't know what cheerleaders talk about any more than I know who my best friend is.

Nicole finally walks out of the gym doors, a black duffel bag slung over her uniformed shoulder. A big maroon *E* is emblazoned across the little V-necked, long-sleeved sweater. Her white pleated skirt sort of bobs and flutters as she walks, and her crisp white socks match her white-and-maroon sneakers. Her legs look tan, tan enough that I think she went to the salon with the rest of the squad.

She's halfway to her car before she notices me, and her step falters. Then she picks up a brisk walk again and makes it to the car before I've figured out what exactly I was going to say. All that time sitting on the hood of her car, and I still don't know.

"I have to go to dinner with all the other girls," she says, walking straight to the driver's-side door.

I don't get off the hood. I just swing my legs around so I face her, and my feet are dangling down by the tire.

I feel like we're the poster children for "Popular" and "Unpopular." We couldn't look more different if we tried. Her ponytail is perfect, perky, with long blonde curls. Mine is lower, boring, my straight brown hair just kind of hanging there. I have no makeup on. She looks like hers was professionally applied.

"How could you not tell me?" I guess I'm going with angry, because my words come out as a cross between furious and bitter. "How could you just ditch me for them and not even tell me? I've been walking around school for weeks and I bet everyone knew but me!"

She looks down at her hands, twists her keys between her fingers. She chews on her bottom lip and glances up at me through her lashes, then back down at her hands.

She looks nervous and shy, like the Nicole I know. It chips away at my anger.

"I didn't think in a million years I'd make it."

When she looks up at me, she's herself again, quiet, pained, my best friend. It melts the ice that was freezing around me, making me hate her, or at least the stranger she'd become.

I cross my arms, try to grasp at some of the anger. Because anger is easier than hurt. "You still could have told me you were trying out."

She laughs, a short, sardonic laugh. "And what would you have said, Kayla?"

I open my mouth to speak, but I can't say the words. I know what I would have said.

"Exactly. Do you even know how hard it can be to talk to you sometimes? You make fun of everything. Of everyone. If I had told you I wanted to be . . . *this*," she says, pointing to her uniform, "can you honestly say you would have been supportive?"

There's no point in speaking. I won't be able to convince her otherwise because I can't deny the truth. I would have laughed. I would have reminded her of how insipid and vapid the cheerleaders are. I would have told her they would never accept her, would never let her on the squad.

And I would have been wrong.

"I just thought I'd try out and get cut, and then I could know I'd tried and feel okay about it and you'd never know the difference. But then I made it, and then I realized you'd be mad if I didn't tell you about trying out . . . and I kept telling myself I'd tell you the next day, and then the next day, and it just snowballed. The longer I waited, the harder it was to tell you."

She's twisting the keys so hard in her hands I think the whole key chain might break. "I don't know, I'm still standing here waiting for you to start making fun of me for this."

And then she looks up at me, and I see that she's genuine, and a slice of pure guilt and sorrow slips through me and takes with it the last of my anger.

Because she really does believe that; she really is waiting for me to start laughing at her.

And it hurts. I don't know if it's because my best friend thinks I'd laugh at her or if it's because two weeks ago, I very well might have.

Before Ann, before the pony, before everything got turned upside down, I really might have done that. Just laughed at her, told her it was all so stupid.

But somehow everything has changed. Somehow I'm not that person anymore.

But Nicole doesn't know that. I guess there's a lot I haven't told her, either.

She closes her eyes for a second and takes in a deep, calming breath. "It's not that I'm a different person, Kayla. It's that I've always wanted this. We both did, in junior high. Remember how we almost crashed Janae's slumber party but lost the nerve? Remember how we used to write down everything they wore in that Look Book we made and then spent the whole weekend at my house replicating their outfits?"

The memories seem to crash into me all at once, and suddenly I know exactly how she feels, exactly how badly she wants this.

Because I wanted it once too. But I buried it, forced myself to forget when it seemed too painful to dream of it anymore. I gave up on everything because it just seemed easier that way.

She shakes her head, and her ponytail bobs. "But it never worked. We were too different, always on the outside looking in.

And then somewhere in the last year or two, you decided that you wanted to be everything they weren't. You didn't even notice that *I* still wanted to be everything they were.

"Before this summer . . . it was impossible. But it's not anymore. And I don't want to be the shy one in your shadow forever. I'm pretty now. I can be the person I want to be. And maybe that's shallow, but I'm tired of sitting next to you and making fun of everything I secretly want."

I swallow the boulder in my throat. "Nicole, I . . . God, I never meant to be that kind of friend."

She just shrugs one shoulder and keeps twisting her keys. "I know that. But you are. You just assume I'll always go along with everything you want, and when I brought up things—like sitting with Breanna at lunch—it never even occurred to you that I was serious, that I really wanted to sit over there. You were too busy mocking her IQ."

I swallow, hating how right she is about all this. Hating that it means she's spent days, weeks, months agonizing over it all, and I've never even noticed. I stuck myself in this box and then expected Nicole to climb right on in with me. "I know. . . . I know. And you're right. About everything."

She gets quiet then. Maybe she's surprised that I'm agreeing so easily. Maybe if the last two weeks with Ann and Ken and idiotic toys hadn't happened, I wouldn't be so open to this. "Because the thing is, I've been hanging out with someone new for the last few weeks. Someone . . . from out of town. And she's opened my eyes to a lot of stuff."

"The girl from Janae's house?"

I nod. "Yeah."

I take in a deep, slow breath and stare down at the toe of my Converse. It's old, dirty, the very opposite of Nicole's perky white sneaker. "And maybe it works the other way, too. Maybe being friends with someone can make you shut yourself off to stuff that you want to be a part of."

She doesn't speak, just shifts her weight back and forth a few times.

I look up at Nicole and give her what I hope is my most sincere look, because she *has* to know that I'm speaking the truth. "I never meant to turn you into someone you didn't want to be. I don't care what you do. If you want to be a cheerleader, then awesome. You can be a nun or a backup dancer for the Jonas Brothers. I don't care. I just don't want you to think you can't be my friend *and* the things you want to be."

Nicole puts a hand on her skirt-clad hip. The other grips her duffel bag, her knuckles turning pale.

Then she smiles the sparkly smile of a cheerleader and throws her arms around me. Her duffel bag whips around and knocks into the car. "I'm sorry. I should have told you sooner about everything. I just didn't know how to, and then you started acting weird. . . . "

I grin. "Yeah. About that. Have I got some stories to tell you. . . . "

She smiles at me. "Do you want to go to homecoming with me tomorrow? I bought two tickets, back when I was going to go with Ben. No zombie costumes, of course, but it might be fun."

My smile falters. "Oh, um, I think I'm grounded."

"Seriously? You never get grounded."

I half smile, half cringe. "I know, I told you the last two weeks have been insane."

"No kidding."

I slide off her car and land in the gravel. "I guess I better get going. We can hang out as soon as I'm off restriction."

I take a few steps, my sneakers crunching in the gravel.

"He's at the track."

I stop, then turn, slowly, to face her. Her words ring in my ears, but I'm afraid to think of what she could mean. "Huh?"

"Ben. He's at the track."

I just blink and stare at her. "Huh?" I say again.

She sighs and stares at the rocks. "I don't know." She shakes her head and then looks up at the sky. She sets her bag down and moves away from me for a minute. "You like him, right? Like *really* like him?"

My mouth feels like I've swabbed it out with a thousand cotton balls and then swallowed them all. "Nicole, I would never—"

"Do you?" she asks, turning back toward me.

I open my mouth to say something, but I don't know what I want to say. I can see Nicole wrestling with this. I just nod.

She takes in a ragged breath and then chews on her lip for a minute, staring at me, her head tipped to the side and her perfect blonde ponytail brushing her shoulder. "I bet you guys would be better than we were. Ben and I, we're totally different."

"But how can you be okay with that?"

She reaches up, plays with that little diamond pendant. I guess if she's still wearing it, it wasn't a gift from Ben.

A car with a broken exhaust drives by the school, seems to

make the moment stretch into infinity as it creeps by. "I don't know. I mean, it was never really about him. I think I knew all along I liked the idea of having a boyfriend more than I liked *him*. It just took me until now to admit it."

I feel myself begin to hope. I feel myself *dare* to hope. "But—"

Nicole heaves a dramatic sigh and gives me a stern look, a look that tells me to stop arguing. "Kayla, I wish I could tell you all the ways he's like you. All his stupid jokes, the way he hates dressing up, that loud track that I hate and you love."

I can feel everything around me, acutely. The uneven rocks beneath my sneakers, the slight breeze across my face, the still-healing spot on my chin where the closet door nailed me on gumball day. "But there's, like, a code, a girl code—"

"Screw some stupid code. I'm standing here telling you that you deserve him."

"You swear?"

"Go," she says, looking at me. "If you're really grounded, then stop spending all your time arguing with me and go see him before your mom notices you're not home."

I race up to her, wrap her up in the biggest hug imaginable, and then spin around and run to my car.

"You're welcome!" she hollers after me.

I smile as I slam the door shut.

My mom will be home in a half hour. I have just enough time.

36

WHILE I DRIVE down the quiet country roads, the radio off as I stare out the windshield, I can't help but wish that the track was more than two miles away so I would have time to figure out a game plan.

But I guess I need to stop wishing for things and just face reality as it comes.

When I pull the truck in at the track, my head is spinning, and it's getting progressively harder to breathe.

Ben and the others seem to be done riding, because they're sitting in the big grassy field. His truck has been backed up to another, so the tailgates face each other, and there are two guys on each, swinging their legs, sipping on Red Bull, eating Fritos. They're still wearing their gear: jerseys, riding pants, boots that have been unbuckled to the ankles.

They watch me as I bump along in the little Ranger, hitting some of the worst ruts in the field because I'm so busy staring at Ben and psyching myself out. By the time I'm climbing out of the driver's seat, I can barely feel my fingers and toes because I'm so nervous.

I don't know what they're talking about because they go silent as I swing the door shut and stare at Ben. He says something to the other guys and jumps off the tailgate, landing in a molehill as a puff of dust rises around his feet. He leans over and buckles the boots back up and then heads in my direction.

I give him the best smile I can manage.

"Wanna take a walk?" he asks, nodding toward the track.

I don't answer, I just turn in the direction he indicated, and we amble toward the track.

"So, what's up," he says, after a moment of silence.

"Oh. Um, so, I, well . . . "

I close my eyes and swallow. This is not how it was supposed to come out.

He stops next to me. I can feel his hand touch my arm. The hairs on the back of my neck stand on end.

I leave my eyes shut for the next part, because the idea of seeing him reject me is just too much. "I like you. And I want to know if you'd like to go out sometime."

Nothing but silence follows. I scrunch up my nose and then open one eye to look at him. He looks amused.

"What are you doing? Taking a nap?"

I smack him on the shoulder. "Don't make fun of me!"

He crosses his arms, gives me a sly smile. "But you make it so easy."

I raise my hand as if I'm going to smack him again and he puts his hands up, a classic surrender pose. "Okay, okay. Sheesh."

"Okay you'll stop making fun of me, or okay you'll go out with me?"

"Weeeellllllll," he says, stretching it out until it seems like at least seventeen syllables.

"*Ben!*"

He laughs and leans into me, until he seems so close I think he's going to kiss me. "Yes. Well, I mean." He stands up again, seems to have second thoughts. "I don't want to hurt Nicole. She might think—"

"I already talked to her."

He stands upright. "Really?"

"Yeah. It's cool."

"Just like that?"

I nod. "I know, it's a little weird to me too. But she swears it's fine."

His smile turns brighter. "So you ladies sit around and talk about me, huh?"

I smack him on the arm again. "Ben!"

He laughs. "Okay, okay. When and where? Because if you say homecoming—"

I laugh. "No, not homecoming. And not the Philharmonic either. I'm grounded for two weeks. I was thinking after that we could do the whole cheesy dinner-and-a-movie thing. If, that is, you want to."

"Do I get to pick the movie?"

"Jeez, you drive a hard bargain," I say. "Will it be horror?"

"No, but it won't be a rom-com either."

"Deal."

We've reached the edge of the track, and I follow Ben through the gate. It's quiet today, no expo or event.

Ben climbs up onto one of the jumps, then turns and extends his hand to me. My nerves jump and tingle and stretch as I put my hand up to his. He grasps my fingertips and helps me up onto the dirt hill. It's the first time our skin has touched since the ill-fated attempt to ride a motorcycle just a couple short days ago.

I scramble up the incline, and when I get to the top, we end up standing face to face, closer than usual. I wonder if Ben notices the way my chest seems to be rising and falling more rapidly than normal as I try to catch my breath.

I'm invading his space, but I don't want to move. We simply stare, inches away from being nose to nose. All I kept thinking is that, *finally*, that stupid helmet isn't in my way.

And for once, those piercing blue eyes are staring straight into mine, waiting expectantly, and I know, without a doubt, that he's feeling what I'm feeling.

This is Ben. The guy I have watched from afar, the guy I have crushed on, the guy I have fallen for. He's standing inches from me, and there's nothing between us anymore, nothing stopping us.

I want to be that girl I was the day I met him, standing on the edge of the cliff.

I want to jump.

I have a surge of adrenaline, of courage, of pure craziness as I shakily lift my arms and wrap them around his shoulders. There is no longer any air between us; his jersey is touching my hoodie.

I blink and my courage falters for one second, and I wonder what on earth I'm doing.

But I want to do this.

Because when I finally kiss Ben, I don't want it to be because of the wish. I don't want Ben to be under some kind of spell, I don't want him to be driven to kiss me because he has to. I want it to be real and I want to know what he'll do, when his head is clear and it's only me, not the wishes.

I press my lips into his, my heart hammering out of control, and I tighten my arms around his shoulders. For just a second, I think I have made a mistake, because he seems so surprised he doesn't move. My chest seems to tighten because I'm holding my breath, waiting for him.

Waiting for his answer.

But then his hands wrap around the small of my back, pulling me closer. I tilt my head as his lips part, just the tiniest bit, and the world slips away.

I'm not sure how long we kiss, but the sounds of wolf whistles are enough to break us apart. I turn to see his friends standing on their tailgates, whooping and hollering at us.

I step away from him and stare at my feet, heat rising to my cheeks.

I *cannot* believe I just did that.

"Hmm." He grins. "So *maybe* I'll let you pick the movie."

37

ANN IS SNORING again. That's the first thing I notice.

The second is the big box sitting on my desk. It's plain, just brown cardboard, with a small red bow on top. The wishes are never this small, this contained, and I smile in relief as I stare at the cardboard.

Then again, a lot of things could be inside that box. For all I know, the Keebler elves are hiding out in there.

I slide out of bed, careful not to pull the blankets with me, and kneel on the floor in front of my desk so I'm eye level with the box.

I rest my hands on the lid, feeling for any vibrations. Maybe I once wished for a rattlesnake. To annoy my brother, of course.

But nothing seems to be moving, so I nudge the lid open and peek inside.

Slippers.

Ballet slippers. They're beautiful: pink satin with delicate bows on the side and soft, pliable soles that would make any girl's feet happy. I know without looking that I won't find a brand name any-where, and also that they'll fit perfectly.

They were custom made for me.

I run my fingers over the bow, smiling a little to myself.

I don't know if there is any rhyme or reason to these wishes, but it seems like they've been arriving in the right order. A week ago I would have seen these and rolled my eyes and shoved them under the bed.

But today, my fingers are itching to slide them on my feet, to dance across the floor, to leap into the air.

I sit down on the floor and tuck the lid underneath the box and pull out the slippers. I peel off the big fuzzy socks I've been wear-ing all night and slide my feet into the pink slippers.

They fit like a dream. No pinching, no tightness, just soft, supple perfection.

I stand in them, pointing one toe and then the other. I look over at Ann for a long moment to be sure she's still sleeping, and then I pick one toe off the ground and hold my arms out as grace-fully as I can manage, and then I spin in a little circle, the sloppiest pirouette the world has never seen.

But the grin doesn't leave my face.

Maybe I could do this. Maybe I could make a go at it.

Nicole tried out for cheerleading. And she *knew* that she wasn't exactly their ideal cheerleader. She still had crazy acne then, still stared at her toes. But it worked out. She was glowing for those moments on the gym floor, her smile from ear to ear as she bounced and cheered and rah-rahed her way to happiness.

If she can do that, why can't I sign up for ballet again?

I spin around again, and then again and again, until I'm so dizzy I can't stand upright anymore and I end up crashing into the bed and then bouncing and falling onto the floor.

I burst out laughing, giddy with crazed happiness.

Because nothing is holding me back anymore.

Ann rolls over and peers down at me from the bed.

"What the heck are you doing?" She rubs her eyes and tries to push a few curly strands out of her face.

"I don't know. Nothing. Everything? I'm not sure anymore."

"Well, at least you look happy doing it," she says, and then groans and lies back on the bed again.

And then I smile to myself, because for the first time in a long time, I am.

Happy.

38

WHEN THE DOORBELL RINGS at noon, I swing it open and see Nicole standing on the stoop, a big gray milk crate in her arms. I smile and take it from her, and she follows me up to my room.

When the door swings open, I see Ann jumping around in big crazy circles, her arms in the air, the middle of her perfectly flat stomach exposed as she dances along to Kiss 106.1, the local pop-radio station. I think the current song thumping out the speakers is Britney's latest.

I cross the room and click the stereo off. "Ann, this is Nicole. Nicole, Ann."

Ann stops jumping up and down and steps forward, her arm sticking out. "Nice to meet you."

Nicole smiles. "Likewise. I hear you have a hot date tonight."

Ann's eyes widen and she nods vigorously. I can see by the tapping of her toe that she's ready to start bouncing around the room again.

"Let's set up in the bathroom and get you ready."

I carry the big crate, which I swear weighs forty pounds, into the bathroom down the hall. I put the lid down on the toilet and set it on top, peering in to see the contents. Blow dryers, a set of hot curlers, round brushes, curling irons, hair spray, and lots and lots of makeup.

"We'll put some hot curlers in your hair and then we can go pick out your outfit," she says, taking charge. "They take a while to set. I'm thinking a partial updo, lots of curls. And you simply *must* wear something green."

I smile as I watch Nicole in her element.

I know she's changed, and she'll never be the girl she was a year ago, but I can't help but think maybe it's not a bad thing, maybe it's a major improvement. She's happy now, ready to take on the world, and I feel a little inspired.

Nicole plugs the hot curlers in and then goes back into my room and grabs my computer chair, rolling it into the bathroom for Ann to sit on. I perch on the edge of the tub, one ankle propped up on my knee, and watch as her skilled fingers set to work, brushing out Ann's hair and then dividing it into sections and rolling it into curlers. Periodically, she sprays enough hair product to kill at least a full foot of the ozone layer.

"So what's Breanna Mills like, really?" I ask, watching Nicole's pretty, flawless reflection in the mirror. Her look is one of utter concentration. I wonder if she wants to be a stylist someday.

"You really want to know?" She looks up at my reflection. I nod. "She's really sweet. Definitely the nicest of the Old Navy dress clique."

I grin, and Nicole realizes she's slipped and referred to them as the Old Navy dress clique. She smiles and shrugs. "She is, though. Her house is, like, a quarter of the size of yours, you know. You'd be amazed the sorts of sales and stuff she finds. Her whole wardrobe probably cost a hundred dollars and she's still one of the best dressed in school."

"Maybe we can all hang out sometime."

Nicole turns and looks right at me. "Yeah. I think that would be cool. She's totally not as bad as you think she is. You might actually like her."

I nod and realize that it might be true.

Ten minutes later, Ann's head is a mass of hot curlers, and we get up and go to my room. I kick all the junk on the floor of my closet into the back so we can find my clothes. Nicole tears through it like a homing pigeon, zeroing right in on the dresses that are of suitable color for Ann's complexion. She hands at least four options to Ann.

Then she holds up a fuchsia sweater with a square neckline and an empire-waist-style tuck. And when I realize she's holding it out to me, I cringe, putting my hands up to stop her.

Nicole puts a hand on her hip and gives me a *Don't even try it* sort of look. "Seriously, Kayla. Give it a chance. I bet it looks great on."

I sigh and take it from her hands. *Clean slate,* I remind myself.

Ann drapes her clothing options over the bed, and Nicole and Ann go back to the bathroom. While they're fussing over her hair, I slip my T-shirt off and pull the fuchsia top over my head.

When I walk into the bathroom to see how I look, Nicole's face lights up. "Told you it would look great on."

When I see myself in the mirror, I can't help but smile too.

Because she's right. The hue of the shirt manages to bring a little color into my cheeks.

Maybe tomorrow, after Ann's big date and homecoming and whatever else Nicole has on that busy social calendar of hers, she can come back and we can dig through my closet.

Somehow I know Nicole won't mind that one bit.

★ ★ ★

A FEW HOURS LATER, Ann and I are sitting at the counter, each of us on a barstool, waiting for the doorbell to ding. My foot resembles Nicole's that day in biology, because it's tapping away against the footrest. I don't know why I'm nervous for Ann, but I am. She's Cinderella, and this is her night. But in *Cinderella*, it's the carriage that turns into something else at midnight.

Tomorrow is the last wish. Tomorrow, this is all over.

I may not be a fairy godmother, but I did have a rather cute dress for Ann hanging in my closet. She looks flawless, more gorgeous than I could have imagined. It's an elegant emerald dress, with delicate spaghetti straps and a slightly flared, flowing skirt that stops just short of Ann's knees. It has a sort of gauzy overlay that gives Ann's pale skin a kind of ethereal quality.

Nicole was right. Green is definitely Ann's color.

Thanks to the hot curlers and what must be a zillion bobby pins, her hair has been completely transformed from her moppy, frizzy look to a smooth, shiny uptwist. The curls that do remain are long, loose, stylish. She looks beautiful, and if Ken doesn't fall all over himself for her, then he's a total fool.

I think Ann is truly nervous as well, because for once in her life, she's not bouncing around like a little kid. She's sitting still, a little pale but serene, occasionally reaching up and touching her hair.

The doorbell rings, and we both jump and then lock eyes and giggle. Nervous laughter. Her green eyes sparkle with it.

I slide off my stool and it seems to screech across the tile.

I can see his silhouette on the other side of the leaded-glass insert in the door. "Are you ready?" I ask Ann.

Her eyes flare a little, betraying her nerves, but she nods.

I yank the door open and step aside so that Ann is the first thing Ken sees.

His lips curl up into a warm, happy smile, showing off those perfect teeth. Today, the smile seems oddly natural, genuine, so much less plastic than it looked a week ago. He steps forward and gives Ann a hug, his big, well-muscled arms wrapping around her, and she stands on her tippy toes to hug him back. I feel a little like a proud parent as I stand there in the foyer, watching them.

Ken looks over Ann's shoulder at me, giving me the faintest of smiles. I can't help but wonder if it's a thank-you, because there's some kind of gratitude in his eyes.

He unwraps his arms from her body and then looks down at Ann, nodding toward his Jeep in the driveway. "Shall we?"

"Don't bring her back too early," I joke. Ann bursts out with another nervous giggle. I think she might melt into a pool of them at any second.

One hand on the door, I watch as they head to his Jeep, which, thankfully, has the top back on today. I would have a serious problem with him messing up her adorable hair.

Ken opens the door for her and she climbs in, careful to arrange her dress so as not to show anything off, nervously smoothing the nonexistent wrinkles away. Ken walks around to his side and climbs in and fires up the car.

Just before they pull out of sight, Ann flashes me a thumbs-up, her lip-glossed lips curling into an all-encompassing smile.

I'm going to miss that stupid doll.

39

WHEN I WAKE the next morning, my room is oddly bright, even through the thick green curtains. I blink a few times, wondering if I've slept in past noon, but the world is silent. Too silent, if it were midday.

I sit up in bed and peek behind the curtain, and what I see makes my eyes flare widely.

Snow.

Huge, fluffy white snowflakes are falling silently from the velvety sky. I can barely see the shed in our backyard between the millions of flakes pouring from the clouds above.

It's barely October.

If it snows in November, it's a rarity. A freak snowstorm.

I bet it has *never* snowed in October before. I blink, staring out at the falling flakes, wondering when I wished for this. I can't seem to tear my eyes away from the sight. Our lawn is no longer green; now it's just a beautiful blanket of pristine white powder.

"Ann!" I whisper, climbing to my feet so that I can press my forehead to the glass. It's cold to the touch. It must have dropped thirty degrees last night. I feel giddy and silly, like a child waking up on Christmas Day.

"Ann! It's snowing!"

I turn to wake her—maybe by walloping her with a pillow—but my stomach plummets and the smile melts off my face when I realize she's no longer in my bed.

The bed is empty. Completely devoid of the freakish redhead I've come to know and like.

Ann is not a morning person. She has not once gotten up before me. She could sleep right through the sinking of the *Titanic*.

I walk to the closet, as if for some reason she's going to be sitting on the floor in there. But she's not. The big pile of toys and junk that I ripped from the shelves a couple days ago is still heaped on the Berber carpeting.

I yank my fluffy robe off the hanger and shove my feet into a pair of thick red slippers and dash out of my room, scrambling down the stairs so fast I nearly topple over before I reach the bottom, and I have to grab onto the railing to catch myself. I scurry out the back door and fling it open, and it's only when standing on the back patio that it dawns on me that it really *is* snowing, and I'm wearing a robe and fluffy slippers.

I look up at the sky, and the snowflakes grace my cheeks and forehead and land in my eyes. I blink a few times and then stick my tongue out and catch a few.

They're real. It is snowing in Enumclaw in October. I turn and look at the foothills around us, but I can barely make out their snowcapped peaks through the falling snow.

This has got to be some kind of record.

I want to marvel a bit longer, but it's *freezing*, so I dash out across the white-blanketed lawn. The snow, icy and wet, seeps through my socks until it feels as if my ankles may break right off.

I make it to the garden shed, where I yank open the latch and fling the door open.

Ann is not there. Neither is the pony. It shouldn't alarm me, because they could have just gone on a walk, but something else is missing too: the bags and bags of gumballs. They're gone, and the shed is nearly empty, pristine, no hoof marks or horse poo or evidence of the wishes at all.

There's just a forlorn looking lawn mower, sitting by itself in the corner. I could run to the garage and look for the dirt bike, but I know that's gone too.

I swallow the lump that is growing in my throat. I turn and look back across the lawn, staring at the blanket of snow, the silence heavy in my ears. Why does the snow make it seem so . . . quiet?

Ann's really gone. They're all gone. This snow is my last wish, and now that it has arrived, somehow, the curse is broken.

This was what I wanted, at least, it *had* been what I wanted. But I feel a little empty as I trudge back toward the house, the snow crunching beneath my rapidly dampening slippers.

I'm going to miss her. And Ken. And that stupid pony.

I glance down. Well, I won't miss my giant boobs, anyway. I'm fine with my barely there chest. I can't believe I used to hate what I had, but I am totally happy to see those giant knockers gone.

I try to think of an Italian word, a phrase, anything, but I can't.

It's really over. Two weeks of insane, topsy-turvy, never-ending craziness, and then it just *ends*.

I walk to the middle of the yard, the icy snow soaking through my slippers and straight to my toes now, and then look up at the silvery-gray sky, nearly blinded by the flakes as they brush my cheeks and land on my nose. There are no cars driving by, no birds squawking, just utter, beautiful, silence.

And then the peaceful tr nquility vanishes as something *splats* across my bare calf.

I whirl around in time to see my brother, his eyes brighter than I've seen them in weeks, balling up another chunk of snow in his hands. He throws it overhand, like a pitcher, and it explodes against my robe before I can process what he's doing.

"Hey!" I burst into a sprint, rounding the side of the shed just as another snowball splats across the wooden siding. Whooping, I scoop up a handful of snow with my bare hands, packing it into a snowball. I peek around the corner of the shed, but my brother is no longer standing near the house.

My eyes follow his footprints in the snow, and I realize belatedly they are heading straight to the other side of the shed.

I whirl around just in time for him to blast me with another snowball, straight to the chest. Without missing a beat, I reel back and let loose of the snow in my hand.

It hits Chase's shoulder and explodes all over him, and I know by the way he arches his back that it's going down the back of his shirt. In a pair of pajama pants, a T-shirt, and a pair of sneakers with no socks, I can see he is just as unprepared for the snow as I am.

My fingers are bright red with the cold, and the belt on my robe has fallen open to reveal the old green T-shirt and matching plaid boxer shorts, but I don't care. I scoop up more snow and burst into a run, turning to throw it at my brother.

I miss, but so does he. I try to reach down and grab another handful of it as I keep running toward the back door, but my slipper catches in an uneven spot in the lawn and my foot slips right out, and before I know it, I'm rolling into the snow.

And despite the fact that my entire body feels like I've been put into a freezer, I burst out laughing.

My brother walks up to me, his hands empty, his chest heaving, and we meet eyes and grin.

Then he reaches a hand out and pulls me to my feet.

"This is crazy, isn't it?" he says, his hands sweeping across the lawn.

I nod, though I don't explain that it's one of the *least* crazy things to happen to me in the last two weeks.

"You want to go sledding? I think our old saucers are still in the garage."

I grin, nodding enthusiastically because sledding sounds like the best idea my brother has ever had.

"Cool. Let's go in an hour or so."

I follow my brother back to the house, and when I realize he's not looking, I can't resist scooping up one last handful of snow and pelting him with it.

"Hey!"

"That's for the cheap shot earlier."

My brother ponders this for a moment, his dark bushy eyebrows all crinkled up, but then he shrugs. "Fair enough."

I follow him inside, and he heads to his room while I plunk

down at the kitchen counter. I shrug out of my wet robe and kick off the slippers, peeling off my wet socks. My skin burns and tingles as it warms back up, and my whole hands are bright red, just like my toes.

There is a pile of bagels in a basket, so I grab one and rip out a big chunk and stuff it in my mouth. I probably look like a chipmunk, like Ann and that Cinnabon, but I still feel a little hollow about all the wishes being over and I want to fill that big gaping hole, and food is the only thing I can think of.

Last night, Ann and Ken decided to sneak the pony out of the shed and take it for a walk. She stayed out for another hour and a half, and when she came back, we gossiped for another hour or so, until past two a.m. We lay on my bed and stared at the ceiling, and I told her everything about Ben and our kiss, and she dished about their date and about how romantic Ken is.

They seem to have really hit it off, which is cool. He bought her a rose from some street vendor, and she hardly put it down all night. Her smile was more genuine and real than any smile I've ever seen.

I don't know where the two of them are now. I'll probably never know. But I hope, somehow, they're together.

My mom walks in as I'm shoving another piece of bagel into my mouth, even though there is no room for more. I probably look ridiculous, but it's making me feel better.

She's not looking at me, she's just shoving some folders into her briefcase. Her hair is in its normal tight and tidy bun, and she's got on a cute purple sweater set with black slacks. I realize, my heart sinking, that she's still mad at me. Maybe the wishes are over, but she remembers our fight, because she's not even looking my way.

She arranges the folders in the briefcase as she simultaneously reads a message on her BlackBerry, furrowing her brow at whatever it says. "I've got a few meetings set up today, so I gotta jet," she says, still not looking up.

I wonder if she has even looked outside yet, if she knows that it's snowing the biggest flakes I've ever seen.

I nod, but my mouth is so full I can't speak. She doesn't notice. She's frowning now, flipping through her day planner. The image—one of total concentration—is one I've seen a million times before.

"Have you seen that business card for the bakery I got your cake at?" She pauses, rifling through her planner. "Did I give one to you? I had a few of them, and now . . . "

My eyes widen and I try to choke down the bagel in my mouth, but I've taken an impossibly large bite.

"Oh, never mind, found it. I'm meeting with Jean later about her daughter's sweet sixteen and thought she'd love a cake from there." My mom pauses, looks up at me. "I think her daughter goes to school with you. Janae? Sweet girl."

My jaw drops, and it probably shows the half bagel crammed into my mouth. My mom doesn't notice, because she's too busy floating out the door. I slap a hand over my mouth to stifle the giggles while I struggle to swallow the food in my mouth.

Let's hope Janae is the type to make birthday wishes.

Really stupid, overwhelming birthday wishes.

I swallow the bagel and wash it down with some orange juice, trying to get enough down that I can speak. "Mom!" I call out, standing up from the stool.

She pokes her head back inside. "Yes?"

I sigh and sink back onto the stool, not sure how to start. I press my fingers against the cold black granite, watching the way they leave warm, foggy little imprints that disappear a moment later. "I'm sorry. About . . . what I said. I know you're doing your best and you give me a lot and everything."

I look up at her, half expecting to see her scrolling through the e-mails on her BlackBerry, but she's not. She's looking right at me.

My mom leans her hip against the countertop and purses her lips. "Thank you. And me too. I'm sorry about forcing that party on you. I knew you didn't want it, but I thought maybe once it started, you'd have so much fun it wouldn't matter. I should have just listened."

I nod and we stare into each other's eyes for a long moment, and I can't help but think maybe a new understanding is taking place.

"I really am running late, though, so I have to go." She starts to turn but then stops. "Oh, and I left a twenty on the table by the door."

My jaw bites down. Even after everything, we're still back to that? Twenty dollars for a pizza, be home late, don't stay up, yada yada yada?

But then she meets my eyes again. "I was thinking maybe you could pick up a movie. Something Chase can tolerate. I'll grab some garlic bread and we can have spaghetti. I'll be home by seven."

Her lips curl just a little bit as we stare at each other.

And then she disappears out the door.

So maybe the wishes are gone.

But I have a feeling life will never be the same.

ACKNOWLEDGEMENTS

Many thanks to my agent, Zoe Fishman, for having all the answers, and to my editor, Lexa Hillyer, for asking all the right questions.

Also, the following people deserve my sincerest gratitude:

My husband, Dave, who always knows how to make me laugh, even if I'm trying stressed about a deadline; Cyn Balog, for the phone calls and the emails and for making this all so much fun; Rhonda Stapleton and Julie Linker, because it really *was* like Summer Camp, and my sides still hurt from laughing so hard; my co-workers, for buying so many copies of *Prada and Prejudice* that they made it a local bestseller, much to the bewilderment of the bookstore; my older brother Brian, because your art never ceases to inspire me; my little brother Danny, because you always show up at a moment's notice to get me out of a jam; my mom and dad for always believing in and encouraging me—your support means everything, and I love you both; Rachel, because life would be half as fun without you and that party animal hat; and my cousins, because I stole your names for this book: Nicole Kaiser, Kayla Harder, and Janae Prince. I promise, aside from the name similarity, the characters are entirely fictional.

A very special thanks goes to Gabriella Forello and her family, who didn't blink an eye when I asked for the Italian translation of "oh my God" and "dang it."

And finally, thank you to those who purchased *Prada and Prejudice* and emailed me to share your thoughts. Those emails always make it easier to get through my latest deadline, and they mean the world to me.

Turn the page for an excerpt from

PRADA&
PREJUDICE

1

It is a truth, universally acknowledged, that a teen girl on a class trip to England should be having the time of her life.

At least, that's what I thought. Instead I'm miserable. It took me two weeks to convince my mom I was responsible enough to go on this trip instead of staying with my dad for the rest of the summer, eight days to rush-order a passport, and precisely twenty-four hours to regret it. It's my first full day in London and instead of seeing Buckingham Palace or Big Ben or the Thames, I'm sitting in Belgaro's café inside my hotel, wishing someone, *anyone*, would give me the time of day.

The point of this trip was to tour all of London's historically significant sights as a precursor to European history. Sophomore year starts next month, and it's supposed to be the *Year We Pad our College Applications*. At least, that's what the pamphlets said.

Last year, I never would have felt this desperate. My best friend Katie and I never wanted to be one of the in-crowd zombies. In fact, we made a sport of heckling the A-list. When the yearbooks came out last spring, we drew mustaches on the popular girls and wrote little quotes of the stupid things they'd said in class.

And then Katie moved away. Without her around, it's nearly impossible to convince myself that I'm happy on the D-list. How can I be? I'm the only one *on* the D-list.

It all started when I called Katie during lunch, two days after she moved. It's probably pathetic to admit it, but I had started eating my lunch in the bathroom. I was miserable, and I needed my friend's support.

So there I was, blabbing away on my cell phone in the corner stall. I had no idea Trisha Marks (cough-SNOB-cough-cough) had walked in. She overheard the whole thing—even the part where I said cheerleaders were modern day courtesans. As you can imagine, it didn't go over so well. At least, not once Trisha looked up the definition of *courtesan* on her handy-dandy iPhone.

Now I'm hated by pretty much every pom-pom-wielding airhead at my high school.

I look up when the door chimes, and to my horror see three of my classmates stride into the room. Angela, the lanky blonde, has no less than three bags with cute little rope handles, *Chanel, Gucci,* and *Armani* proudly emblazoned across each one. Summer, her petite best friend, walks quietly in her shadow, a *Juicy* bag in hand, her dark wavy hair cascading down her shoulders. Mindy walks beside them, looking like the normal American teen she is: her messy brown hair is in a bun, and she's wearing a lace-embellished pink tank top and destroyed denim jeans. The three of them laugh at something I can't hear.

Basically, they look like they're having the trip I dreamed of. The three girls might not *be* the A-list, but they're certainly *on* it. And since Angela Marks is Trisha-the-demon-cheerleader's little sister, she's sworn in blood to defend her honor. Or, you know, give me the evil eye and ditch me, even though we're assigned travel-buddies. It's her fault I can't leave the hotel without breaking Mrs. Bentley's golden rule: Safety in pairs. Never go anywhere alone. Blah, Blah, Blah.

And now they'll see me wallowing in misery like a total loser. I shrink back in the leather booth, hoping the big leafy palm next to the table is enough to obscure my face. They *cannot* know I'm sitting here, two empty glasses of Coke next to me, like I've been here all day. Because the truth is, I *have* been here all day.

The group activities won't start until the day after tomorrow. We'll be visiting museums and palaces and going on double-decker bus tours. I can't decide if things will improve then, or just get worse. Sometimes I feel more alone when I'm surrounded by my classmates than I do when I'm actually by myself.

Why did I think this trip was going to be different?

It was supposed to be my chance to change everything. I guess I thought if we were thousands of miles from home, I'd be just as far from my old reputation. I was wrong.

For the record, I don't think it's humanly possible for me

to be friends with Angela. She definitely shares Trisha's gene pool, if you know what I mean—all the way down to the sneer she makes every time someone annoys her. But Mindy is usually in a bunch of honors classes with me, and last year sometimes we'd end up as lab partners in Chem. Maybe if I was a little more outgoing, Mindy and I would be friends by now.

She seems cool, I think, as I watch her roll her eyes at Summer when Angela's not looking. If I'd been assigned as *her* buddy for this trip, she wouldn't have ditched me. I just have to get Angela to begrudgingly accept my presence, and then maybe we could all hang out as a foursome. If I'm lucky, maybe we can switch buddies entirely.

The trio of girls set their shopping bags in a heap on the booth next to mine, oblivious to my presence behind the leafy palm. I can't see what they're doing, but I imagine Angela is picking up the menu and trying to decide between the spinach salad with no dressing or a glass of water. I'm pretty sure she's anorexic, which is easier to handle than the idea that she's naturally perfect. I mean, really—her collarbone could cut glass.

"So, should I wear this red one, which shows more cleavage, or my sparkly yellow tube top tonight?" Summer asks. She must be rifling through a bag, because all I can hear is crinkling plastic.

"Yellow tank. Definitely. It's more clubby," Angela says. "But what shoes can you wear with it?"

Seriously—clubby? Figures they're going to break all the

rules and hit a club. I never would have the guts to do something cool like that. All I have on my schedule is an in-room movie rental, which is sounding more pitiful by the minute.

Summer sighs, this great melodramatic heave that makes it seem like she's just found out she flunked sophomore year before it even started. I picture her frowning her big pouty lips and wrinkling a perfectly groomed brow. "I dunno. I swear I packed my black Guccis, but they weren't in my bag."

"Those aren't Guccis. They're knockoffs," Angela says in a sharp voice.

Oh, snap. I look down at my Old Navy flip-flops poking out from under the table, and then slide them further underneath me.

"So?" Summer says, her voice rising an octave. "Do they look that bad?"

Mindy says, "Well, it's not like guys can tell the difference."

Angela makes a growling sound. Her minions have spoken back, so she must be trying to assert her dominance. I don't speak *Angela*, so I can't know for sure. I imagine right now she's flipping her platinum blonde hair over her shoulder while rolling her eyes. "Well, *I* can. Did you see that girl at the coffee stand this morning? She was wearing fake Pradas. I mean, seriously. Does she really think she's fooling someone?"

Yeah. Angela is seriously the most stereotypical Valley Girl I've ever met. She's a walking cliché. It doesn't stop people from worshipping her, though. With flawless skin, sparkling blue eyes, and the bounciest hair I've ever seen, I can't really blame them.

Now I imagine Mindy rolling her eyes, wishing they were having a more intelligent conversation. The kind she could have with me, for instance. We could be strolling up and down the fancy walkways and admiring English architecture while we debate the theory of evolution. Or at least how much we hate Mr. Thomason, our Honors Chemistry teacher from freshman year. During our first lab together, I almost burned off my hair with a Bunsen burner and all I got from him was a lecture in front of the entire class. The man has no sympathy.

"Fine. Let's go find a good pair of heels after lunch," Summer says. "But you have to help me with the conversion rate. I think I might have overspent already."

"Like I can figure it out either. I'm just charging everything," Angela says. Rumor has it Angela comes equipped with a black, limitless AmEx card.

"I'll help you," Mindy says. "It's pretty simple."

It *is* simple, but whatever. There's a reason I'll be voted "Class Brain" and Summer will get "Major Catch," and it's not because she's good at math.

"What's this place called, anyway?" Summer asks.

"I don't know. It's at the end of Sloane Street, where it dead-ends at Hyde Park or something. We're supposed to meet up with the guys at the backdoor at nine," Angela says.

I can't believe this. They're crashing a nightclub while I'm stuck in the room. This isn't fair. Why can't I go too?

The waitress strolls up to take their order (Angela shocks me by ordering a cheeseburger), and I develop a game plan as

I nervously jiggle a spare straw between my thumb and index finger. I'll saunter slowly by, and then when I look over and see Mindy, I'll act surprised. Then I'll ask her if she's gotten any reading done on Mr. Brown's summer reading list. If at all possible, I'll segue into how boring London has been so far, and maybe they'll invite me out with them. My plan is flawless.

My stomach is already twisting and flopping around in protest, but my mind is made up. I have to get this over with. I fish my mango lip gloss out of the pocket of my Levis and smear it on, and then smooth over my slightly frizzed-out blonde hair.

No time like the present. I slide quickly out of the leather booth and am almost to my feet when someone slams into me from behind.

Oomph. I'm knocked to my knees, but I manage to catch myself before face planting.

That's when I feel a chill seeping through my shirt, spreading so my entire back is covered in icy-coldness, and goose bumps pop up all over my arms. I twist my head and see a woman holding a half empty pitcher of iced tea, a black apron tied around her waist.

"Are you okay, love? Oh blimey, you're soaked! I'm so sorry. I was just walking by and you jumped out in front of me," she says, more to herself than me. "Let me help you up."

"Uh, I'm okay, really. No biggie."

I take a deep breath and look up at the trio of girls next to me. Angela is fighting a huge grin (and losing) but Mindy is just staring, her face blank of all expression. Summer is hiding behind a menu, her face turned downward so all I can see is her highlight-streaked dark hair.

"You okay?" Mindy asks.

"Smooth move," Angela says. "Very graceful."

Summer's tiny shoulders shake with silent giggles as my face nearly bursts into flames.

"Oh. Uh, I'm fine. I'm just . . . soaked. I, uh, I'm fine. Thanks."

And then I bail. There's no way I can talk to them now. Like they're going to invite me to the club? Ha. Right. I've just confirmed the reason they don't hang out with me. God, I'm a walking disaster.

I bolt through the café's side-door and duck into the hotel lobby bathroom, the closest door to the scene of my humiliation. I go into one of the fancy pink wallpapered stalls and sit down on a toilet for a few minutes, my face buried in my hands, trying to compose myself. There's a lump in my throat, but I won't cry because it's not worth it. This kind of stuff happens to me all the time, and tomorrow it won't sting so much. I'll block it from my memory like it never happened.

My mom has always told me I have two left feet, but I think that's giving me too much credit. I'm so clumsy I deserve my own cliché. I'm sure eventually falling flat on your face will be known as "pulling a Callie Montgomery."

I get up and leave the stall, the automatic toilet flushing behind me. I shuffle to the sinks, sniffling back the last few tears that still threaten.

Once in front of the gilded mirror, I twist around to survey the damage. My white tee is totally soaked through so you can see my black bra strap. The ends of my lifeless blonde hair aren't exempt from the iced tea treatment, either. They even smell like lemon.

I sigh and grip the edges of the sink as I stare back at my reflection. It's not like I'm horrendously ugly. I'm just kind of plain. Straight, narrow nose. Average cheekbones. Dull blue eyes. Could I *be* anymore average?

It's no wonder I've never even been kissed. My lips are sort of thin. Not full and kissable like Angela's.

The door swings open and I look up to see Mindy stride in. I yank back from the mirror so she won't know I've been staring at myself.

She's retying the knot in her charcoal-gray shrug when she sees me, and her glossy lips part—and then freeze like that—a tiny little *o* of surprise.

I drop my hands to my sides and try to ignore the prickling feeling of the wet shirt glued to my back.

"Oh," she says, and then stops at the door, halfway into the bathroom and halfway out, like she might get bubonic plague from me if she gets too close.

"Hey," I say. My hands are suddenly in need of a good washing, so I stare at the soap dispenser as I pump it five times, filling my palm with pink suds. I'm overly aware of her presence in my peripheral vision, and have to force my eyes to remain on the ultraimportant task of personal hygiene. Why is she staring at me like that?

Mindy finally walks into the bathroom stall as I switch the faucet off and reach for a few paper towels. I use them slowly, one square at a time, until she comes back out.

I toss the paper towels and pretend to fix a few strands of hair as she walks toward the sinks. She stops halfway there.

"Oh, um, Callie?"

I perk up and turn to look at her. She's smiling at me.

This is *it!* My ticket out of the hotel.

"Um, I just wanted to, well—" she pauses for a second.

My heart is going crazy. I knew Mindy would come through if I gave her the chance. I just know we'd click if I could stop acting like a freak for more than five minutes.

She clears her throat. "You have toilet paper stuck to your shoe."